THE SLAVE'S LOVE
(*Adimayin Kaadhal*)

Ra. Ki. Rangarajan, who was with Tamil magazine *Kumudam* for forty years, left a mark on almost every genre of Tamil literature. He even wrote on the occult. He was perhaps the author with the most pseudonyms—as many as ten! He also tried his hand at translations, capturing the flavour of Sidney Sheldon and Jeffrey Archer for the Tamil reading public. His translation of Henri Charriere's *Papillon* was serialised in *Kumudam* and was a huge hit. Ra. Ki's short stories with a surprise twist in the end were compiled under the title *Twist Kadaigal*, and were inspired by Jeffrey Archer's *A Twist in the Tale*. Ra. Ki.'s magnum opus was *Naan Krishnadevarayan*.

Suganthy Krishnamachari is a Chennai-based journalist, and has written articles on history, temple architecture, Sanskrit, mathematics, literature and music. She has written a series of books for schoolchildren on mathematics and English grammar. One of her short stories, published in a leading newspaper, is being used by an educational publishing company which is bringing out two English Language Teaching (ELT) series for school students. Another story was translated into Tamil some years ago, and published by an educationist in a magazine he edits.

THE SLAVE'S LOVE

*(Adimayin Kaadhal)
in Tamil*

Ra. Ki. Rangarajan

Translated by
Suganthy Krishnamachari

Published by
Rupa Publications India Pvt. Ltd 2023
7/16, Ansari Road, Daryaganj
New Delhi 110002

Sales centres:
Bengaluru Chennai
Hyderabad Jaipur Kathmandu
Kolkata Mumbai Prayagraj

Copyright © Ra. Ki. Rangarajan 1998

This is a work of fiction. Names, characters, places and incidents are either the product of the author's imagination or are used fictitiously and any resemblance to any actual person, living or dead, events or locales is entirely coincidental.

All rights reserved.
No part of this publication may be reproduced, transmitted or stored in a retrieval system, in any form or by any means, electronic, mechanical, photocopying, recording or otherwise, without the prior permission of the publisher.

P-ISBN: 978-93-5702-810-3
E-ISBN: 978-93-5702-677-2

First impression 2023

10 9 8 7 6 5 4 3 2 1

Published in English by Rupa Publications India Pvt. Ltd
in association with Mysticswrite Pvt Ltd 2023

The moral right of the author has been asserted.

Printed in India
This book is sold subject to the condition that it shall not,
by way of trade or otherwise, be lent, resold, hired out or otherwise
circulated, without the publisher's prior consent, in any form of binding
or cover other than that in which it is published.

ONE

With his elbow he pressed the door that led to the backyard, while he opened the latch. The door opened noiselessly, and he stepped out.

The gold coins he had tied to his dhoti jangled. He tightened the knot, so that the coins wouldn't make any sound.

A bullock cart stood in the yard, with two bullocks harnessed to it.

"Are you upstairs, my boy?" a voice called out from inside the house.

His mother.

He hesitated for a second.

He then got into the bullock cart, and loosened the reins. He picked up the whip. The bullocks sensed that they would soon be moving.

The cart started to make its way down the lovely streets of Kanchipuram.

"Where are you off to so early in the morning?" some people asked him.

He didn't bother to reply. Nor did he stop the cart. He just gave them a smile.

The looms were at work. One could tell by the sound. One could hear the squishing of feet in the fields, indicating that people were at work transplanting seedlings.

The temple towers and palatial houses of Kanchipuram could no longer be seen.

"Good bye," he said, leaving the city.

"I am leaving, father. I do not want to guard your safe. My dear cousin, I cannot marry you. Golden bowls, and the rich porridge in them! Forgive me. I am sick of your sweetness."

He kept bidding farewell to everything in the city.

Chennai, the city of freedom beckoned. The city of opportunity called out to him.

He began driving on the road that led to Chennai.

The rays of the early morning sun were soothing. The polished brass ornaments that decorated the horns of the bullocks shone in the Sun. The breeze ruffled his curls.

Back home, father would have finished his morning prayers. Mother would be waiting near the staircase, and calling out, "My son, please come down. I am waiting here with the kumkum and sacred ash. I find it difficult to climb the stairs, my dear boy."

Her "dear boy" wouldn't come down. Mother would go upstairs to find out why. A few minutes later...

He bit his lip, and gave the tails of the bullocks a gentle twist. Unaccustomed to such treatment, the bullocks picked up speed.

◆

The roadside rest for head-loads indicated that he was in Sriperumbudur.

It was noon. The bullocks had slowed down. That was when he realised he hadn't eaten anything since morning.

He unharnessed the bullocks, and spread some hay before them. He led them to a pond nearby, so that they could slake their thirst.

He then harnessed them again and drove on. But he wasn't able to drive fast, because of the crowds on the streets.

"What's happening? Why is there such a crowd?" he enquired.

"It's the weekly market."

"Where?"

"Behind the Vishnu temple. Go and have a look."

He entered the market at the place where cattle were being sold. This place wasn't noisy. Sellers and buyers were transacting their business in silence. Their hands were covered by their dhotis. Each finger represented a certain sum of money, and when the seller touched a finger of the buyer's, that meant he was willing to buy at that price. Kanchipurathan knew all about these transactions. He was amused by this supposedly secret transaction. He sat beneath a peepul tree and watched the proceedings. He clapped his hands. That attracted the attention of a few men.

"I plan to sell a pair of bullocks, together with the cart, for three gold sovereigns!"

There was a clamour to buy the bullocks and cart from him. Men jostled and pushed to seal the deal. He took money from the first man who approached him, and handed over the reins to him.

"Good bye," he said to the bullocks and gave them each a gentle pat on the back.

The smell of food that wafted from an inn nearby drew him to the place. He bought some food, and sat down near the pond to eat. When he finished, he washed his hands in the pond, and as he was coming up the steps, he heard an animated discussion going on in the pavilion nearby.

"He looked quite regal. But he must have been an idiot. Will anyone be fool enough to sell two bullocks and a cart for just three gold sovereigns?"

That was the man who had bought the bullocks and cart. The young man from Kanchipuram smiled. He tapped the shoulder of the man who had bought the bullocks. He signaled to him to follow him. He took him to the cart. He pointed to one of the bullocks. "Look," he said.

"Oh my God! It has an inauspicious mark!" exclaimed the buyer.

"Yes. This bullock will bring disaster to the one who buys it. My father said he would have to give it away to someone."

He walked away.

The man who had bought the bullock came running after him, but the young man ignored him and turned his attention to the festivities that were on.

He could hear the laughter of women and girls in the place where bangles and beads were being sold. He walked in that direction. He came across a little girl who was crying. "Go away," the shopkeeper was saying to her.

"What does the child want?" the young man asked.

"She wants these beads. But she doesn't have enough money to pay for it," the bangle seller said. But before he could say anything further, he was cut short by the sound of a coin that fell before him.

It was the young man who had flung a coin at the seller. "Give the child whatever she wants," he said. "Stop crying, little girl. Buy whatever you want."

He walked on...

The Sun's duty for the day was done. He was taking leave of the beating waves, as he began to go down.

Was this Chennai? The young man enjoyed taking in the sights of the city.

He had walked all the way to Chennai and had reached just when the Sun was about to set. His feet must have ached because of his unbelievable feat! As if they understood this, the waves caressed his feet.

Catamarans being dragged ashore. Huge fishes struggling to breathe. Women waiting to welcome the fish and their husbands. Huts here and there. Yachts in the distance.

Coconut palms, with their green fronds forming a canopy. The Triplicane temple tower that could be glimpsed through this canopy. The new fort. It had been built by the Company recently. The frightening cannons that peeped out from the ramparts of the fort.

Soldiers in red uniforms standing on guard outside the fort.

Until recently, Chennai had been a pilgrim centre, frequented by the elderly. It was only with the advent of the white men that it had become a city that drew youngsters too.

He felt a surge of enthusiasm. An uplifting of his spirits.

Suddenly, he felt something crawl over his feet.

"Moses. You mustn't bother strangers. Come here," he heard someone say.

He turned round to see who it was. There were more surprises for him in store. The creature that had crawled over his feet was a chameleon. There was a little collar around its neck. A small silk rope was tied to the collar. A white man was holding the rope. He had brought the chameleon for a walk, like a dog being taken on a walk!

But unlike the white men he had seen in Kanchipuram, this man did not speak French or English. He spoke Tamil.

The moment he called out to the chameleon, the creature ran up to the white man, clambered onto his shoulder and perched there.

"Are you new to the city?" he asked Kanchipurathan.

The young man nodded.

"I live inside the fort. I am a chaplain. That means I am a priest."

"This man cannot be a Catholic priest. Had he been a Catholic, he would have been wearing a cassock, and would have had rosary beads as well," the young man thought.

"Shall we go, Moses?" the white man asked his chameleon. Whether it understood the question or not, one could not tell. But it nodded its head. The priest left.

"Not all white men are cunning. There are also lunatics like this man!" the young man thought. He walked in the opposite direction.

It was getting dark, and he was hungry.

He walked to the North of the fort. The Company had turned the area into a business district. A little further away was the village of Royapuram.

He walked through the area that the white men referred to as Black Town. There were separate streets for the Telugus, Tamils and Muslims. He saw weavers with skeins of thread draped around their shoulders.

He saw the nouveau riche, who fancied themselves rich white men, and who therefore rode in coaches.

A tower was being built for the temple of a goddess. He saw workers climb down nimbly from the scaffolding. Sailors returning home. Women—babies straddling their hips, and baskets of flowers in their hands—hurrying to the temple. He saw all these people on the road, as he made his way to an inn.

♦

"Some more rasam, please."

He was eating food served on a plantain leaf.

The lamps suspended from the ceiling swayed. The walls built of black rocks made the place appear like a prison.

Every now and then, he lifted his head, and listened keenly. Was he imagining it, or was it real? He could hear something from nearby. He couldn't tell what it was, but every time the people in the inn heard it, they looked at each other in fear.

What was it that frightened everyone?

Suddenly, everyone in the inn fell silent. They picked up their plates hurriedly. The inn keeper and his assistants stood aside, with their arms folded.

A tall man, entered, twirling his moustache. He swished his whip, and struck the ground with it. The coarse hairs on his chest and hands looked like metal wires.

"What shall I bring for you?" the inn keeper asked the man.

"Rasam."

The man smelt what was brought and said, "Even a dog won't drink this." He flung the cup away. "Get me some food."

No one cleaned up the mess. A black cat began to lick the spilt rasam.

Kanchipurathan summoned a waiter. "Please get me some more rasam in another bowl. Cats and dogs have had a go at what I had."

Kanchipurathan's sarcasm was wasted on the newcomer with a thick moustache. He began to eat.

"Hot water," the newcomer ordered.

"Sure," said the inn keeper.

The moustachioed man finished eating, and asked Kanchipurathan, "Where are you from?"

"A place where men treat others with respect."

"Cheeky, are you?"

"You haven't had an opportunity to witness how cheeky I can be," said Kanchipurathan.

A man who had just come in went up to the moustachioed man and said, "It would help if you could come there. Some business has turned up. But our men have left for the day."

The moustachioed man laughed loudly. He ran his hands lovingly over the whip, and left.

♦

Dinner was over. Kanchipurathan lay down outside the inn. But he couldn't sleep. He could still hear those mysterious sounds from nearby. He looked at the building from which the sounds came. It had high walls, very much like a fort.

He heard footsteps on the road.

A man, with his hands manacled, was being led into the building.

"Is that a jail?" asked Kanchipurathan.

"No, it is the place where people are whipped," said the waiter in the inn.

"A place reserved for whipping people?"

"To whip slaves," said the man bitterly.

"Slaves? Are you speaking the truth?"

"I am speaking the truth. There is a flourishing slave trade in Chennai, didn't you know?"

Kanchipurathan's eyes dilated in wonder.

"This is the place where slaves who have displeased their masters are whipped. Those who carry out the punishment are paid according to the number of lashes they give the slaves."

A slave who had been whipped was coming out.

Kanchipurathan's eyes burned with anger. The slave's back and shoulders bore the marks of the whipping. So many red welts, resembling millipedes!

Kanchipurathan looked around. There was no one to stop him. He entered the building from which the slave had come.

There were flaming torches fixed in brackets on the wall.

A long passage. On one side was a pyol. Beyond that was a pavilion with an iron sheet for a roof. To the right another passage. A huge well. Beyond that a peepul tree.

He kept close to the wall, and moved slowly.

He had never seen anything like this before.

Some slaves were tied to pillars. Others had their hands and feet tied to iron rings fixed to the wall. Huge whips came down heavily on the backs of the slaves.

Two men stood beside each slave—one on either side of the slave. As the whip came down, one of them counted the lashes. Another had a cup of water. Every now and then he sprinkled some water on the wounds.

An old man was seated at a table in the middle of the pavilion. There was a candle on his table. He was making some entries in a palm leaf, and counting the coins on the table. He must be the accountant. Every few minutes, the moustachioed man whom Kanchipurathan had seen in the inn, came to the accountant and gave him figures about the number of lashes. He seemed to be the head of the team of men whipping the slaves.

Suddenly…

"Oh, my God… Oh…"

The voice of a woman!

Kanchipurathan looked around keenly.

At the far end of the pavilion he saw her—the woman slave.

Did her skin always shine like burnished copper? Or was her skin glowing because of the blood from her wounds? Her disheveled hair was plastered to her forehead because of sweat. She was young. Her shoulders were smooth like bamboo.

The whip came down. "Twenty one. Twenty two…" the man counted.

She screamed in pain.

Kanchipurathan ground his teeth.

A bell pealed somewhere.

The men dropped their whips.

"Let's go. There's the bell. Time for our break," the men said. They washed their hands. The accountant continued to sit at the table.

Kanchipurathan looked around. In a corner of the room there were pots piled up one on top of the other. He hid behind them, and tapped the pots. "Who is that?" asked the accountant. He tapped again. The accountant left his seat and came to investigate. It took Kanchipurathan just a second to push the accountant down and tie him up. He pushed the accountant behind the pots.

He ran to the girl who had been whipped. He untied the rope around her hip. He pushed aside her hair. What a beautiful girl she was! He gently ran his hands over her cheeks.

Broad forehead. Huge eyes. Perfect nose. Rosebud lips.

When he touched her lips, his heart missed a beat. He wiped the blood on her lips. He quickly untied her.

"No. Please go away. Don't put yourself in danger," she begged. What a lovely voice she had!

The other slaves hurried him, "Hurry. They will be back soon."

The accountant was struggling to free himself. A few pots rolled down.

"Quick. Quick," the slave girl too was in a hurry now, and twisted her body. This only tightened the knots Kanchipurathan had loosened.

"Stay still. Don't wriggle," he said to her. Using his teeth, he loosened the knots in the rope that bound her hands. Her fingers brushed against his chin. They conveyed her anxiety and her gratitude.

"Hey!"

Kanchipurathan heard someone behind him roar with anger!

The girl turned pale with fear.

TWO

An uneasy silence prevailed in the Singavaram palace. The servant took off his footwear and tiptoed down the corridor. A maid dropped a jar in her nervousness, and turned pale with fright as if she were guilty of murder, when it rolled down the steps noisily.

King Krishnappa was unwell. He had been in bed for the last fifteen days. He was a little better now. But he needed rest.

The chief of the palace guards called out to the solider guarding the cannons, "The physician will be here any minute. Is the boy ready with a torch?"

"He's gone to get a torch," replied the solider. It was day time. But the palace convention was that every time the royal physician made a visit, a boy with a flaming torch in his hand had to lead the way.

The chief guard toyed with the idea of accompanying the physician. He took off his jewel encrusted turban.

But he hesitated, because the 'old man' was with the king. The 'old man' was Raghunatha, the father-in-law of King Krishnappa. Raghunatha was also the King's advisor.

The chief guard made his way slowly in the direction of the King's room. He opened the pearl studded door, and moved aside the silk curtains. The palace was on top of a small hill, and a pleasant breeze kept the palace cool.

He peeped into the King's room anxiously.

He felt reassured, for the King was no longer in bed, but was seated. He looked distinctly better. His eyes were beginning to show some brightness. He had lost weight, of course.

The royal physician felt the pulse of the king. He opened his brass medicine chest, and took out some medicinal powders. He began to mix them in a dollop of honey.

Raghunatha was pacing up and down. "How is the King's health?" he asked the physician. Raghunatha was stout; he spoke in measured tones.

Krishnappa gave a dejected laugh. "Why do you encourage the physician to tell lies? What will he say except that I will soon be all right?"

"No, no. I really do think that, that..." stuttered the physician. He put the medicinal mix in a betel leaf, folded the leaf and handed it to the King.

"No, I do not want any more medicines. Medicines cannot save this sinner," the King said.

"You mustn't refuse to take your medicines..." the physician pleaded.

The chief guard who was outside the room could no longer remain silent witness to this scene. He wiped his tears, and entered the King's room. "Please take the medicine, Your Majesty. The welfare of your subjects depends on your welfare."

Raghunatha indicated to the physician that he should leave.

Krishnappa said to the chief guard, "Veeranna. I am glad you have so much affection for your king. The physician can do nothing for me. But you can…"

"I await your command, Your Majesty," said Veeranna.

Raghunatha asked the King not to strain himself.

"No, no, please do not interrupt. I have to unburden myself. Veeranna, do you remember I entrusted a task to you and to the chief mahout years ago? I think the mahout's name was Vel Pandithan."

Veeranna became nervous. "We carried out your orders, Your Majesty."

"Yes, you did. And that was when I lost my mental peace. Veeranna, go and fetch Vel Pandithan."

The chief palace guard was confused. Why was the King raking up the past, and now, when he was unwell?

All the same, he had to obey the king's orders. He ran to the elephant stable. Vel Pandithan was drawing water from the well. "Vel Panditha, the King wants to see you."

Vel Pandithan and Veeranna hurried to the King's room.

"Come close to me, Vel Pandithan," said Krishnappa. Vel Pandithan hesitated.

"Please come close to me. I am not your superior in any sense of the term," Krishnappa said. "Moreover, I am on the brink of death..."

"Your Majesty mustn't say such things."

"What is the use of self-deception? I know I am going to die soon. Wait a minute..." said Krishnappa. He strained his ears to listen, and then said to Raghunatha, "Is that the sound of cannons?"

"Yes. Zulfikar Khan has laid siege to the Senji fort," said Raghunatha.

"Soon, I will be in the same position as Rajaram— the King of Senji."

"That is unlikely. Rajaram is a sinner. He imprisoned his sister and her son, so that he could be king. He is being punished for his sins."

"And if that were true, then what would you say of a man who killed his brother, sister-in-law, and niece, so that he could seize the throne?"

"Who did that?"

"I did."

"No, no. That's a lie," shouted Raghunatha. "They went on a picnic, and the royal elephant threw them off in a fit of rage..."

"...That's the story I cooked up for public consumption. The truth is that I asked the mahout to annoy the elephant, so that it would throw them off. I murdered my brother and his family. And these two men here helped me do it."

"What? Is that true?" asked Raghunatha, in disbelief.

"I am being punished for my sins," said Krishnappa. There were tears in his eyes. "And I am in agony, because I will never be able to atone for my sin. Vel Panditha, I have a question for you. Try to recall what happened. Are you sure the King, Queen, and the princess died when the elephant threw them down?"

"I saw it happen, Your Majesty. The elephant picked them up and flung them down a cliff. I will never forget that terrible scene."

"Oh my God! I was hoping that one day I would be able to put the princess on the throne of Singavaram. But now my hopes have been dashed. Tell me, Vel Panditha. Do tell me, Veeranna, if it is possible that my niece Meera, who was two years old then, may be alive somewhere. Is it possible?"

Vel Pandithan and Veeranna looked at each other. "One word of assurance from you will help ease my conscience. Just tell me that there is such a possibility. Your words will be like nectar to this dying man," cried the King.

Veeranna and Vel Pandithan fell at his feet.

"Forgive us, Your Majesty," said Vel Pandithan. "We can no longer conceal the truth from you. That child is alive somewhere…"

"Alive? Is she alive?" Krishnappa jumped up. He embraced Vel Pandithan.

"You mustn't get emotional," Raghunatha said to his son- in -law. "All right, old man. Tell us what happened," he said to the chief mahout.

The chief mahout was overwhelmed by emotion, and it was a while before he could speak. "As we had planned, the King and Queen were flung down by the elephant, and they died instantly. But the princess landed in a bush. She lay there crying. We didn't have the heart to leave here there. So we took her..."

"Where did you take her?"

"We took her to Trichinopoly that night."

"So she is in Trichinopoly. Go there at once and bring her here," said Krishnappa.

"That's not so easy," said Vel Pandithan. "The Dutch were there to buy slaves. We sold her to them."

"Did you at least make a note of the child's identification marks?" asked Raghunatha.

"Yes, we did."

"So it is quite possible that she is alive somewhere in Chennai, in the house of some rich man?" asked Krishnappa.

"Yes."

"I want both of you to go to Chennai at once. I want your trip to be kept secret. You must bring the princess back. That's the only way you can save my life."

"We will leave at once, Your Majesty."

As soon as the two men left, Krishnappa's wife Chennamma entered. She was furious.

"Are you mad?" she asked her husband. "Will a sane man try to find a girl who was lost years ago, and make her the queen? What is to happen to our son Srirangan? Do you plan to make him a beggar?"

Krishnappa laughed maniacally.

Chennamma was taken aback by his reaction. "Father! What is the meaning of all this? Should you not have advised your son-in-law to be sensible? Don't you care for your grandson Srirangan? Don't you want your grandson to be the next king?"

Raghunatha smiled. "My dear daughter, don't you know that the ways of God and the ways of a king are inscrutable? These arrangements are to secure the throne for your son."

"How can that be?"

"Explain our plans to your daughter," Krishnappa said to Raghunatha.

"We had assumed that we had got rid of your brother-in-law's family. But we had some information that the girl Meera was alive somewhere. We were not sure if this information was correct. But if it were, then we knew we had to get rid of her. The only way to find out was to question those two men. If we had threatened them, they would never have told us the truth. This whole drama—your husband's sickness, his tears— was to get them to tell us the truth. Our plan has worked.

They will find that girl for us, and we will finish her off."

♦

The man who had made an unexpected entry was the moustachioed man! He recognised Kanchipurathan. "So it's you!"

"Who had you been expecting? Yama, the god of death, perhaps?" asked Kanchipurathan.

"Yama? You? What arrogance!" said the moustachioed man, and pushed down Kanchipurathan. He sat on his legs, so that Kanchipurathan couldn't move. He dashed Kanchipurathan's forehead on the floor repeatedly, until he passed out. The slave girl couldn't bear to look, and cried silently. Blood from Kanchipurathan's forehead splattered over her feet. Her tears mingled with his blood.

The moustachioed man warned the other slaves that this would be their fate if they attempted to escape. He sat down, and pulled out a wad of tobacco. But what was that? Was the young man wriggling? Had he not fainted? Before he could check, he heard Kanchipurathan say to the girl, "Run." The slave girl shook off the ropes and ran into the adjacent room.

Kanchipurathan laughed. He had only faked a faint, so that he could remove the knots in the rope that bound the girl's feet.

Now that the girl was free, Kanchipurathan turned his attention to the moustachioed man. He wrestled with him, and knocked him down. Having taken care of him, Kanchipurathan wasted no time. He ran into the room where the girl had taken refuge. She was shivering with fright.

"Don't be afraid," he said to her.

The room had a window, with two iron bars across. He began to bend one of them. Soon there was enough space for them to escape through the window.

He lifted the girl. "Quick. Get out through the window."

He followed her, and jumped out.

It was very dark outside. "Come on. We'll have to leave quickly."

He held her hand and led the way.

They reached the market, and invited curious stares. When they reached a junction of four streets, Kanchipurathan said, "Good bye."

"Good bye? But where am I to go?"

"Go to your house."

"I have no house. I am a slave. My master's house is the place where I used to stay. Now after what has happened, I cannot go back there."

"So what do you plan to do?"

"You rescued me. You are my master now. Please don't tell me to go away." She held on to his feet, and wouldn't budge.

THREE

She held on to Kanchipurathan's feet and refused to let go. With her doleful eyes and quivering lips, she presented a piteous sight. Kanchipurathan helped her to her feet.

He showed her the gold coins he had. "I am not encumbered by anything, except this bag of money. Maybe I should throw this away too." He lifted the bag of gold coins and was about to throw it away. She stopped him.

He could see the silhouette of ships in the distance. A journey across the seas. Visits to foreign lands. Trying the foods of different countries. How could he give up his dreams?

"I rescued you from slavery. Are you suggesting that I should be bound by ties now?" he asked her.

"All right. Let me not encumber you," she said, and began to walk away.

Kanchipurathan watched her leave, and didn't try to stop her. But what was that noise that he heard? The clutter of horses' feet, and it was clear the horses were coming towards him. Behind him was a mango orchard.

"Shh. Don't make a sound," he warned, and pulled the girl towards the orchard. They hid behind a tree.

Two horses went past them.

"They are looking for you," he whispered. He was standing close to her, his hand resting on hers. He noticed her broken glass bangle, crushed it and threw away the pieces.

"We are close to the beach. This is a dangerous place. Let's go," she said.

"Why is it dangerous?"

"I've heard that this is the place where people from the Santhome Church and those in the fort fight."

"Let us wait for those two men to leave. And then we too should get away from this place. What's your name?"

"Thamarai."

He was holding her hand. "Thamarai", he said to himself. "Where do you want to go? I'll escort you there."

"You were about to fling your coins into the sea. That's where I should be," she said.

"Why do you sound so dejected?"

"Death is preferable to going back to Peria Pedhu's house."

"Who is Peria Pedhu?"

"He is my master. The man who owns me. He bought me when I was three years old."

"Where were you before that?"

"I don't know. But I vaguely remember a doting mother. I remember a father who would give me rides on his shoulder. I can't recall anything else."

"Shh!" he said, covering her mouth with his hand.

The men on horseback had returned. They waited for a few seconds, and then went on their way, their search having proved futile.

She whispered to him, "Let me go with them. I'll go back to Peria Pedhu's house."

"And?"

"I'll be given a few more lashes, for running away. My name and my owner's name are branded on my thighs. If I return, they will punish me severely, or will probably send me to Goa."

"Why Goa?"

"The biggest slave market in the country operates in Goa. In Goa, holes are bored in the palms of slaves and ropes that pass through these holes keep them bound. Slaves are exported to foreign countries from Goa."

"How can you be so calm when you talk of such horrors?"

"I am inured to suffering."

Kanchipurathan, who had been leaning against her back, moved away.

She moaned.

"What is the matter?" he asked, and touched her shoulder. Blood! "Are you bleeding because of the whipping?"

"No. A thorn lodged itself in my back, when we hid behind the tree."

"And you have been patient for so long?"

She pointed in the direction the men on horseback had taken. "So what do you think I should have done? Betrayed you—my saviour?"

He rubbed his palms with sand. That got rid of the blood stains. With the tip of her saree, he wiped the blood from her back.

"I've made up my mind. I'm going to take care of you," he said.

She looped her arm through his, showing she trusted him.

The city was asleep. Kanchipurathan avoided the bigger streets, and walked through the small by-lanes. They moved furtively, keeping to the shadows.

He laughed softly.

"What are you laughing for now?"

"I see my future as lightning. I see your future as thunder. And if lightning and thunder get together, well, Chennai is going to be flooded!"

"It's the darkness of the night that makes you think along those lines. Just wait until morning. You'll come up with a plan."

They came across an inn, which was brightly lit. Kanchipurathan approached the inn keeper, and asked, "Do you have a room for two?"

"Husband and wife?"

"Yes," said Kanchipurathan.

And old man came from inside the inn. "Wife? What a lovely wife you have!" he said, and pinched Thamarai's chin. Kanchipurathan knocked his hand away. Kanchipurathan could see that the old man was drunk. "This is not an inn. It's a tavern. Let's go," he said to Thamarai.

Thanmarai was tired. She couldn't keep pace with him. She wanted to, but simply couldn't. He had to literally drag her.

"Thamarai. Don't lose hope. Look—the sign of hope."

He was pointing to the tower of the Kapaleeswara temple. The fronds of coconut palms rustled in the wind. He could see the reflection of the stars in the limpid water of the temple tank.

"Look! Here is a place where you can spend the night," exclaimed Kanchipurathan. He was referring to a coach! It was an old coach, with hay spread on its floor. It did indeed look like a room, with its two doors, and the soft hay that could serve as a bed.

"There, look—it even has a bed. Have a good night's rest," he said.

"And you?"

"You haven't had anything to eat. I will buy some fruits for you."

"Wait. Don't go. I hear someone coming. "

"You're frightened. That's what makes you think someone's here. I'll be right back."

Thamarai was reluctant to let him go, and held on to his hands. He slowly disengaged her hands, and left.

♦

Were they ordinary horses? They sped like the wind. The path down the Singavaram hill was sheer, and the horses thundered down the slope. At the place where the slope met the plains, a cloud of dust was kicked up by the speeding horses. Was that the sound of hooves? No. It sounded more like a fast beat on a mridangam.

The Sun was setting. "Mahout, that isn't the road that leads to Chennai," Veeranna said to Vel Pandithan. Vel Pandithan did not reply. "This is the road that leads to Thanjavur," said Veeranna.

Vel Pandithan smiled. "I know, Veeranna. Just follow me."

"Raghunatha asked us to look for the princess in Chennai."

"I know. I heard him say that. I may be old, but my hearing is quite good."

Kunimedu, Puducherry, Devanampattinam, Parangipettai, Palayamkottai—these were areas the white men had colonised, and through these areas their horses sped. That year Tamil Nadu was in the grip of a severe famine. Heavy rains, floods, damage to standing crops—a combination of factors had led to the famine.

The men from Singavaram saw people leaving their villages in search of work. They reached

Chidambaram, where the local ruler had ordered that free food be provided to the poor. The two men sat down to eat. The king came on horseback and enquired if the people there had eaten well. "What a conscientious ruler!" the two men remarked.

The Kollidam River was full, because of the heavy rains.

"Will you not tell me why we are proceeding towards Thanjavur?" Veeranna asked.

"Be patient. You will soon see why we are going to Thanjavur."

They reached a rest house. But they couldn't find a boat to take them to the other side of the river. No one was prepared to take a risk, because of the flooded river. Dark clouds were gathering and it looked as if more rain was in store. This didn't help matters either.

Finally, Veeranna shook a bag of gold coins, hoping the gold would tempt someone to take a risk. A teenager came forward to take them across the river in his coracle. "But we must be back before dark," the boy said.

"Forget coming back. Forget all about your coracle. I will get you a job in the palace."

The teenager untied the coracle. He **manoeuvre**d it deftly. The wind howled. But they managed to cross the river. "Tell me now," pleaded Veeranna. Vel Pandithan smiled mysteriously. He walked towards the Siva temple. But he stopped, and said anxiously, "Have I come to the right place?"

"Are you looking for someone?" enquired the temple priest.

"I am looking for a Havildar called Nalla Devan. He was appointed havildar by Shivaji Maharaja, and his palatial house used to be here."

"But that was so long ago!" exclaimed the priest.

"That means…" The tension in Vel Pandithan's voice was palpable.

"That means, the palatial house you are referring to was demolished long ago. Nalla Devan went chasing a Dutch ship in Parangipettai, and barely managed to escape alive. While he was away, Sher Khan Lodi's men demolished his house. The last I heard of him was that he was a beggar somewhere."

The priest left.

Vel Pandithan was devastated. "Oh my God! What has happened to the princess?"

"All right. Let us return home. I hope you will tell me the whole story on the way back," said Veeranna.

The water in the river had risen. There was an old man seated in the coracle now. He was shivering in the cold, in spite of the shawl draped round his shoulders.

The rain had let up. But it was dark, and the coracle made slow progress. Vel Pandithan sighed and wiped the tears from his eyes. "I wasn't sure if the princess' foster father would part with her. After all, she would have been pampered and doted on in a rich household, if things had gone right. I was afraid he would have to be coaxed to part with her. That is why I lied to the king that the princess had been sold into slavery. But now Fate has played a trick on me. What am I to do?"

"I know you rescued the child. I saw you leave with the child. But where did you leave her? If you believed that she would live luxuriously, then you must have left her with some rich man. Who was he?"

"I took the child to the Chidambaram temple. There was no one in the temple. I didn't know what to do with the child. That's when I heard a voice saying, 'Oh God, will you not bless me with a child?' I turned round to see who it was. It was Nalla Devan. At once…"

But Vel Pandithan could not complete the sentence.

"Are you Vel Pandithan?" said a voice. The old man in the coracle hugged Vel Pandithan. "You? Is that really you?" Vel Pandithan asked, in surprise. They were in the middle of the river, where dangerous whirlpools were a threat to anyone who fell into the water.

"Please, please don't rock the coracle," the boy begged. The rope he was holding slipped from his hands. The coracle shook, turned and toppled. The boy got a hold of the coracle and hoped to reach the shore safe. Vel Pandithan was trying his best to save Nalla Devan. Veeranna began to swim towards the shore. "Vel Pandithan! Come on. Hold me. Let us swim to safety," called out Veeranna.

Nalla Devan was going down, and Vel Pandithan was unable to save him. Nalla Devan managed to say between gasps for breath, "Thamarai. My dear child. The rascals. They ransacked my house. But I managed to save the child. I ran away to Thanjavur. There…"

"Yes. Go on. What happened in Thanjavur?"

"My dear child. Thamarai. At that time Peria Pedhu had come to Thanjavur. He is a slave owner in Chennai. He is engaged in the slave trade. Thamarai… Peria Pedhu."

"Did you hand over Thamarai to him? Is she a slave in Chennai?"

There was no reply. Nalla Devan was lost in the waters of the Kollidam River.

Vel Pandithan summoned up the energy to swim to safety.

Now that they knew Thamarai was in Chennai, they did not want to waste any more time.

They knew what they had to do, Go to Chennai. Find Peria Pedhu's house.

They bought two horses, and rode hell for leather towards Chennai.

They reached Peria Pedhu's mansion the night Thamarai escaped from it. They overheard the conversation of the guards.

They wasted no time. They followed her trail. They went to the place where slaves were whipped, discovered that Thamarai had escaped from there.

When they reached the Kapaleeswara temple in Mylapore, they heard voices. "Listen," whispered Vel Pandithan. "Let us move closer, so that we can hear what they are saying."

♦

It was midnight. All the shops in the market were closed. Kanchipurathan didn't want to go back empty handed. He had to get Thamarai something to eat. He walked on. His foot touched something soft and slippery. A banana skin! A fruit shop! He began to work on the locked door. The lock gave way. He helped himself to some fruits.

He felt a stirring of his conscience. Wasn't it wrong to steal? He took some gold coins from his bag and placed them on the counter.

He closed the door to the shop, and returned to the grove.

Shock. Disbelief.

Where was the coach? Had he come to the wrong place, perhaps? How foolish he had been! She had warned him that she could hear someone there, but he hadn't paid heed. He threw away the fruits he had brought, and began to walk. But where should he go? He would have to go Peria Pedhu's mansion.

But where did Peria Pedhu live?

He remembered having seen many palatial residences in Poonamallee. He ran along the road that led to Poonamallee. A night watchman told him the way to Peria Pedhu's house. "It is like a fort," he told Kanchipurathan.

♦

Yes. It was certainly like a fort. There were guards keeping watch over it. Dawn was breaking over the horizon. Kanchipurathan began to think of a way to get into Peria Pedhu's well-guarded house.

"Curd! Thick set curd!" – a man selling curd was calling out.

Kanchipurathan had an idea. "Give me your pot of curd, and wait here," he said to the curd seller. He borrowed the curd seller's turban, and wrapped it round his head. He was now ready to attempt an entry into Peria Pedhu's house.

"Stop," said a guard to Kanchipurathan.

"I have been asked to bring curd for a death anniversary," he lied.

The guard laughed. "There are 200 cows in this palace. And you want us to believe that you have to fetch curd from somewhere else? Have all the cows here stopped yielding milk?"

"Quiet. The master is coming out," warned another guard.

From inside the mansion, a horn was blown. "Keep out of the way," the guard told Kanchipurathan, and gave him a push. The pot slipped from Kanchipurathan's hands, and broke.

"What have you done? The master will be here soon," said the guard agitatedly. He began to clean the spilt curd.

A band played various musical instruments, and an ornate palanquin came out. A bejewelled, beautiful girl was in the palanquin. She looked at the spilt curd, and at Kanchipurathan. She threw a rose at him, as the palanquin moved past him.

Kanchipurathan picked up the flower, and chewed it thoughtfully. Disappointed, he went back to the curd seller. "So your plan didn't work, did it? You couldn't get in," the curd seller commiserated with him.

"There is no way anyone can get in," said Kanchipurathan.

"You're wrong. There is a way to get in."

"What's that?"

"Follow that palanquin. You will come to the place where the Company does its business. There you will find a way."

Kanchipurathan ran after the palanquin.

The beach was abuzz with excitement. "What's happening?" he asked a boy.

"Slaves are going to be sold," replied the boy. "Peria Pedhu will choose the best slaves and take them to his mansion."

Kanchipurathan was delighted. He had found a way to get into Peria Pedhu's house.

He ran up to the row of male slaves and stood there with them.

FOUR

Kanchipurathan joined the row of slaves.

The slave market was close to the Company's fort. Weak men. Poor men in search of work. Elderly men begging the youngsters to make way for them. Youngsters telling the elderly, "Please make way for us. We looked for work the whole of yesterday, and found nothing." Kanchipurathan paid no attention to these conversations.

Where was Thamarai? Had she been recaptured and taken to Peria Pedhu's mansion? Was she lying there, trussed up? Was she going to be whipped again?

In the distance, outside the fort, he could see men from the Company, in their red coats, buying clothes and grains. Other white men, not employed by the Company, were also there, haggling with the sellers.

It was the scene of a battle. The battle of wits. The battle between cleverness and money.

That was a market where goods were bought and sold. But this one— the one where Kanchipurathan stood— was a market where human beings were bought and sold.

The man next to Kanchipurathan whispered to him, "Look at the Company's flag on top of the fort!"

The man on the other side of Kanchipurathan responded, "The white man is clever. There is no point envying him. Just you wait. One day he is going to rule over the entire country."

"Aren't you ashamed to say we will be the slaves of the white man?"

"Shh. Are we in a position to discuss these things? There come the buyers. Stop arguing."

Peria Pedhu got down from his palanquin. He was wearing a silk turban, and his thigh length tunic was made of silk too. Strands of rubies adorned his neck. He had a thick moustache, the ends of which he twirled every now and then. It was obvious that he lived in the lap of luxury.

Beside him was his accountant, ready with a palm leaf and stylus.

Another palanquin arrived. "Who's that girl?" Kanchipurathan asked, looking at the girl who alighted from the palanquin. "You seem to like courting danger," said the slave beside him. "That's Peria Pedhu's daughter."

"What's her name?"

"Deivanayaki."

"I like the name Thamarai."

"If you have a daughter, give her that name. Now just be quiet."

Deivanayaki went off to have a look at the female slaves. Kanchipurathan couldn't bring himself to look at the female slaves. Women anxious to be bought as slaves. Slavery at least held out the assurance of two square meals a day, and a roof above their heads. But the price they had to pay for that was lashes with the whip, if they displeased their master. They didn't know what they were letting themselves in for.

Was Thamarai being whipped now? How foolish it was to have left her alone!

"I can no longer stand up. Water. Can no one give me water?" an old man collapsed at Kanchipurathan's feet.

One of the palanquin bearers mocked the old man. "How can you complain that there is no water here? Can't you see the huge ocean?"

Kanchipurathan helped the old man sit up. "Wait here. Let me fetch some water for you."

Next to the palanquin stood one of Peria Pedhu's servants, with a silver flask of water for his master. Kanchipurathan grabbed the flask and ran back to the old man, who took a few sips of water.

Peria Pedhu's guard snatched the flask back from Kanchipurathan, and said, "How dare you! A man about to become a slave—and you offer him water from a silver flask, which belongs to the master!" He gave Kanchipurathan a lash with his whip. The old man ran away, afraid that he would be punished. Kanchipurathan went back to the line of slaves awaiting scrutiny by prospective buyers.

"Why do you invite trouble?" asked the slave next to Kanchipurathan. "We are people with no food to eat, without proper clothes to wear. We are here hoping we will get at least one good meal a day. And you dare to touch the master's silver flask!"

Kanchipurathan lost his temper. "You are all absolutely shameless. Is it necessary to be someone's slave to survive? There are so many carpenters, textile weavers in the city, who are paid by the Company. Maybe they can employ you."

"We explored all those avenues, and we drew a blank. That's why we are here."

"I have a question for you," said another slave to Kanchipurathan. "Since you seem to disapprove of our being slaves, why are you here? To enjoy the sea breeze?"

"I have my reasons."

"Look at you. A silk jacket. A gold ring. Who will buy you if you are dressed like a rich man? Remove your jacket and ring. Try to look like a poor man."

Kanchipurathan did as the man advised, and waited to be bought.

There were thirty men in his row. He was the third in the row.

Peria Pedhu was a man of few words. He lifted the chin of each slave with his walking stick. "Let me have a look at your palms," he said. He inspected their nails. He asked some of them to run. He asked some to dance! He lifted the eyelids of some with the tip of his walking stick, and examined their eyes. When he decided to buy a slave, he merely grunted. The accountant immediately made a note of the slave's name.

It was now Kanchipurathan's turn to be assessed by Pedhu. But Pedhu ignored him and moved away. The slave next to him and the one after that—Pedhu inspected them, and moved on.

Kanchipurathan didn't know why he'd been rejected. He ran ahead of Pedhu, and stood in line again. But Pedhu ignored him again, and moved on! Kanchipurathan was not going to give up. He ran after Pedhu, and again waited to be examined. But again Pedhu ignored him. Kanchipurathan could not be patient any longer. "What's wrong with me? I have the right height, weight and strength a slave needs," he said to Pedhu.

"But you have a quality that does not sit well with a slave."

"What's that?"

"Arrogance!"

The slaves burst out laughing. After all, one of them had already warned Kanchipurathan about his attitude.

Peria Pedhu walked back to his palanquin, the day's business having been done. He threw a shawl around his shoulders. He had used some perfume, but the fragrance was hardly noticeable, because of the overpowering smell of the slaves' sweat.

Kanchipurathan had a look at Pedhu's palanquin. It was obvious that it was heavy. It was decorated like an opulent chariot. Its doors were made of iron. Kanchipurathan lifted the palanquin with ease. He put it on his shoulders, and set it back on the ground after a few seconds. "Let me see if any of the slaves you picked today can do what I did," he said to Peria Pedhu.

Peria Pedhu did not deign to reply. His fingers kept twirling his moustache.

A man from the fort came up to Peria Pedhu. "How is he?" asked Peria Pedhu.

"He is still in prison. But he gets ample food and even liquor."

"Good. Tell him help is on the way."

Another man came running to Peria Pedhu. "Your daughter wants to know if it is time to leave."

"Yes," said Peria Pedhu.

Kanchipurathan was desperate. He looked at the palanquin of Peria Pedhu's daughter. She was looking at the Company's fort. The palanquin was about to be lifted. Kanchipurathan ran towards her palanquin, and pulled out a cushion from her palanquin. "How dare you!" she slapped him. Kanchipurathan did not reply, but opened the palm of his hand. Deivanayaki screamed. He threw away the crab he had picked from the palanquin. Peria Pedhu was there in a trice. "What's the matter, Deivanayaki? Why did you scream?"

"This man saved me…"

"This lazy man?" laughed Peria Pedhu.

Kanchipurathan's cheek bore the marks of her fingers. "Forgive me for slapping you. I didn't know…"

Kanchipurathan laughed. "There is something you can do for me. That will cancel out the slap."

"What is it?" she asked.

"Let me be a slave in your palace."

Deivanayaki turned to the accountant. "Include him."

"Deivanayaki, you are making a mistake. This man's a lazy fellow. It will just be a waste of money to employ him."

"Let us give him a try," she said, as her palanquin moved away.

"Clever man! I wonder if he picked up the crab from the palanquin, or merely pretended to have!" said Peria Pedhu.

Kanchipurathan joined the slaves who had been selected by Peria Pedhu. They would be taken to a place where they would be registered as Pedhu's slaves, and paid half a rupee each.

♦

Peria Pedhu's mansion. It was not easy for anyone to enter it. But ironically, a slave could do so. Kanchipurathan tried to enter the mansion, but was stopped by a guard. "There is a separate entrance for slaves," he said, pointing to a passage.

Kanchipurathan groped his way down the dark passage. He could see the slaves entering a room. He could hear screams from the room. There was a look of pain on the faces of the slaves who came out of the room. They were unsteady on their feet. They staggered through a passage that led out into the backyard.

What was going on in that room?

Kanchipurathan soon had an answer to his question. There was a fire burning in the room. The branding iron was being heated in the fire.

"Turn," said a man to Kanchipurathan, and branded Kanchipurathan's right shoulder with the hot iron. Kanchipurathan bit down on his lip. He could taste the saltiness of blood. There was the smell of burning skin…. Despite the pain, Kanchipurathan still had his wits about him. He could tell what was being branded on his back—the letter 'P', short for Peria Pedhu.

"Are you thick skinned? Didn't you feel the pain? You didn't utter a sound," said the man brandishing the iron rod, and shoved Kanchipurathan out.

Kanchipurathan found himself in an open courtyard. Beyond that was a cowshed, and next to it was the horse stable. A huge garden lay beyond. There he found wood cutters, people who were dyeing cloth, men giving cows a bath, those tending to the horses, those who were busy washing vessels or clothes. Hundreds of people at work.

A supervisor arrived. "Go and fetch water from the well, and water the plants," he said to Kanchipurathan.

"Where are the women?" Kanchipurathan asked.

One of the slaves laughed bitterly and said, "We are slaves. We command even less respect than dogs. And you dare to dream of women!"

Kanchipurathan wasn't in the mood to carry out the supervisor's instructions. The slave who was beside Kanchipurathan had a leather bag full of water. Kanchipurathan picked up a stick with a sharp tip, and poked a hole in the bag, when the slave wasn't looking. Water began to leak out of the punctured bag. "Oh my God, your bag's sprung a leak! Let me sew it up. Do you have a needle?" said Kanchipurathan.

"Ask the supervisor," said the other slave.

The supervisor said, "Am I a woman, to have a sewing needle? Borrow one from the women."

"I have the answer I wanted," Kanchipurathan said softly to himself, and slowly moved in the direction pointed out to him by the supervisor.

The women slaves were busy threshing and winnowing rice grains. Kanchipurathan asked an old woman if she knew Thamarai.

Tears welled in her eyes. "They took her to the whipping centre. I was told that someone abducted her from there. She is a very sweet natured girl. Are you related to her?" she asked.

"But she was recaptured and brought back here."

"No, she hasn't been brought here. She isn't here. Who told you she was here?"

"Are you sure she isn't here?"

"I swear, she isn't here. Why would I shed tears if I knew where she was?"

Kanchipurathan could see that there was no point in continuing to stay in Peria Pedhu's mansion. Where had Thamarai been taken? Had she been taken back to the whipping centre? He had to find out at once. At once.

Of what use was money to him? He had with him the coin he had received when he had been bought as a slave. The price for his being sold into slavery. He gave it to the old woman, and walked away. He came to the entrance, and was about to step out, when he was stopped by a guard. "Where do you think you are going?"

"I can go where I please."

"Slaves can't do as they please."

"Send him here," called out Peria Pedhu from the balcony of the mansion.

Kanchipurathan went up to the first floor. "So, you want to be free?" said Peria Pedhu. He gave Kanchipurathan an appraising glance, and then said, "Hmm. You are strong. You also seem to be cunning. I think you will be able to accomplish the task."

"What task?"

"Getting into the Company's fort."

"And what should I do, once I gain entry into the fort?"

"My relative Siva Chidambaram used to be a trusted aide of the Nawab of Golconda. The men from the

Company took him prisoner and have imprisoned him inside the fort. I want him to be rescued and brought here. Can you do it?"

"Why not?"

"Go to the entrance. I will join you presently."

As Kanchipurathan crossed the courtyard, he heard the snap of fingers. It was Deivanayaki. "Come here," she summoned. "Do you want to be freed?"

"Yes."

"I would have freed you, if you'd asked me."

"Why would you do that?"

"All I want is for you to do something for me."

"What do you want me to do?"

Deivanayaki lowered her voice. "I want you to enter the Company's fort."

Kanchipuarathan controlled his laughter. "And what should I do, after I enter the fort?"

"A relative of ours is imprisoned there. His name is Siva Chidambaram."

"Do you want me to rescue him?"

"No,' said Deivanayaki. She drew her hand across her neck, indicating she wanted Siva Chidambaram's throat slit. "And if you can't do that…" her gestures indicated she wanted Siva Chidambaram's hands and legs chopped off! "I don't care what you do. Just make sure he never sets foot here."

FIVE

Delighted, Kanchipurathan awaited further instructions from Peria Pedhu. Peria Pedhu walked towards the well laid out garden.

"You must bring Siva Chidambaram here. I will tell you when to leave," he said to Kanchipurathan.

"When should I leave?"

"I don't know what would be the best time for you to try and rescue him. It may be a month from now. Or it may be in just four days. But you must be prepared to leave whenever I tell you to leave."

"Is it likely to take a month? And if it does, what will I do until then?"

"You can go out. Have a look at the town. No one will stop you from leaving. But you cannot escape. Remember you have been branded with my initial."

"Don't worry. I will earn my freedom."

"I trust you. Feel free to go where you please."

♦

The plangent waves were bidding farewell to the setting Sun. Kanchipurathan walked on the beach, steeped in thought. He had set out to find Thamarai, but see what that search had led to! Here he was trying to locate a prisoner in the Fort!

Outside a hut, he saw a visually challenged girl trying to find something. "What are you looking for?" he asked.

"I have to make some chutney. I am looking for the roller of the grinding stone."

"Let me do it for you," offered Kanchipurathan. In a few minutes, the chutney was ready.

"Please let me pay you for your help," said the girl.

"Do you think I will take money from my sister?"

"I wish my brother were as affectionate as you are."

"What does your brother do for a living?"

"He is a boatman who ferries the white men of the Company. Is it dark?"

"It's twilight."

A sailboat stood anchored some distance from the shore. Since Chennai had no natural harbour, ships could not come close to the shore. Boats used in fishing, called masoolas, were used to fetch passengers and goods from the ships.

Kanchipurathan saw a masoola boat on its way to the shore. When the masoola boat drew up some distance from the shore, trunks, bags and bedding from the boat were carried to the shore. A white woman was calling out warnings to the men. Kanchipurathan didn't know English, but guessed that she was telling them to be careful with her luggage.

Two Indian soldiers came out of the Fort, and behind them came a bearded Englishman. He had a ruddy complexion because of the heat of the tropic sun.

The white man waved a handkerchief, and called out to the woman, "Mary!" Kanchipurathan could not understand what the man was saying, but he could guess that the white man wanted to know if all the luggage had been brought ashore safely.

"Pay them,' the white man instructed his servants.

"They've missed out some luggage," said Kanchipurathan.

"No, we have not," said the boatmen.

"I'll show you what they have missed," said Kanchipurathan, and swam towards the boat.

It wasn't such a good idea, though, because the salt water made his wound smart.

He reached the boat, and dived into the water. The white woman wondered what he was up to. She asked him something, and naturally he didn't know what he was being asked. He stirred the water with his hands—sand, sea shells...

There!-

He found what he was looking for— an iron chest.

He swam to the shore with it. The white woman called out after him. She seemed to be concerned about the chest. Perhaps it contained valuables.

The white man was furious with the boatmen.

"So this is what you always do—fling something into the sea, and retrieve it later? Thieves!" the white man said angrily, in broken Tamil.

"No, no. We didn't even know this chest had fallen into the water."

"Shut up! Can't you see my name on this chest? Luckily, this young man noticed that you had dropped the chest into the water. Sepoy! Pay them only half the wages we had agreed to pay."

"Master… Please… Don't be swayed by this young man's…" the boatman pleaded, and looked daggers at Kanchipurathan.

"Why are you angry with me? I didn't know you had thrown the chest into the water deliberately. I thought it had slipped out of your hands. Go home soon. Your sister is waiting for you," Kanchipurathan said to them.

"Wait, Mary. Don't step into the water. Don't get your feet wet. The chair will be here soon," said the white man to his wife.

A sepoy brought a chair from the Fort. It was a chair, but resembled a palanquin. "Take this man with you too," said the white man, pointing to Kanchipurathan. "You'll need four men to carry the chair."

"We do not know who he is," objected the men.

"At least, he is honest. That is obvious. If you take him with you, you will get at least half the wages I had offered to pay you. If you refuse to take him, you will be paid nothing."

The men acquiesced, albeit reluctantly.

When they reached the boat, Kanchipurathan lifted the white woman from the boat, and seated her in the chair. It was a cold night, but she was fanning herself with a paper fan.

The white man had a smattering of Tamil, but she couldn't speak a word of Tamil. Fully aware of this, the boatman said to Kanchipurathan, "Don't think you can get away after what you have done. We will have our revenge."

When they reached the shore, they set down the chair. The white man and woman seemed to be husband and wife who were meeting after a long gap. Kanchipurathan looked away. He was decent enough to know that he shouldn't disturb them.

They were now outside the fort. Kanchipurathan wondered how he could get in.

The Englishwoman said something to the sepoy. The sepoy translated for Kanchipurathan, "That chest that you retrieved has the lady's jewels. She is very pleased with your alertness."

The white man and his wife were about to enter the fort. The white man had his arm around his wife's waist.

Here was an opportunity Kanchipurathan did not want to miss. If he were to wait for Peria Pedhu to make plans, it might be years before he stepped into the fort.

The white man asked the sepoy if the barber was ready.

"Barber? What for?" the woman asked her husband.

"You need the services of one. You have no idea how hot this place can be in summer. The first thing our women do when they arrive, is to shave off all their hair."

He repeated his question to the sepoy.

"No barber has turned up," said the sepoy.

"Why?"

"There is some disturbance in the city. A fight between the right-hand castes and left- hand castes. The barbers didn't want to be caught between the two sides. So, they have all run off."

"What a shame! We have appointed an officer, with fifty assistants to ensure riots don't break out. But still, we are unable to stop these caste quarrels. Now where will I find a barber?"

Kanchipurathan, who had been listening to this exchange, ran into the fort and said to the white man, "I can do the job. I know how to shave off the lady's hair. All I need is a knife."

The white man looked at him in astonishment. "You seem to be able to do a lot of things. All right. Follow me."

Kanchipurathan followed him enthusiastically.

Well planned streets. Elegant houses. Silk curtains. Flower vases. Pictures of Jesus on the walls. Some families were seated in the open verandahs of their houses, so that they could enjoy the sea breeze. They all stood up when the white man entered the fort, a mark of respect to him.

Kanchipurathan wondered where Siva Chidambaram was kept prisoner.

They reached the white man's bungalow. "Here's the knife you asked for," the white man said to Kanchipurathan.

Kanchipurathan was not a snob. He had never considered any job infra dig. Besides, one of his childhood companions was the son of a barber, and Kanchipurathan had seen the barber at work. So he had a fairly good idea of how to go about the job. He sprinkled water on the lady's head. He massaged her hair for a few seconds, and then began to shave off hair. It just took him a few minutes. "Lovely hair," he remarked. There were tears in the lady's eyes.

The white man pressed a coin into his hands, and said, "Leave the fort at once. It is against the rules for an Indian not employed inside the fort to stay on after dark. If the President gets to know, there will be trouble."

Kanchipurathan saluted the white man, thanked him and left his house.

But he did not leave the fort. He kept to the shadows and began to explore the area.

SIX

Dark corners seemed to welcome him. He inched his way forward.

It had rained and the frogs kept up an incessant croaking. The metal of the cannons felt cold against his skin. Kanchipurathan paused.

It was silent all around.

The pavilion seemed to be a place where the Right Honourable President of the Company received guests and important officials. Kanchipurathan could hear musical instruments from there, but they sounded strange to him. He had never heard these instruments before.

Where were the streets? Where should he look for the secret chambers? He kept close to the wall and kept moving.

He stopped in shock. Someone was tugging at his dhoti. He turned round and laughed to himself, for there was nobody there. His dhoti was caught in the thorns of a bush! He began to walk faster. His back brushed against the rough walls of the fort.

He could hear something, from the top of the walls.

He looked up, and...

A man landed on him! Was this indeed a human? Or was it a statue made of iron that had landed on his back?

Kanchipurathan's back hurt. He felt as if his back had broken under the impact. The man who had jumped on his back rolled off, and before he could pick himself up, Kanchipurathan was on his feet. He could see that the man who had jumped on him was a sepoy. A Tamilian- who worked as a sepoy for the Company. He gripped Kanchipuarathan's hand and dragged him along.

Kanchipurathan could tell that they were close to the sea. He could hear the roar of the sea, and even felt a few drops of salty water on his back.

The sepoy bent close to Kanchipurathan's nose. "Can you smell alcohol on my breath?"

"It can be smelt miles away," said Kanchipurathan, as he wiped his nose.

"Then I am done for," said the sepoy. He held Kanchipurathan's hand tightly and said, "Mannaru, please help me."

He was so intoxicated, that he couldn't even tell who he was talking to.

"That's not my name," protested Kanchipurathan.

"Now is that fair? The moment I ask you for help, you pretend you don't know me." The sepoy now fell at Kanchipurathan's feet. "Mannaru, you know how strict the Durai[1] is. Yesterday, I pledged my uniform and had a drink at the toddy shop. Today, I had to redeem my uniform. And I couldn't resist the temptation to drink. I just had a little bit to drink.

---

1   *Durai- A respectful term Indians used to refer to or to address Europeans.*

And then I found I was late for work. So I scaled the wall and jumped in. Mannaru, Mannaru, please you must..."

♦

"I must..?"

"I want you to substitute for me, Mannaru... But where is your uniform? Have you sent it to be laundered? All right. Have mine." The man took off his uniform, and shoved it into Kanchipurathan's hands. "Go, go."

"All right. But where should I go? What are my duties?"

"Mannaru. This is not the time for you to have a joke at my expense. As if you don't know what my duties are. You and I take turns to do the same thing every day, don't we? Go, go."

The sepoy left.

Kanchipurathan walked on.

"Pandiya! What are you doing there?" A voice from the kitchen. But it seemed to be a kitchen where food was prepared for those of a low rank. The kitchen was dark and dank. Pieces of fish and vegetable peels lay scattered all over.

The old cook had only one eye. Was this the 'duty' the sepoy had spoken about—kitchen duty?

"Pandiya, you lazy man. Where have you been? Do you have to wander off every day?"

"Actually... I..." Kanchipurathan stuttered.

"I know where you've been. There was an announcement that there were many pigs in town, and that those who captured pigs would be suitably rewarded. And you went off to make some extra money, didn't you? Did you think of that poor man who is waiting for his food? His food is ready. Take it to him."

There were many plates with food on them. Kanchipurathan picked up one of them, taking care not to let the cook see his face.

The cook stopped him, and whispered, "How can you give him the food you and I eat? Put it back there. Now take this," he said, and handed to Kanchipurathan a plate that he had kept behind a cupboard. Kanchipurathan walked out of the kitchen.

But for whom was the food intended? Maybe he should just tip the contents of the plate into the drain. No, no, how could he do that? There was someone waiting for the food.

A little girl came running out of a room. What lovely, curly hair the child had! And what a mischievous, bold little girl! Everyone was asleep, but she wasn't afraid to be out alone.

She was playing with a ball. She bounced it and it fell into a tub of water. And there it lay floating in the water. The child tried to retrieve her ball, but she couldn't. There were tears in her eyes. Kanchipurathan retrieved it for her.

The child was very pleased. She curtsied and said, "Thanks."

Kanchipurathan tried to do what the little girl had done, but his bow wasn't as graceful as the child's curtsy, and she laughed.

She pointed to the plate in his hands, and said "Saapaad, Saappad..." Now where had she learnt Tamil, Kanchipurathan wondered.

"I know for whom the food is being taken. I see it being taken to him- everyday," she said in broken Tamil.

"To whom is it taken?" Kanchipurathan asked.

"I'll show you," the child said.

She pointed to a house on the next street. "Upstairs," she said, and ran off bouncing her ball.

Kanchipurathan entered the house, and went upstairs. All he had to do was to put the plate there and leave quietly. He opened the door. The room was dark, and he groped in the dark and found a table. He put the plate on the table and was about to leave, when he heard a voice.

"Who is it? Stop."

An authoritative voice. But it wasn't a white man who was speaking. The perfect diction couldn't have come from a white man. Was it that priest who had a chameleon for a pet?

"Are you a newcomer?"

"All right. The game's up", thought Kanchipurathan.

The moonlight was streaming in and he could see what seemed like iron bars. He reached out and he could feel the iron bars. He could feel iron chains too and a lock.

His heart began to beat fast. Anxiety. Curiosity. Could this be a prison? Inside was an emaciated man. But there was pride in his voice. "Are you Sivachidambaram?" Kanchipurathan asked.

"Yes. Who are you?"

Kanchipurathan ran to the balcony, to make sure there was no one to overhear their conversation.

He found a cannonball lying in the room. He picked it up, and struck the lock with it a few times. The lock opened and he removed the chains, and opened the door. "Come on, quick. We don't have much time." But Sivachidambaram did not budge.

"Come on," Kanchipurathan tugged at Sivachidambaram's hand. But Sivachidambaram didn't move.

Sivachidambaram then spoke in stentorian tones, "I do not want to be freed now. When I want to be free, I will not need your help. I have many people here, who will help me…"

People to help him? Was this the secret behind the cook serving good food to a prisoner?

"Now tell me, why are you so keen to free me?" Sivachidambaram asked.

"Peria Pedhu's orders."

"I see. Do you know why he wants to free me? To make me his son-in- law!"

"That is a very good idea."

"I am past the marriageable age. Nor am I interested in marriage. Pedhu is happy to be a shameless sycophant of the men of the Company. He thinks I will do the same. I never will, my boy. Never."

Sivachidambaram paced up and down his prison cell. He spoke about many things. Kanchipurathan understood only some of what he said.

Madurai Mangamma, Senji Rajaram, Marathi Yesubai, Ramanathapuram Sethupathi—all of them saw only the Mughal Empire as a threat. But actually, the Mughal Empire was not likely to last beyond Aurangazeb's time. The new enemies of Bharat were these white men. And this Fort St. George was the foundation for their Empire. They came as traders and merchants. Stopping them from becoming the rulers of India was Sivachidamabaram's goal.

Some time ago, Lingappa, the representative of the Golconda Sultan, felt that one way to make trouble for the Company was to stop the supply of rice to Chennai. He also threatened those who worked for the Company. But what this resulted in was hardship for the ordinary citizens of Chennai. And Lingappa ended up being labelled a rowdy.

Sivachidambaram ended his long narration with an outline of his plans, "I plan to attack this fort.

Peria Pedhu is afraid that this will harm his business interests. That is why he wants to give his daughter in marriage to me and pack me off to some godforsaken place. But that is not going to happen."

"Even if you won't let me free you for the sake of Peria Pedhu, you must allow me to free you for the sake of my love."

"Who is your love?"

"Thamarai." Kanchipurathan narrated briefly how he had met Thamarai.

"Thamarai. Now I remember hearing some sepoys mention that name this evening."

"What did you hear?"

"I heard some sepoys say that they were on the Vellore to Chennai road. That's a road infested with dacoits. So they kept warning everyone on that road to be careful. And they saw two men on horseback travelling towards Vellore, and with them was a girl. That girl, the sepoys said, was very beautiful. 'She said she was thirsty, and I gave her water', said one of the sepoys. He said her name was Thamarai."

"The Vellore road! I must go at once..."

"Wait. I know that sepoy. Let me find out if it was your sweetheart they were talking about. Or else..."

Sivachidambaram did not complete the sentence.

"Shh. Someone's coming up. Quick. Get into the prison cell. That's the safest place for you to hide in," he said, and dragged Kanchipurathan in and pushed him to a dark corner of the cell.

Sivachidambaram closed the door, and put the chains and the lock back in place.

Two sepoys entered. "There are two fools here," one of them said.

Kanchipurathan was taken aback.

"The man who brought the food tray must be a fool. He forgot to lock the door. And the prisoner is an even bigger fool. He didn't escape."

Kanchipurathan was relieved.

"What do you want? Why have you come here now? I suppose the Durai wants to make some enquiries of me. Your Durais have so many ways of spending the night. Do they have to question prisoners at midnight?" asked Sivachidambaram.

"We know you are quarrelsome. But we have no intention of arguing with you. The Durai has sent us to fetch you," said the sepoys.

Sivachidambaram went out of the prison cell. The sepoys closed the door and locked it.

After they had left, Kanchipurathan tried to open the door, but couldn't. He was locked in.

SEVEN

The palms of his hands smarted, for he had been holding on tightly to the rusty bars of the prison cell. He had thrust his face between the bars of the prison and his skin had turned red.

When would Sivachidambaram be back, Kanchipurathan asked himself.

He was restless. When was he going to get out of this prison? But his hopes seemed to die out like the flame of the lamp in the wall. And then just as he almost gave up hope, he heard footsteps.

No, it was not Sivachidambaram. He could hear two sepoys engaged in conversation.

"Why are you walking past that cell? Aren't you supposed to be on guard duty for the cell where that revolutionary is imprisoned?" asked one of the sepoys.

"You mean Sivachidambaram? They didn't want to keep him in the same place. He's been moved to another place."

So Sivachidambaram wasn't coming back. That meant the door to the cell would not be opened. Kanchipurathan had to find a way to escape. Now where was that cannonball he'd used earlier to break open the lock? There it was, and he tried to draw it towards him. But he couldn't get a grip on it. He was just able to touch it with his nails. His fingers hurt with the effort, and his arms were getting tired.

He decided to give it one last try, and when he did, the ball rolled away. There was nothing to stop it, and on it went down the wooden staircase. There were a total of 18 or 19 steps. What if someone had heard the noise?

And someone seemed to have heard it, for he could hear footsteps on the staircase. But they were not the harsh footsteps of a man in a hurry. They were gentle footsteps. The person who came in was not a sepoy. Nor was it Sivachidambaram. It was the little girl whose ball he had retrieved a while ago.

"Did you drop that ball? You're a good man. Why have they put you in prison?" the child asked Kanchipurathan.

"You are a good girl too, aren't you? I dropped that ball. Can you fetch it for me?" asked Kanchipurathan.

"Certainly," said the girl, and ran off.

She came back a few seconds later and said," I couldn't lift it. Too heavy."

Kanchipurathan begged her to try again. "Please, please try again. I am sure you can do it this time."

The little girl ran off, and stopped when she got to the landing. "I'll bring my father. He should be able to lift it," she said.

"No. Please don't bring anyone here," Kanchipurathan called after her, but she was out of earshot. It was easy fooling that child. But what was he going to do if her father turned out to be an important official? How was he to escape then?

"Sivachidambaram, do you want something to read? My daughter said you wanted something."

Kanchipurathan greeted the man. "How is your pet, the chameleon, Moses?"

"What a surprise!" the priest exclaimed, upon seeing him.

"I too am surprised. And since when did Christian priests start having families?"

"I am not a Catholic priest. I am a Protestant priest from England. I will explain the difference between the two to you, when you become my disciple. Now tell me your story. You are wearing a uniform that is not yours. You are in a place where you shouldn't be. Is this why you came to Chennai?"

"I am not in prison because I did something wrong."

"I can see that. A man who makes such a good first impression on a child cannot be wicked. And you've won my daughter's affection."

Kanchipurathan narrated his story briefly to the priest. The priest smiled. "I have heard of men giving up their kingdoms or their lives for the sake of their love. But I have never heard of a man who became a slave because of his love. So, do you plan to remain in this prison until Sivachidambaram returns?"

"I overheard two sepoys say that he will not be brought back here."

"He isn't coming back?" The priest looked crestfallen. "Young man, do you see that stone there in that dark corner? Now move it."

"What's under the stone?" Kanchipurathan asked.

"Do as I say. Move that stone."

Kanchipurathan slowly dislodged a jutting stone. And underneath it he found something he had never seen before. What were they?

"Bring them to me," said the priest. "These are called books. You write on palm leaves. We print on paper. If we had lost these books..." The priest hugged the books to himself.

Books? Print? Kanchipurathan had never heard those words. "Give me those books," he asked the priest. Yes, the letters were Tamil letters. But he was not holding a palm leaf manuscript.

"Did you do this?" he asked the priest.

"Yes, I did this with European technology. Efforts are on to set up a printing press in Tarangampadi. In another ten years, Tamil books will be printed here." He wrapped the books in his tunic. "I would have lost these treasures. Thank you, young man."

"Why did Sivachidambaram hide these books?"

The priest went to the landing to make sure there was no one there. He then came back, lowered his voice and said, "Sivachidambaram is a revolutionary. I am in the opposite camp. But we share a common interest in Tamil literature. But the officers of the Company have forbidden me from having any contact with him. That is why I had to pass on the books very carefully to him and the books had to be kept hidden. Thank you once again, young man."

He made his way down the stairs.

For a few seconds Kanchipurathan was thinking of the paper and the books he had just seen. It took a while for him to realise that he had not asked the priest to get the cannonball for him.

And then he began to wonder how it was that he could remove that stone in the wall so easily. He went back to check. He tugged at the stone next to it. After some effort, he was able to move that stone too. Then he managed to move a third stone, and he found that he was looking down at a flight of steps! He went down them, counting the steps as he climbed down. He had counted 150 steps. And then the passage stopped abruptly. He was sure there must be another passage that led out. But he couldn't find any steps leading up. He looked for stones that he could dislodge, found one, and moved it aside, and found a narrow hole. He looked down the hole, and could see the floor beneath. And then he realised that he had been imprisoned on the first floor of the building, and so he must now jump down through the hole. Looking through the hole, he saw what was like a huge warehouse. There was a pungent odour in the warehouse.

All was quiet in the warehouse. He jumped in. The hard floor hurt his feet.

Chests. Huge ones, everywhere. Wooden chests. Had he come into the treasury, perhaps? But what was this nauseating smell? There was an itch in his throat. He felt the urge to cough. But he controlled himself with great effort. He could see a door on the opposite side of the warehouse. He opened the door carefully. But the moment he opened the door, he turned his face away. There was a European woman on a bed. He couldn't bring himself to step into a woman's bedroom. Besides, even assuming he overcame his reservations, what if she woke up just as he was crossing the room?

He closed the door, and went back into the warehouse. What was he to do now? There were huge doors on the other side. There was no way to open them. Should he go back up the secret passage? But to do that, he would have to climb a height of ten feet. Should he pile up some chests to climb back into that passage?

The urge to cough was difficult to control, but he managed to control himself.

Starlight filtered in through the cracks in the door. He had a look at a chest. "Danger, explosives", red letters in Tamil, etched on the chest.

He broke out in a sweat. And he also realised what Sivachidambaram's plan was. He knew explosives were stored beneath the cell where he was imprisoned. His plan was to somehow set off the explosives or smuggle them out!

Kanchipurathan walked up to the huge door. He placed his hand on it. He could sense that there was someone on the other side. As the door opened, Kanchipurathan, kept close to it, and the two men who entered did not see him. He slowly slipped out the moment their backs were turned.

What a relief it was to be in the open! To feel the breeze! But he couldn't savour the breeze. He had to find some place to hide. There was a cart stationed in the courtyard. There seemed to be no one in it. He decided to hide in it. He sprinted to the cart. But the two men who had entered the warehouse were now out and making their way towards the cart. Kanchipurathan jumped in. Chests inside the cart! The two men from the warehouse brought two more chests and shoved them into the cart. They were going to drive the cart out of the fort. He would be able to leave the fort, if he stayed inside the cart. The smell of the explosives in the chests irritated his throat.

The cart began to move. The streets were silent. All he could hear was the rattle of the cart and the hooting of an owl somewhere in the distance.

They were now near the village of Tiruvallikkeni. He could tell from the sound of the swaying trees.

"Stop." Someone had stopped the cart.

"These chests have to reach Zulfikar Khan. You know that, don't you?"

"Yes, we do."

"Have you made sure the chests are secure and won't fall off?"

"Of course, we have."

Kanchipurathan's nerves were on edge. What if the man opened the doors of the cart to check if everything was in order?

"All right. You may go," said the voice that had stopped the cart.

Luck seemed to be on Kanchipurathan's side. Kanchipurathan waited until the cart got close to a densely wooded area, so that he could jump off.

The driver of the cart and his friend were silent for a long time. Then one of them broke the silence, "Have you forgotten the way to Senji? Why are we on this road?"

"Don't you know that Rajaram's men are on the road to Senji? Do you want to be caught by them? This is the Vellore road. We have to take a circuitous route to Senji," the other man said.

Kanchipurathan was about to jump, but when he heard that they were on the Vellore road, he stepped back. The Vellore road! He was unable to bear the overpowering smell of the explosives. But he had to put up with it. It would be far easier to catch up with Thamarai, if he travelled in this cart, than if he walked. He rested his head on one of the chests and his feet on another. The gentle swaying of the cart, the lack of sleep for two nights, the ache in his legs, the lack of food—a combination of factors made him drowsy, and he was soon asleep.

He could sense that the cart was ascending a slope. He could feel the heat of the rising sun. But he lay there in the cart, only half conscious.

Suddenly, he felt a constriction in his chest. He found it difficult to breathe. He realised that since he had been asleep for so long, he had inhaled fumes from the explosives.

His hands and legs felt weak. And the cough that had been threatening to erupt could no longer be held back. He also remembered that he was in company uniform. Who knew what problems that would bring? He removed it and bundled it up.

He opened the latch. The dust on the street gleamed like silver. The cart was moving adjacent to the wall of a temple. He knew he mustn't jump, because that would cause the cart to quake and that would give the game away. He held on to an iron rod near the axle, and put his feet on the ground. Without letting go of the rod, he put his feet on the ground. His feet hurt as they were dragged along the hard ground. Carefully and dexterously, he manoeuvred his body, so as not to be caught under the wheels of the cart, and then he let go of the rod. He fell to the ground with a thud, but the rattle of the cart, muffled the sound of his fall.

Kanchipurathan waited till the cart had turned the corner, before getting up. He let the coughs have their way. He then drew in the fresh air. But it didn't really help him get rid of the toxic fumes he'd inhaled. He staggered and was unsteady on his feet.

"Are you unwell? There is a physician near the temple tank. Go and consult him," said a goatherd.

Physician... He wasn't so much in need of medicines, as he was in need of water and some food.

He was still wobbly on his legs, but he was able to locate the physician's house. There was a group of people outside his house. Kanchipurathan went past them, and entered the physician's house. But there was no sign of the physician. There were jars of potions and pills on a table.

"Hello. Can't you hear me calling you?" That voice came from behind Kanchipurathan.

"Come here. Aren't you the physician? Come with me," said the man, and dragged Kanchipurathan to a palanquin.

Kanchipurathan could see a hand outside the palanquin, the hand of a woman, but the curtain of the palanquin kept her face hidden from view.

"Why are you hesitating? She is from a rich family. A woman from a rich family will never let strangers see her face. She will only let you examine her pulse. Didn't you know that? Go on. Check her pulse, and see what is wrong with her."

Was this really the hand of a woman? Or was it the work of a sculptor? Was it sculpted out of sandalwood?

Kanchipurathan stared at the hand, and then he saw tattooed on it the name Thamarai!

EIGHT

Her hand trembled. It reminded him of rice stalks trembling in the wind.

Did the tremble mean that she too had recognised him? Her fingers were so slender, that it seemed as if they would turn red under the slightest pressure. Her nails looked as if they had been polished red.

His mind quickly went through all that had happened in such a short span.

His drive out of Kanchi in a bullock cart; meeting the priest who had a chameleon for a pet; seeing a woman in a place where slaves were whipped; rescuing her, and the few pleasant moments spent in her company; being branded by a slave owner; the secret passage under Sivachidambaram's prison cell; a journey in a cart carrying explosives; and when he was recovering from his dizzy spell, once again a pleasant meeting!

"Quick. Attend to her," said the man to Kanchipurathan.

In order to make sure that it was indeed Thamarai who was in the palanquin, Kanchipurathan asked, "How long have you had fever?"

"Since this morning," replied the man who had fetched Kanchipurathan.

"Let her answer," said Kanchipurathan.

"Since this morning. I think the water from the temple tank didn't agree with me," said the lady inside the palanquin.

Kanchipurathan felt as if he had just had nectar. That sweet voice. It was she! Thamarai had cleverly indicated that it was indeed she!

And since she was guarded in her reply, Kanchipurathan guessed that the men she was with were strangers and that she was being taken away forcibly. Kanchipurathan had to rescue her.

He felt her pulse. Even as he did so, his eyes took in the scene around him.

The house had an open courtyard. There was a door that led out from the backyard. There was an almond tree in front of the house. Under the tree was a raised platform. An old man seated on the platform coughed. The guard scolded the old man, "Listen old man. The physician is busy. He will attend to you once he has finished attending to the lady here. You don't have to signal your presence by coughing."

The old man stopped coughing.

Kanchipurathan took count of the number of men accompanying Thamarai. There were four palanquin bearers. There were two guards too. He would have to get them out of the way. And then he would leave with Thamarai.

"Come here," he said to two of the palanquin bearers. "I need your help..."

"What do you want us to do?"

"I have had no help for the last ten days. I want you fetch two big stones from near the river. I need them to grind medicines. I am unable to lift huge stones."

"Certainly." The two men left.

"Why don't you go with them? They could do with an extra pair of hands," he said to another palanquin bearer.

"Did you see a tamarind tree at the entrance to this street? I want you to get me two sprigs from that tree," he said to the fourth palanquin bearer. "I think you should take this guard with you. There is a mean tempered bull there. So you will need help."

The guard and the remaining palanquin bearer left.

Now all he had to do was to get rid of the remaining guard.

The old man coughed again. "I told you to stop coughing. Have you no sense?" said the guard.

Even as he was ticking off the old man, a woman went up to the old man and said, "I've run out of medicines. Can I have some more of that medicine you gave me?" she asked the old man.

"Here is the physician. You are talking to the wrong person," said the guard.

"Are you mad?" the woman asked the guard angrily. "I've been living in this village for 30 years. Don't I know who the physician is? You are new to this place and so is the man standing next to the palanquin."

Kanchipurathan usually never lost his equipoise even in the most trying circumstances. But when the old man got up and walked towards him, he was nervous.

"Young man, are you trying to compete with me?" the old man asked Kanchipurathan.

"So you're an impostor!" exclaimed the guard and gripped Kanchipurathan's hand tightly, and twisted it behind his back.

"Let go of my hand," said Kanchipurathan, and managed to shake off the man's hold. "Is there a rule that says only a man who is racked by coughs can be a physician? I too am a physician. I used to practise in Chennai."

"Where did you study medicine?" asked the physician.

"In Kanchipuram."

"Who was your teacher?"

"Chokkanatha Pandit."

"You would have been born after he died. So you could never have learnt from him."

The woman who had exposed Kanchipurathan chuckled.

"You packed off some men to fetch sprigs from the tamarind tree. Some have been sent to fetch stones from near the river. What were you planning to steal, after getting everyone out of the way?" the old man asked.

"I too am a physician," said Kanchipurathan.

"Wait," said the old man, and went into his house. He returned with a spoonful of some powder. "Open your mouth. Even a badly trained practitioner of Siddha medicine, will be able to say what powder this is. Now tell me, what was it I put into your mouth?"

Kanchipurathan had no time to think. He had to make a guess. He came up with the name of some medicinal powder he had heard of. He was, of course, wrong.

"Tie him up to that tree. We'll have to hand him over to the village chief," the old man said to one of the guards.

By now the two men sent to fetch sprigs from the tamarind tree were back. The men sent to fetch stones for grinding were also back. They tied him to one of the pillars in the verandah of the physician's house. "This man took us in with his clever acting! But you found out he was an impostor so easily!" said one of them to the physician.

"That was easy. All I put into this rogue's mouth was sacred ash, and he said it was a medicinal powder. Rogue!"

The physician then said to Thamarai, "Let me examine your pulse."

Kanchipurathan realised that he had to be careful in dealing with the situation. "Listen. I was only trying to have some fun. I didn't mean any harm," he said to the physician.

"Having fun? You cannot have fun playing with other people's lives."

Kanchipurathan tried to free himself, but he couldn't.

He turned towards the palanquin. The curtain was moved aside for just a few seconds, and he saw Thamarai. There were tears in the corners of her eyes.

The guard said to the physician, "She is from a very influential family. We have to take good care of her. Unfortunately, she came down with fever and we had to seek help."

The physician admonished the guard and told him to be quiet for some time.

Suddenly a woman came running from inside the physician's house.

"Come on, quick," she said.

"What's the hurry?"

"Come and have a look at our son. He is playing with a gun. And close to him is the baby Jothi. Please come…"

The physician ran into the house. The crowd that had gathered round Kanchipurathan ran into the house too. In just a second, almost everyone had moved away.

Kanchipurathan looked at the palanquin. Thamarai stepped out and ran to him. She untied the ropes.

"I untied you the other day, and now you have untied me," he said.

He noticed that she looked worn out. "Thamarai, what is the matter with you?"

"You pretended to be a physician, but you were found out. I pretended to be sick and I have been successful," she said. "I knew you would come in search of me. I wanted to delay things by pretending to be ill."

"Who are these men and where are they taking you?"

"I don't know. But they treat me like royalty. I don't know why. They treat me as if I were a queen."

"You are a queen enthroned in my heart."

Thamarai wiped the tears from her eyes. "That is all I want. Take me with you. Let's leave now, before they come back."

"Be patient, Thamarai. We can't escape in broad daylight. I'll come up with some plan for us to make good our escape at night."

"But what if they leave this evening, before dark?"

"I won't let them leave. You go back to the palanquin. I will hide somewhere in the village. If they ask you how I managed to escape, tell them I managed to untie the ropes myself and ran away."

As Kanchipurathan slowly left the verandah of the physician's house, where he had been tied to a pillar, he could hear a cacophony of voices from inside the house.

"Please, darling. Drop it."

"No, no. Don't tell him to drop it. He may drop it on the baby."

What was it the boy had? Kanchipurathan decided to find out. He peeped into the house.

The physician's eight year old son was jumping up and down, brandishing a gun! On the floor close to him, was a baby, which was bawling.

The physician's wife begged the boy to drop the gun. "Aren't you a dear boy? Please drop it, and come here."

"No, I will not. I am going to shoot."

The baby continued to scream.

"Let me go. Let me go," shouted the physician's wife. Two men were holding her back.

Everyone kept as far away as possible from the boy. Most of them had never seen a gun and what they had heard about guns filled them with dread.

One of the villagers asked Kanchipurathan. "What is it that the boy has in his hands?"

"That's called a gun. But how did this boy get a gun?"

"The physician's eldest son was in the white man's army. He is no more. When he died, the white men sent this gun to his parents, so that they could keep it in memory of their dead son. Now this boy thinks it is a toy. And he refuses to give it up," said another villager.

"Why is the boy unsteady on his feet?"

"The physician had a vat of country arrack, for his patients. The boy has drunk some arrack from that barrel. It's very strong arrack. Adults get drunk even if they imbibe only a small quantity. Imagine what will happen to a boy who drinks that arrack."

The physician was begging the guards who had accompanied Thamarai to help. But they refused. They said they didn't know how to handle guns, and besides, the boy had his finger on the trigger. What if he should accidentally shoot one of them?

The baby screamed. Kanchipurathan could no longer be a silent spectator. He pushed aside the crowd.

"Hey, you! You cheat! How did you come here?" shouted a guard.

In the batting of an eyelid, Kanchipurathan snatched away the gun from the boy.

The physician's wife came running to him. "You are my saviour. You are God incarnate," she said.

The physician shook his son who was still under the effect of arrack, and asked one of his assistants to give the boy a lot of water to drink.

He turned to Kanchipurathan. "You have saved my family. You are a very clever man."

"The only thing I do not know is medicine," Kanchipurathan laughed.

"You are a very good man. I am sure you pretended to be a physician for some good cause. I am bound to help you. What can I do for you?"

"Thanks a lot," said Kanchipurathan. He looked round. Most of the crowd had dispersed. He whispered something into the phsyician's ears.

♦

The physician went back to the palanquin. One of the guards said "It would help if you could do something soon. It will be difficult to travel after dark. We have to cover a considerable distance."

"Where do you have to go?"

"If we could tell you that, we would. But we are not supposed to. All we can say is this involves an influential person."

"You keep saying that again and again. But you have been careless. She has lung congestion. I will not be responsible if travel at night aggravates it."

"What do you want us to do?"

"Stay here this night and leave tomorrow morning."

"Here?" the two guards asked.

"Don't worry. You won't lack for comforts in my house."

One of the guards asked Thamarai if she didn't mind spending the night there.

Thamarai had been taken aback when the physician had diagnosed lung congestion. When the physician suggested that she spend the night there, she was amused, and since she could guess whose plan it really was, she was pleased.

The physician's wife arrived and took Thamarai into the house.

One of the guards brought her some hot water. He dusted the bed. Another lit some incense sticks. Thamarai was served fruits and milk. When the guards had left, Thamarai heard someone singing! Who was that?

"It's me, Thamarai," said Kanchipurathan. "The guards had forgotten something, and I made sure you had that too."

"What did they forget?"

"To sing a lullaby for you."

Thamarai laughed softly.

"The physician's wife said you had risked your life to save her children."

Kanchipurathan laughed. "Since they didn't know anything about guns, they were scared. It's an old gun. It wouldn't have fired."

"Courage or presence of mind—whatever you want to call it—you have it in ample measure. All right, shall we leave now?"

"Leave through the back door. Keep walking through the street. You will come to a Ganesha temple. Stay there. I will bring a cart and pick you up there."

Kanchipurathan left too, to look for a cart. He came to what seemed like a market. He saw a horse there, saddled and ready to leave. To whom did it belong? He looked round and saw one of the men who had accompanied Thamarai. He was buying sweets in a shop. The horse seemed to be his. But why and where was he going alone on horseback? Kanchipurathan saw a little wooden container tucked under the saddle. It was one of those containers used to keep manuscripts.

To whom was this man taking a message? And in such haste too? It took Kanchipurathan just a second to pull out the container from under the saddle. He quickly made his way to the pyol of a house. He sat down there, and began to read in the light of the lamp there.

To His Royal Highness, the King of Singavaram,

We found the princess and with great difficulty we are bringing her there. We haven't told anyone who she is. We haven't even told her the truth. On the way, we had to halt, because she had fever. The physician felt it would be better if she rested for a couple of days. In two days, we will be there, with the princess.

Princess!

Kanchipurathan read the letter again and again.

His heart felt heavy with sadness.

What a foolish thing he had been about to do!

He walked on, but not in the direction of the Vinayaka temple, but towards the physician's house.

He woke up the other guard who was asleep on the pyol of the physician's house. "The girl you have brought here is trying to escape. She is near the Vinayaka temple," he said to the guard.

The guard ran towards the temple. Kanchipurathan sighed and stared at the room where Thamarai had been housed.

He then began to walk towards Chennai.

♦

And in Singavaram, on an open terrace, close to a watchtower, three restless people paced up and down. They were Raghunatha, Krishnappa and Chennamma.

A guard came down the winding staircase of the watch tower. "Did you see anything?" Raghunatha asked anxiously.

"There is no one either on the road from Chennai or on the road from Trichy," the guard replied, and went back to the tower.

Chennamma was furious. "How foolish you have been!" Chennamma said. "You have revived a dead cobra. You needn't have done that."

"Who are you referring to?"

"Your niece, your brother's daughter, of course. She had disappeared from our lives, and was a slave somewhere. You wanted to finish her off, but your dreams have proved to be nothing more than day dreams."

"Just wait. Wait and watch what happens when she arrives," said Krishnappa.

NINE

The sky began to lighten. It was early morning. Kanchipurathan stretched his limbs. He sat on a load relieving stone.

Something fell on his head. It was a jujube fruit. He looked up. It was a monkey that had thrown it on him. "Why don't you throw some more down for me to eat?" he said to the monkey. The monkey shook down more fruits, as if it understood what he was saying. It seemed to like Kanchipurathan. It jumped down and sat beside him. It seemed to be asking him why he looked sad. "She's gone," Kanchipurathan said. "The woman I was in love with."

The monkey rolled its eyes, as if to say, 'Why did she part from you?'

"She didn't leave me. I came away from her. She is a princess. Is it right for me to seek the hand of a princess?"

The monkey nodded, as if it approved of Kanchipurathan's words. It then jumped on to the tree.

Thamarai's palanquin would be on its way. She had a pleasing personality. Someone would have offered her food.

Kanchipurathan jumped down from the load relieving stone, and began to walk. Where should he go now? To Chennai?

Yes, that's where he should go. He shouldn't break his promise to Peria Pedhu. He looked at the sign board. 'Kanchipuram'—it said. And that's where his mother was. He hesitated for a second. A bullock cart drew up beside him. "Get in, young man," said the driver of the cart.

The cart was stacked high with sacks of rice. A girl was perched on top of the pile of sacks. She laughed and said to Kanchipurathan. "Are you surprised? You are going to Peria Pedhu's house, aren't you?"

Kanchipurathan was taken aback. "Who told you that?"

"Your back." Pat came the reply from the driver of the cart. "Did you think that villagers are not smart enough to know? Get in. This cart is bound for Peria Pedhu's house."

Kanchipurathan clambered into the cart and covered himself with his towel.

The branded letters 'P.P.' could be hidden from view, but they could never be gotten rid of, Kanchipurathan realised.

The girl was chewing a piece of sugarcane. She tapped an old man seated beside her and said, "Grandfather, move over. There is another man getting into the cart."

Kanchipurathan looked at the old man. The old man's face was completely covered with a cloth, leaving just a small slit for his eyes. Why was he keeping his face covered? Kanchipurathan was puzzled.

"A young man going to Chennai? Good." Then he said to his granddaughter. "Thangamma. I am sure we will be able to sell it to this young man."

"He seems to be a good man. Should we get him into trouble?"

Kanchipurathan pretended to be frightened. "Your conversation is so cryptic, it fills me with dread. Let me get down. Stop the cart," he said.

"There is no need to be scared. Grandpa wants to sell something to you."

"What does he want to sell? I am even more frightened now. Anyway, let me see what your grandfather wants to sell."

The cart driver asked, "Has the old man pulled out the sword?"

Kanchipurathan's surprise vanished in a trice. The old man had pulled a sword from beneath the sacks. It was an old, heavy sword, with a beautiful carved handle.

"Will you buy this sword?" asked the old man.

Kanchipurathan picked up the sword. The handle bore the emblem of the Madurai Nayak kings.

"I would like to buy it, but I don't have the money."

"All right. Then just take it. You don't have to pay me anything. I am tired of asking people if they want to buy it."

The girl called out to the cart driver, "Grandpa has decided to bid goodbye to the sword."

"Good. Now no head is in danger," replied the driver.

"Don't be so sure, now that I have the sword. Old man, now that I have a sword, I want to join some army," declared Kanchipurathan.

"No, no. You mustn't entertain such ambitions. About sixty years ago, I would have said that serving in an army was a good idea. Not anymore. Wars then were fought according to rules. What we now see is nothing but savagery. The downslide began when the Mysore Nayak King began the 'nose war.'"

"What is the 'nose war'?" Kanchipurathan asked.

"Wait. I will ask the driver to stop the cart. I will go and sit beside the driver. Grandpa will remove the cloth that covers his face."

The old man said, "Forty years ago, there was a war between the Mysore Nayak king and the Madurai Nayak King. I was in the army of the King of Madurai. War means one side wins, and soldiers from the losing side are captured. That is understandable. But what the Mysore troops did to the captured soldiers was unforgivable..."

"Did they kill them?"

"If only they had. Death wouldn't have been so bad. The soldiers chopped off the nose and upper lip of all the captured soldiers, and sent the chopped parts to the Mysore King. And the Mysore king was happy with what his soldiers were doing. That made the soldiers so happy, that they began to chop off the lip and nose of not just soldiers, but of anyone they came across. Sacks full of noses and lips were sent to the Mysore King. The Mysore Nayak King paid by the nose. A solider would receive payment for every nose he sent. If the moustache above the upper lip was black, then the soldier received more money, because a black moustache meant his victim had been a young man."

"How cruel!"

"Yes, cruel indeed! Some, like me, managed to find herbs, which we used to heal the wounds. But we had to keep our faces covered, because anyone who saw the disfigured faces would be frightened..."

The cart was entering the city of Chennai.

Peria Pedhu was pacing up and down, with his hands behind his back. Occasionally, he twirled the tips of his moustache. The accountant stood there quivering with fear.

"Do you mean to say that that slave girl Thamarai, who escaped, has still not been found?"

"Thamarai...she..."

"You were employed in Kasi Veeranna's company, and you drew a measly salary there. I gave you a post in my business, with a decent salary. Why did you think I did it? Tell me. Why did I hire you for a good salary? So that you would help me expand my business. Not to let my slaves escape."

It was when Pedhu was ticking off the accountant that Kanchipurathan entered.

"This seems to be the season for slaves to run away. I am glad at least you have returned," Pedhu said to him. "Now tell me, has your mission been successful?"

"Sivachidambaram refuses to come."

"You should not have made such a hasty entry into the fort."

"I am sorry. An opportunity presented itself, and I didn't want to miss it."

"But what was the use?"

Deivanayaki entered and cast an enquiring glance at Kanchipurathan.

"What do you want?" Peria Pedhu asked her.

"Madasami tried to punish those at the whipping centre, for letting Thamarai escape. That enraged the people there and about seven or eight of them thrashed him soundly, and he is badly injured."

Madasami was the one who supervised the slaves. He was a eunuch.

"What did he expect?" Pedhu asked. "Did he expect royal treatment such as members of the Beri Chetty caste receive, when they enter the fort during Pongal? Who asked him to create a disturbance at the whipping centre?"

"How can you be so unsympathetic, father? He wants to tell you something."

"I am busy."

"Father, he has been a pillar of strength to you. How can you be so unkind?"

"All right. I will be kind. If he dies, I will give him a decent burial."

"You are cruel, father. He wants to say something to you. Please come and see him, father."

Peria Pedhu left. Deivanayaki signaled to Kanchipurathan that she wanted a few words in private with him.

But Peria Pedhu made a private meeting between the two impossible, because he insisted that Deivanayaki accompany him.

♦

In the garden, a huge crowd had gathered around the peepul tree. Madasami was badly hurt.

The crowd moved aside for Pedhu. Peria Pedhu looked round at the unhygienic surroundings with disgust. One of Pedhu's servants said, "Madasami has been moaning in pain, but he keeps saying every few minutes that he wants to tell you something about Thamarai."

"Find out what it is."

The man shouted loudly into Madasami's ears, "The master is here. What is it you want to say?"

But Madasami didn't utter a word.

"Deivanayaki, you find out what it is," said Pedhu to his daughter.

She bent near the injured man and asked him what he wanted to convey to her father.

"Father, he refuses to tell me. He says he will only convey it to you."

Pedhu had no option but to bend down to hear what Madasami had to say.

"That girl Thamarai—we bought her 17 years ago… in Thanjavur…She is the heir to the Singavaram throne… Her misfortune that she was sold as a slave…Forgive me for not telling you the truth all these years."

What shocking news!

"Take this man to the hospital, and attend to him at once," ordered Pedhu.

He was steeped in thought, as he walked back.

There was a warehouse at the end of the garden. A cart was parked outside it, and rice sacks were being unloaded. Thump. The sacks were being flung down from the cart. Pedhu was furious, when he saw how the men handled the sacks. How dare they throw down the sacks!

"Listen, you fellows. How dare you treat sacks of rice so carelessly? Every grain of rice is like Goddess Mahalakshmi Herself. How many grains have been spilt because of your careless handling?" He looked down angrily to check how much grain had been spilt, when his attention was caught by a palm leaf manuscript.

He picked it up. "Who put this here?" he asked.

"There were so many people who hitched a ride in the cart. How can we tell who dropped it?"

Pedhu didn't listen to the cart driver's explanations. He was absorbed in reading the message on the palm leaf. He read it again and again, *"We found the princess and with great difficulty we are bringing her there. We haven't told anyone who she is. We haven't even told her the truth..."*

Madasami's secret... Thamarai's disappearance... And now this message...

So, was it really a princess who had lived in his house as a slave?

Pedhu was excited. Here was a treasure that he knew he could unlock. But what was the key to it? He had an idea.

"Ask Deivanayaki to come here," he ordered.

"Did you send for me, father?"

"Do you have to amble in so slowly? Are you a queen?" Pedhu asked her angrily.

"Do you have any doubts on that score?" Deivanayaki smiled. "Peria Pedhu's daughter is like the queen of a minor principality, isn't she?" she asked.

Queen!

Pedhu's eyes gleamed, for he now knew what he had to do.

"Accountant, come here. What was the route that this cart took?"

"They came through Vellore."

"Quick. Send two men there on horseback. That slave girl Thamarai is on her way to Singavaram. She must be stopped. And you must do this as soon as possible."

"I will send two men right away."

"Wait a minute. Does Thamarai have any identifying marks?"

"Yes. On her right wrist is a tattoo of a lotus."

"All right. Now bring someone who knows how to do a tattoo."

"Father, what is all this about?" asked Deivanayaki.

"Your luck, my cleverness and the state the country is in— all of these are working together to our advantage." There was a smug look on his face, as he tapped his moustache.

TEN

"I have enslaved the Queen!" laughed Raghunatha.

"Yes, you have," Krishnappa joined in, slapping his thighs in joy. "Yours is indeed a significant achievement, because these days, slaves become queens, not the other way round."

"Talk, talk—that is what you do all the time," grumbled Chennamma. Chess was a game she didn't like. She was sipping a glass of fruit juice. Her eyes were red with anger.

Raghunatha moved the chess board away. He smiled at his daughter. "Criticism, criticism all the time. Chennamma, you mustn't speak against the art of conversation. If you ask me, speech is the only way we can get back at God."

"I don't understand," said Krishnappa.

"God has kept all our other sense organs in open view—our eyes, nose, ears—all of them can be seen. But he has kept the tongue hidden inside the mouth. Isn't that unfair to the tongue? Now it's only by talking that the tongue defies God!"

"True... true!" said Krishnappa. "Do you know who commands the most respect in Tamil Nadu today? It's a woman called Shanta. Many scholars have lost to her in debates. Such is the power of speech."

Chennamma looked out through the window and then said to her father, "Now here is a challenge to your power of speech. You sent two men to look for the lost princess. Only one of them is back. Now let me see how you use your power of speech to explain that."

Krishnappa stood behind Chennamma and looked out. Raghunatha was worried. A man on horseback could be seen riding through the special path intended for those employed at the palace.

"He has a wooden manuscript container in his hands. That means Vel Pandithan has sent us a message."

The man jumped off the horse, and said, "Long live the King! The mission was successful, Your Majesty. Here's the message from Vel Pandithan."

Krishnappa took the container from him. He opened it, and was shocked to find it empty.

"Are you playing a trick on me? Or is this Vel Pandithan's idea of a joke?" the king asked angrily.

"He put it in... It must have fallen out..." the man stuttered in fear.

Raghunatha was the only one who was calm. "Never mind if it is lost. Just tell us what the message contained," he said to the messenger.

Krishnappa intervened, "How can he be so careless with something so important?"

"Yes, it is unforgivable. But we must not concern ourselves with that now. We need to know what the message contained."

The man shot a look of gratitude at Raghunatha. "We found the princess, and we were bringing her here.

But she fell ill. So we were forced to halt in a village near Vellore. She will be here in two days."

Raghunatha darted a meaningful glance at Krishnappa, who understood what he had to do. He launched into another bout of crying. "Have they found my darling? Is she on her way here? Go at once and make arrangements to receive her. Light lamps in the palace. Let musical instruments be played. Let there be special prayers in the temples…"

"The King mustn't be in a hurry," said Raghunatha. "It is better to keep the matter a secret until the princess is safely inside the fort."

"You must escort Vel Pandithan and the princess safely to the fort. Here is a gift for your efforts," said Raghunatha, and flung a strand of pearls at the messenger.

Chennamma was fuming. As soon as the messenger left, she burst out, "He has lost the palm leaf with the message. Who knows whether he is spreading news about the princess' arrival all over the town? He should have been punished for his carelessness. You not only did not punish him, but rewarded him! How stupid!"

Raghunatha smiled. He sent for a soldier. "Are the servants of the palace training for the contests to be held during the festival?"

"Yes. Even now they are training in the Vasantha Mandapam," the solider said.

Chennamma was annoyed. "Why do you ask, father? Is it because you want celebrations for the princess' coronation to begin right away?" she asked.

Raghunatha said to the soldier, "One of the men training in the Vasantha Mandapam, cannot speak. Fetch him."

Now Krishnappa was beginning to lose patience too. "Is this the time for us to celebrate?" he asked angrily.

Raghunatha smiled. The man who couldn't speak arrived. He was hefty. He had a bow in his hand.

Raghunatha patted him on his back. "Are you training well? Can you hit a target from a long distance?"

The man nodded.

"The target may not be stationary. What if it is moving? Can you still hit it?"

The man nodded again.

"All right. Now look there." Raghunatha pointed out through the window. Not just the archer, but Chennamma and Krishnappa also looked out. The messenger on horseback could be seen in the direction in which Raghunatha pointed.

"That is your target. Let me see how good you are," he said to the archer. The archer shot an arrow, and it found its target. The messenger, who had brought the empty container to Raghunatha fell from his horse.

"Brilliant," said three voices in unison.

"I just rewarded that man with a strand of pearls. You are more deserving of such a gift than he. Go and take it from him," said Raghunatha, and the archer smiled. "Vel Pandithan is travelling through the Vellore road. He is bringing a girl to the fort. Bring them through the secret passage to the palace."

What perfect arrangements! Not a single detail was forgotten! Two pairs of eyes looked at Raghunatha in admiration.

♦

The unsuspecting Thamarai went to the Vinayaka temple. After some time a palanquin arrived. "I thought you would fetch a horse. But you have brought a palanquin," she said, as she emerged from the temple.

A shock awaited her. Instead of her dear one, she found the old man who had kidnapped her! It was the same palanquin, and the same palanquin bearers.

"Get in. We have to leave," said Vel Pandithan respectfully.

"He...he..."

"You mean that young man from Chennai? He has returned to Chennai."

Why? Why? Thamarai felt dizzy.

"We have a long distance to cover. Please get into the palanquin," the old man urged.

Thamarai was livid. "I refuse to get into the palanquin. I have no intention of coming anywhere with you," she said.

"If you refuse to come, a life will be lost here," the old man warned.

"You mean my life, don't you? My very life has left for Chennai. All that is left here is this shell – my body," Thamarai said.

"I did not mean your life. I meant my life," said Vel Pandithan. His sword was now near his neck. "If I don't take you to the place where you should be, then I would have failed in my duty. If I fail in my duty, then what is the use of my being alive?"

Thamarai sighed and got into the palanquin. Where was he? Why had he left? He was a master in planning things. If he had left, then there must be a reason for it. He must be biding his time. He would soon come and rescue her. Thamarai took comfort from such thoughts.

Around noon, she heard someone stop the palanquin. That must be Kanchipurathan! She looked out, and had the feeling of getting out of the frying pan only to land in the fire, for the palanquin had been stopped by Peria Pedhu's men! The palanquin bearers were unarmed. They were all killed in a matter of minutes. Vel Pandithan did fight valiantly, but he was vastly outnumbered. He fell down bleeding. There was a look of deep sorrow in his eyes. It seemed as if he wanted to tell Thamarai something. Thamarai was terrified. But she thought of how respectfully the old man had treated her, although he'd known her only for a short period.

She thought of getting down from the palanquin, to be by his side. But the old man breathed his last before she could get down.

"Lift the palanquin," commanded the man in charge of Peria Pedhu's guards.

Thamarai wondered where Vel Pandithan had planned to take her. What was the carefully guarded secret he hadn't told her about?

But even before she could get over her shock at the rapid turn of events, there was another shock in store. She could see some men on horseback coming from the opposite direction. That must be he, her dear one, thought Thamarai. She cheered up, but her hopes were dashed once again, when she saw that he wasn't one of the men attacking Pedhu's men. A fierce fight ensued between Pedhu's men and the newcomers. It was a gory scene, with heads being chopped off. Thamarai fainted.

♦

A cool breeze. The fragrance of wild flowers. Thamarai woke up. She could see a fort on a hill. She was being carried towards it.

Whose fort was it? Had the old man planned to bring her here? What was the connection between her and this palace? She had the answer soon.

"Thamarai, my darling. You're here at last. I can't tell you how happy I am to see you!" King Krishnappa came running towards the palanquin.

Raghunatha signaled to the palanquin bearers to leave.

"Welcome to the palace. You are back after 18 years. May God bless you with long life," he said to Thamarai.

The Queen Chennamma kissed Thamarai's forehead.

Krishnappa explained to Thamarai, "This is your palace. This is your kingdom. These are your people. Fate separated you from us. You are my elder brother's daughter. I have been on this throne all these years. But you are the one who should be seated on this throne. At last you are here and I no longer need to sit on that throne of thorns."

Thamarai was overwhelmed, and didn't know what to say. She looked around. The palace seemed familiar. Perhaps she had been associated with the place in a previous birth, she thought.

"The coronation must be held tomorrow," said Raghunatha.

Two maids from the palace were entrusted with the task of escorting Thamarai to her room.

Krishnappa asked Chennamma to accompany them and attend to Thamarai.

But Chennamma stayed back. She waited until Thamarai was out of earshot. She then burst out against her husband and father, "Son-in-law and father-in-law have gone mad. Such a warm welcome for a girl who should have been killed-, the moment she was found. But you bring her. At least, if you had killed her as soon as she arrived, it would have made sense to me. Why do you allow a poisonous weed to flourish?"

Raghunatha laughed. "Have you seen a cat corner a mouse? Killing someone is easy. That's the job of a butcher. Planning the act of murder is the work of an artist. Go, Chennamma. You too have a role to play in this drama."

♦

Rose water was sprinkled on Thamarai. Sandal paste was rubbed on her body. Two women fanned her with peacock feathers. There were eight mirrors on the wall, which captured Thamarai's beauty from different angles. Gold jewellery and silk clothes were laid out before her. Surprise, joy, amazement – Thamarai experienced a whole gamut of emotions. A slave girl was being treated like a queen. The body that had been whipped was now being pampered with sandal paste and rose water and silks.

Chennamma plaited Thamarai's hair, and decorated the plait with flowers.

"Chennamma, how dare you! You are unwilling to give up your position as the Queen. You do not want to see to my brother's daughter on the throne. I am not surprised. You don't belong to our family. You are no blood relation. That is why you are jealous," Krishnappa shouted at Chennamma...

"I have done nothing wrong," Chennamma said.

"Uncle, she has done nothing wrong. Why do you scold her?" Thamarai interceded on behalf of her aunt Chennamma.

"You keep out of this, darling," said Krishnappa to Thamarai. Turning to Chennamma, he said, "Don't you know the practice to be observed the day before the coronation? What should the queen in waiting wear? Don't you know?"

Thamarai was touched. "Uncle, you don't have to prove your affection for me through adherence to conventions. I was a slave somewhere. You took the trouble to search for me, and you found me..."

"No, no. Please don't remind me of that. I want you to forget your life as a slave. I too want to forget that dark chapter in your life. Get some rest. At midnight, you have to go for a ceremonial bath."

"At midnight?"

"Yes, at midnight. To the South of the palace, is a moat. The water there is called Kasi Theertham. It is customary for the one about to be coronated to have a ceremonial bath there at midnight. After the ceremonial bath, there will be a procession. I've bought excellent Persian horses from the Company for the procession. Now rest for a while."

Krishnappa and Chennamma left Thamarai's room.

Thamarai looked at herself in the mirror. The gem studded necklace gleamed in the light. She playfully gave her ear drops a tweak.

If 'he' saw her now...

Even as Thamarai was admiring her jewellery, in another part of the palace, Chennamma was seething with fury. "That gem studded necklace is so precious, that I haven't worn it even once. And you give it to that slave girl."

"You'll get it back soon. When we take her to Kasi Theertham for her bath, she'll have to take off all her jewels."

"As if a ceremonial bath is necessary for a slave! And what happens after that bath?"

"After that? Nothing happens after that. That will be the last bath in Thamarai's life," laughed Krishnappa.

"Please don't be cryptic. Explain what you mean."

Krishnappa took Chennamma through a secret passage.

"Our moat has been patterned after the Vellore moat. You do know that, don't you? Do you know the significance of what I am saying?"

Krishnappa smiled. He didn't utter another word till they reached the moat.

He clapped his hands. A guard came running. "Lift that goat," he ordered. The guard had a goat in his hands. He held it over the water. The moment its shadow fell on the water, seven huge crocodiles swam towards the shadow, and opened their mouths wide. "Throw it in," commanded Krishnappa. The man obeyed. The crocodiles tore into the goat. In a matter of seconds, nothing of the goat was left, not even its horns.

"This is where Thamarai is going to have her bath," said Krishnappa.

ELEVEN

"Stop daydreaming. Start working."

The supervisor gave Kanchipurathan a shove.

Kanchipurathan hadn't slept for the last few days—he had been searching, grieving. How many things could he put up with? Was his body made of flesh and blood or was it some kind of mechanical contraption? His limbs ached and he craved rest. He was, in fact, looking for a suitable place to rest for a while, but before he could, the supervisor was back.

"You are the one who gave us the slip, saying you were going to fetch a needle. Go and help out there."

Kanchipurathan looked in the direction in which the supervisor pointed.

And what he saw made his blood freeze in horror. A mechanical water lifting device was being operated, but instead of the usual bullocks tied to it, in this case it was a boy who bore the weight of the yoke on his neck.

"What are you staring at? I've decided to rest the ox. You and that lad there have to do duty instead of the beast, till tomorrow morning, when the ox will be back. Go on." The supervisor gave Kanchipurathan a push.

"I will take care of this. You just pretend to be working," Kanchipurathan whispered to the boy. Kanchipurathan placed the yoke on his shoulder and pulled. A potful of water was scooped up. Another pull, and another potful of water was scooped up.

It wasn't very hot yet, because it was forenoon. Peria Pedhu's garden was noisy, with slaves at work. And then Kanchipurathan recalled that it was the day for selling and buying slaves. Some slaves were going to be sold off and were taking tearful farewells of their friends. Some of them were leaving for kingdoms to the South of Chennai. Some were leaving for foreign shores. New slaves had arrived and were trying to make friends at the place.

Suddenly there was a scream.

"No. I will not. Let me go," screamed a man.

Kanchipurathan stopped pulling the water lift. "'What's that?" he asked the supervisor.

"That is the sound of wedding drums being played for your wedding. You dog, how dare you ask questions? Get on with your work," the supervisor said angrily.

Again another scream. Kanchipurathan dropped the yoke and ran to have a look.

A crowd had gathered around the man who was screaming. A vat of oil was boiling over a fire.

"Let me go," screamed the slave, struggling to break free.

A supervisor was holding him. "What is happening?" Kanchipurathan asked.

"Look who's here! A man who questions us!" the supervisor tried to push Kanchipurathan away.

But Kanchipurathan didn't budge. So he decided to answer Kanchipurathan. "All right. So you must know what is happening? This man has been stealing goats and hens and selling them. But he says he has done nothing of the sort."

"And so?"

"I've asked him to stick his hand in a vat of boiling oil. If he is speaking the truth, then the boiling oil will not hurt his hand."

"How just you are! But I have a doubt," said Kanchipurathan.

"What is your doubt?"

"Who is the witness to what this man is supposed to have done?"

"I am the witness. I saw him steal the goat and hens," said the supervisor.

"In that case, we have a solution to the problem," said Kanchipurathan.

"What do you mean?" the supervisor asked.

"You swear that you saw this man steal. So why don't you stick your hand in the boiling oil? If nothing happens to your hand, then that means you are telling the truth, and this man is lying. Go on! Stick your hand in the oil," said Kanchipurathan.

"Yes, yes. This man is right," many approving voices greeted Kanchipurathan's suggestion.

"Shut up, all of you," said the supervisor, and tightened his grip over the slave who was wriggling.

"If you touch him, I will tear you to bits," growled Kanchipurathan.

"What are you all staring at? Bring this man to the master. Let him decide what punishment he deserves," the supervisor shouted.

Four men held on to Kanchipurathan, and took him to Peria Pedhu. "Bring a whip," shouted the supervisor.

When they reached Pedhu's mansion, the supervisor said, "Master, this man is a bad influence on the rest of the slaves…"

But before the supervisor could complete his complaint, he was cut short by Pedhu.

"He's mischievous. That's all. And you have come here to complain about that, you idiot," said Pedhu. "If only you were at least half as hardworking as this man, I would be happy. Now go away, and stop wasting my time," Pedhu said. The supervisor and his men dispersed. "Thank you," Kanchipurathan said to Pedhu.

The accountant arrived and said, "The Governor has sent word from the fort. He has asked you to come there."

"What for?" asked Pedhu, and then read the invitation from the Governor. "The Prince of Sumatra has arrived. There is going to be an official dinner this evening… A welcoming procession… The men of the Company do not welcome anyone, unless they can get something out of him. Now this prince is surely going to lose some of his territory to the Company."

♦

A beautiful pavilion. Polished floor. Pleasant breeze. Flowers that seemed to fall with some hesitation, like poor relatives making a diffident entry into a rich relative's house…

Suddenly, Kanchipurathan felt a constriction around his throat. He woke up with a start. What was the matter? Why was his heart beating so fast? His fingers twitched. His body was drenched in sweat. His heart pounded so much, that he felt it could be heard miles away. He sat up.

"What is wrong with you?" the boy beside him asked.

"I had a nightmare… There is some danger to Thamarai's life…"

"Do you know Thamarai? She is a very nice lady. No harm will befall her," the boy assured Kanchipurathan.

"No. She is definitely in danger. Otherwise I will not feel so agitated."

"When you were asleep, you kept saying 'Crocodiles,'" the boy said.

"Did I say crocodiles? Yes, no doubt about it. Crocodiles. I saw them…"

Pedhu, who had been hiding behind a pillar, slid away quietly.

"Crocodiles..." Kanchipurathan muttered. "I must go and see Thamarai at once."

♦

The 'crocodile' went back to the mansion. His eyes were bloodshot. His moustache twitched in anger.

A gypsy was tattooing Deivanayaki's arm. She had drawn the picture of a lotus on her arm, and was now pricking the outline with needles dipped in dye.

"Ooh," groaned Deivanayaki, in pain. "Father, is it he?"

"Yes, it is he. Their description fits him." Pedhu sent for the accountant. "You can ask the man in charge of the whipping centre and the driver of the cart to leave. We no longer need them. Bring the gardener Mookkan to me."

To his daughter he said, "You go elsewhere and continue with the tattooing. I thought Kanchipurathan could be trusted. But the cart driver tells me that he brought Kanchipurathan here and that he picked him up on the road to Vellore. ... But the important question is— does Kanchipurathan know that Thamarai is the princess of Singavaram? If he does, then he must be killed..."

Mookkan entered and saluted his master.

"Have you fixed the wall of the well in the coconut grove?" Pedhu asked Mookkan.

"No, I haven't. Half the wall has collapsed. If anyone going down the steps touches the wall, it will collapse on him and he will be surely crushed to death," replied Mookkan.

"That's what I want. I have my suspicions about a man. If my suspicions are confirmed, that is what I want you to do to him. Crush him under the wall," said Pedhu.

Pedhu had hardly completed the sentence when Kanchipurathan made his entry into the room.

"Oh, it's you. I was just thinking of you," said Pedhu. He wondered if Kanchipurathan had heard what he had said to Mookkan.

"I have to leave at once. I will be away for two days."

"You have my permission to go," said Pedhu, with a smile. "Oh, by the way, I found this palm leaf with a message on it. I don't know for whom it is intended," Pedhu said, and handed over to Kanchipurathan the letter that had been addressed to Krishnappa.

Pedhu watched Kanchipurathan keenly, when Kanchipurathan took the palm leaf and read it.

"This is mine. I dropped it, and have been looking for it," said Kanchipurathan, tucking the palm leaf into his dhoti. "Let me take leave of you."

"Are you in such a hurry? There's something I want you to do for me."

"What is it?"

Pedhu pointed to the gardener and said, "This idiot here has dropped his spade into the well. Please retrieve it for him, and then you can leave."

Mookkan noticed the signal from Pedhu. Kanchipurathan, in his state of agitation, failed to notice this exchange of glances between the two men.

♦

The procession was moving towards the town. It had been organised by the Governor to welcome the prince of Sumatra. The cannons in the fort fired twenty three times.

Men on horseback led the procession. They held aloft the Company's flag. On one side were all the rich merchants of the city and officers. Peons were on the other side. Elephants with highly ornate decorations followed the horses. Men seated on elephants were playing kettle drums. Trumpeters followed on foot. Behind them came three companies of sepoys.

In a coach drawn by white horses, came the Governer and the Prince of Sumatra. White women came in palanquins. All the prominent citizens of the city were part of the procession—Alangatha Pillai, alderman of the Corporation of Madras, and Nagappan, a merchant who dealt in explosives.

Chinna Venkatadri, who built houses with well laid out gardens and let them out to white men. Merchants Kala Chetti, Soori Appanna, Kannappar; Peria Pedhu; the lawyer of the Company—Gopal Panditar...

But suddenly, the procession stopped. The governor asked his assistant what the matter was, and the assistant asked Pedhu to find out. Pedhu assigned the task to the alderman, who went away to find out and came back with the information that many people had climbed a tree to witness the procession, and that half the tree had broken and fallen on the road. The road was blocked and efforts were underfoot to remove the tree.

But it was taking a long time and everyone was beginning to lose their patience.

At last came the message that the tree had been removed. Nagappan, who had been sent to supervise the operation, returned and said, "Wonders never cease! So many men struggled for so long to get that tree out of the way. And then comes a man, who pushes it aside with ease. What so many men couldn't do, this man was able to do single-handedly!"

"Is that so?" asked Gopal Panditar, in amazement.

The governor conveyed the information to the Prince of Sumatra.

"Isn't it amazing that one man could do what so many couldn't do?" said Soori Appanna to Peria Pedhu.

"Indeed. Who is he?"

"He is one of your slaves."

"My slave?"

"Yes. You have earned the governor's goodwill because of this slave. There he comes," said Soori Appanna, and moved away to talk to the governor.

Pedhu saw someone bringing Kanchipurathan!
"Let me go. I have some work to take care of," Kanchipurathan was protesting.

Peria Pedhu's eyes narrowed.

"You...you... went to the garden with Mookkan."

"I will tell you what happened later. I have to go somewhere now. I am in a hurry."

"Did you not go with Mookkan?"

"Oh yes, I did. Poor old man. He slipped and fell into the well. I jumped in and rescued him. I left him at the physician's house, and then I left your house. On the way I saw this tree blocking the road and I helped to remove it."

The alderman came to Pedhu and said, "The Governor and the Prince of Sumtara want to see this man."

Peria Pedhu was good at masking his emotions. He didn't show his anger, but smiled and went to meet the governor.

The dubash[2] translated for Pedhu, "It appears that rice cultivation was not known in Java and that it was slaves from the Tamil country who taught them rice cultivation."

"Is that so?" said Pedhu.

"The prince says that generally Tamilians are shrewd and hardworking people, and that he is very happy to have met a strong man like your slave."

---

2 *Dubash- someone who knew both English and Tamil. Dubashes were employed by the British as interpreters and translators.*

"I am honoured. Since the prince is so impressed with my slave, I would like to offer him a gift. Ask him if he will accept my gift."

"He says he will gladly accept any gift from you."

"Here, this man—he is my gift to the prince," said Pedhu, pointing to Kanchipurathan. He then turned towards his supervisor and said, "Take this man to the prince's ship. Quick."

TWELVE

Thamarai rested an elbow on the bed and rested her chin on her hand. The soft bed dimpled; where she rested her elbow. Thamarai had never enjoyed such luxury before. But she was here alone. She wished he were there beside her.

She looked at herself in the mirror. "Do not cry, Thamarai. You wouldn't have dreamt that you would one day become a princess. But you have. And one day he too will be yours. The moment you become the queen, instruct your men to find him and bring him. Will they not carry out your command? You mustn't cry..." she told herself.

What was that? Was it someone crying? Yes, it was. No doubt about it. Someone was sobbing. Someone was trying to control her sobs, but couldn't.

Who could it be? In a palace that was like something from heaven, who could be so sorrowful?

Thamarai opened the door. She could see someone there. It was a servant girl.

"Come here," said Thamarai. The girl came running to her. "Why were you crying?"

"I wasn't crying," the girl said.

"I will reward you if you tell me the truth. But I will punish you if you tell me a lie. Now come on, tell me why you were crying."

Tears rolled down the girl's cheeks. Her voice broke. "My husband is dead."

"When did he die?" asked Thamarai.

"A little while ago."

"How?"

"Ask me who was responsible..." the girl wiped the tears from her eyes. "He was a loyal servant. He was one of the most important officials of the king. He and the old man Vel Pandithan were the ones who brought you from Chennai..."

Thamarai remembered the young man the girl was talking about.

"What happened to him?"

"They have killed him. They have killed him!"

"What? Who did it? When? Why?" asked Thamarai, in shock.

"No use talking about it."

"Listen. This is not a kingdom where people can do as they please. I will find out who killed him. I am the queen of this kingdom. I am going to be crowned tomorrow morning."

The girl laughed pathetically. "If your head is still on your shoulder," she said.

"What are you saying?"

"I think I have said too much. Let me go."

She tried to slip away, but Thamarai held her back and said, "Tell me the truth. Please don't keep anything from me."

The serving girl looked at Thamarai sadly. "I do not know the details. But they have not brought you here to make you the queen. Please escape from here as soon as you can."

Thamarai was shocked. "What are you saying? They told me that they were going to make me the queen. What danger can there be to me? Why?"

The servant said nervously, "I have been here talking to you for too long. There is a secret passage that leads out from here. Let me see if the coast is clear."

She stepped out and let out a scream. Raghunatha had her firmly by the hand. "Let her go," commanded Thamarai.

"My respects to you, Queen. It is my duty to punish traitors."

"It is for me, the queen, to punish. It is not your job."

Raghunatha let the girl go, and she ran as fast as she could. Poor girl! She didn't know that Raghunatha had already signaled to a guard who was at the end of the corridor. He was waiting for the servant girl.

"The Queen is very kind hearted," Raghunatha said to Thamarai.

Thamarai was furious. "Yes, since there seems to be no one in this palace who knows what kindness means, it is just as well that I have brought some kindness into this palace."

"When the Queen's kindness is followed by wrath, I am reminded of a blue sky illumined by a bolt of lightning."

He noticed that she was wearing silks and jewels. "It would help if you removed all your jewels and got ready for the ceremonial bath."

"I need explanations," said Thamarai.

"All right. I will give you explanations. We have the whole night before us. The coronation is only tomorrow morning. I will give you explanations till then," said Raghunatha, and sat down in Thamarai's room.

♦

King Krishnappa and his Queen Chennamma were in a happy mood. She was resting her feet on his lap, and he was popping pomegranate seeds into her mouth. One of them slipped from his hands and landed in a bowl of milk. "You are adept at letting things slip away," Chennamma teased.

"What are you referring to?" he asked.

"You showed me the moat and the crocodiles. But is that enough?"

"What haven't I done?"

"It is almost midnight. Something tells me Thamarai will slip away."

"I might let her slip away. But your father is more careful."

"My father?"

"Yes, look there."

Chennamma looked out through the window. She could see Raghunatha escorting Thamarai to the moat. "What a relief! Our prayers have been answered. If father is in charge, then we can take it for granted that the mission will be accomplished."

"And now, it's time for us to make the most of the night, as the Delhi kings do," Krishnappa said and gave her a tight embrace.

Chennamma smiled. "What's so special about the Delhi kings?"

"Come here," said Krishnappa, and took her to the terrace. "The Delhi kings enjoy the moonlight and the beauty of the Taj Mahal. We have no Taj here. But there is the moon... And look. Can you see the moat? Raghunatha is there. Can you see him there?"

"Yes, I can. My God, how many crocodiles. How frightening!" Chennamma hugged her husband.

"You don't have to look. I will describe the scene for you. There are four crocodiles swimming towards her. They are tearing her to bits. What terrifying teeth they have! What huge jaws! Our enemy has been torn to pieces. Can you hear her screams?" Krishnappa laughed. He was overjoyed.

♦

"**V**ery well, Payria-pedhu!"

The governor who was in his coach praised Pedhu. The prince conveyed his thanks to Pedhu for such a thoughtful gift to the Prince of Sumatra.

Kanchipurathan realised the trick Pedhu had played on him.

He bent before the prince, and touched the prince's sword. He shed copious tears and said, "How blessed I am to be your slave! What do you want me to do for you?"

Through the dubash the prince conveyed that he wanted strong men like Kanchipurathan to be by his side in Sumatra. He asked Kanchipurathan to go to the ship.

Kanchipurathan displayed no emotion. He turned to Pedhu. He fell at his feet and sought his blessings. "I will never forget that you looked after this slave well," he said to Pedhu.

Pedhu could not tell if Kanchipurathan was faking it, or whether he was sincere. "Do well in the country to which you are going. Bring credit to Tamil Nadu," he said to Kanchipurathan.

Kanchipurathan walked with the supervisor to the seashore. A masoola boat was waiting there. Kanchipurathan was surprised to find that there were already five or six slaves there! The supervisor explained that Pedhu hadn't done anything unusual. It was customary to gift slaves to visiting dignitaries.

"Who gifted these other slaves?" Kanchipurathan asked.

"Thimmappa Nayak and Angappa Nayak, who have been asking the company to make them administrative chiefs, gifted these slaves to the company and the company has in turn gifted the slaves to the prince of Sumatra. Now get into the boat."

When Kanchipurathan stepped into the boat, one of the men on the boat said, "Welcome, welcome. Kannayiram, do you know who this man is? If the trunks of European women were to fall into the water, he will retrieve them. He is the right hand man of officials of the Company."

Kanchipurathan bit his lip. These were the men whose enmity he had earned on his first day in Chennai. "Take this man to the ship too," said the supervisor and left.

"So, our hero is going to cross the sea to a foreign country. How blessed is my boat."

The boat began to move towards the ship anchored some distance away. "Kannayiram. You shouldn't row the boat. Hand over the oars to our hero. He should be the one to row," said the boatman to his friend Kannayiram. He gave his oar to Kanchipurathan and Kannayiram gave his oar to another slave.

Kanchipurathan rowed silently. The coast began to recede. They were getting closer to the ship. Kanchipurathan made eye contact with the other slaves, and their eyes exchanged a hundred messages in a trice. The other slaves knew what Kanchipurathan wanted them to do. They thwacked the boatman and his friend with the oars, and dumped them into the sea. The two men struggled to get a grip on the boat. "Quick, start rowing," Kanchipurathan shouted. Two slaves plied the oars. Other slaves used their hands as oars. The boatman and his friend couldn't catch up with the boat.

An old slave said, "Young man, what is the use of setting us free? The moment we land on shore, we will be captured again."

"That is only if you land on the shore here. Steer the boat towards the South. We mustn't mind hunger or thirst. We mustn't fear storms or rains," said Kanchipurathan.

On the third day, a European ship gave chase and caught up with them. But they didn't capture Kanchipurathan or the others in the boat. "They are pirates. They will not attack paupers like us," explained one of the slaves.

"They have been captured and branded as pirates. I saw the letter 'P' branded on their foreheads. That means they are pirates."

Three days and three nights were spent on the boat. Kanchipurathan's arms felt weak and tired. The pain in his back was unbearable. Three of the slaves were so hungry and thirsty, that they could no longer sit up. "If we had been slaves, we would at least have been given something to eat. I wish we hadn't paid attention to you," complained one of the slaves.

"Look – land!" one of the slaves shouted.

Yes, they could see land. The men's spirits revived. They took turns to ply the oars. When land was still a few feet away, Kanchipurathan jumped into the water and swam ashore.

He asked a fisherman, "What place is this?"

"Cuddalore."

Kanchipurathan smiled. "How do we go to Singavaram from here?"

The man gave him directions. Kanchipurathan walked towards Singavaram. He reached Singavaram and the path that led to the moat in Singavaram. He looked down, and what he saw there made his blood freeze in horror, for floating in the water that swarmed with crocodiles were clothes— Thamarai's clothes!

THIRTEEN

Kanchipurathan was speechless with horror. Were those Thamarai's clothes? They did look like her clothes. But something told him she wasn't dead. But how was he to find out?

On the other side of the moat was a tent that housed the guards. He clapped his hands to draw their attention. But no one seemed to have heard. "Is anyone there?" he called out. He wondered how he could attract their attention. He broke off a branch from a tree nearby. He sharpened one end of it. He then threw it across the moat like a javelin. It pierced the tent. "Who did that? Who dared to do that?" asked a guard who came out of the tent.

"Forgive me," said Kanchipurathan deferentially. "Can you tell me if a girl slipped and fell into the water here?"

"No one slips and falls into the water. They are pushed in. Just as thieves are punished in Vellore."

"Was anyone pushed into the water recently? A girl perhaps?"

"I do not know. But I can help you find out, if you wish."

"What should I do?" The guard's words revived Kanchipurathan's flagging spirits.

The guard laughed. "The King's father-in-law Raghunatha is the only one who has the authority to order that someone should be pushed into the water here. Go and ask him. He will push you too into the water, and you can join that girl you are so worried about."

If the guard had been within reach of Kanchipurathan, he would be dead by now, for Kanchipurathan wouldn't have spared him. But the moat and the crocodiles in the water saved him.

Who was Raghunatha? And how was Kanchipurathan to enter the place? Kanchipurathan had to find out.

He went into the town and made enquiries. He was told that there was to be a festival the next day, and that he would get many opportunities to get into the palace then.

It was dark. Kanchipurathan was tired. He lay down in a Kali temple. Devotees came there to worship. The temple bell was rung. But Kanchipurathan was unaware of any of this. He had fallen into deep slumber.

When the din subsided, an old woman began to wail, and Kanchipurathan woke up with a start.

"Goddess Kali! I do not know how to cure my son's fever or his obstinacy. Please show me a way, Divine Mother!"

Kanchipurathan rubbed his eyes. He could see an old woman lighting a lamp and then genuflecting before it.

Kanchipurathan threw his voice, so that it seemed as if the words came from the sanctum sanctorum, and said, "Old lady. Go home now. A young man will soon visit you. He will get rid of your worries."

The old lady thought it was a divine command that she had heard. She prostrated before the lamp she had lit, and ran back home. Kanchipurathan followed her silently.

She entered a small tiled house. Kanchipurathan could hear her pleading with someone, "Listen! You are in no condition to go anywhere. Please listen to me."

"No, I have to go, mother. I do not want to give up the hereditary right our family has."

"Grandmother," called out Kanchipurathan.

The old lady came out to see who it was. Kanchipurathan fell at her feet. "What an unbelievable thing happened today! I was asleep on the bank of the river. I felt as if someone was waking me up and directing me to your house."

The old lady looked pleased. "I knew you would come. Come on in."

As soon as Kanchipurathan entered the house, he realised that it was the house of a nagaswaram exponent.

A man was seated on a mat, and he was holding a nagaswaram in his hands. It was obvious that he had been ill for a long time. He looked emaciated, and hadn't shaven for many days.

"This is my son, Rathnavelu. He insists that he will go to the festival that is to take place tomorrow. He has been ill for more than a month. Can he play this instrument? You tell me if he can, young man," the old lady said to Kanchipurathan.

"An artiste knows no illness, grandma," said Kanchipurathan, and sat beside the nagaswaram artiste. "You cannot impose restrictions on artistes."

"You're absolutely right," said the artiste, approvingly. "And it's not just a question of the art. It's also a matter of family honour."

"Then you should not be stopped."

"Get up," said the old lady to Kanchipurathan. "Is this your idea of helping me? Get out."

Kanchipurathan laughed, and took the nagaswaram from Rathnavelu's hands. "What is your problem, grandma?"

"This is the problem," she said, pointing to the nagaswaram. "When the king comes to the court hall, during the festival, it is customary for someone from our family to play the nagaswaram. This year, my son Rathnavelu has fallen ill. But he insists that he will go to the festival."

Rathnavelu said, "How can I be indifferent when family honour is involved?"

"You are right," said Kanchipurathan, as he picked up the nagaswaram. Here was a way for him to gain entry into the palace. "Grandma, will you adopt me as your elder sister's son?"

"What are you suggesting?"

"Just tell people I am your sister's son." Kanchipurathan smiled. "I will go to the palace tomorrow. I will play instead of your son. I am not an accomplished player…"

Rathnavelu said enthusiastically, "It is enough if you hold the instrument, young man. I am anxious that our hereditary right should not be lost. That's all."

They heard the sound of approaching footsteps. The old lady went out to have a look.

"It is the thavil player—Suruli Muthu. Come on in Muthu."

The thavil player asked Rathnavelu if he felt better. The boy who was to play the cymbals also came in.

"Grandma, everyone says there are going to be a lot of surprises at the festival this year."

"What is this boy talking about?"

"Is there anyone as good as our king? He has a rough exterior. But he has a heart of gold," said the thavil player.

"Go on. Tell me what you heard."

"Krishnappa had an elder brother, and a niece. You do know that, don't you?"

"They died when an elephant tossed them down."

"Krishnappa's brother and sister-in-law died in the accident, but their daughter Thamarai survived."

"Thamarai?" Kanchipurathan forgot himself for a minute and shouted out.

The Thavil player continued, "Wait... There is more news that is shocking. The princess who survived that accident was a slave in the house of a rich man in Chennai. The king came to know of this only recently. He at once made arrangements to bring her here."

"And what is he going to do?"

"He is going to make her the queen. How magnanimous our king is!"

"No doubt about it. He is indeed magnanimous. Had anyone else been in his position, would they have been willing to let go of the kingdom? Is the princess here?"

"I do not know. But that's the latest buzz in town. The people are anxious to see their princess."

Kanchipurathan was reeling under the effect of a series of shocks.

Thamarai had been brought secretly to Singavaram. How then did everyone get to know of her presence there? And if indeed it was Thamarai who had perished in the moat, then what would the king tell the people of the country?

He would have answers to his questions, only if he met Raghunatha.

Kanchipurathan had been in the boat for three days and had no idea about what had happened in the interim. He had to meet Raghunatha.

♦

When Peria Pedhu returned home after attending the Company's procession to welcome the Prince of Sumatra, he ordered that sweet porridge should be made the next day and served to all the slaves.

Deivanayaki was surprised. "Have you already come into possession of that kingdom?"

"I have packed off my enemy to another country. I no longer need to fear anyone," said Pedhu.

"He knows how to trick even Yama, the God of death. I am sure he will surface somewhere."

"Impossible," said Pedhu, and examined the tattoo on Deivanayaki's arm. "The gypsy has done a good job. Did she rub the juice of herbs on it to make it look like an old tattoo?"

"Yes."

Pedhu was pleased. He then went to the hospital where Madasami was being treated.

Madasami brought his palms together in supplication, and expressed his gratitude to Pedhu for saving his life.

"You have a chance to show me your gratitude," said Pedhu, and signaled to the others to leave.

"The girl we bought in Srirangam was not Thamarai, but Deivanayaki. Is that clear?"

"But the Singavaram princess…"

"The Singavaram princess is Deivanayaki. You will have to say that when the need arises."

The spy who had been sent to Singavaram returned the next morning.

"Thamarai was taken there so that she could be killed," he said to Pedhu.

"And?"

"Krishnappa, the King, entrusted the task of getting rid of Thamarai to his father-in-law, Raghunatha. Raghunatha pushed her into a moat full of crocodiles."

"So Krishnappa has got rid of the real heir to the throne. Very good. You will have to send ten men to Singavaram. They should be good at spreading rumours and they should be clever in propaganda."

"What should they do?"

"I will explain to them myself."

♦

The bazaar in Singavaram. "Why is rice selling for so much?" asked a man.

"The yield from our fields has been poor this year," replied the shopkeeper.

"This year the monsoon will not fail. Wait and see. When a righteous king is in power, can the rains fail? Is there a king to equal our king? He searched for and found his brother's daughter and is going to make her the queen."

"This is news to me," said the shopkeeper.

"That is what I heard. What happened was…"

♦

A blacksmith's workshop in Singavaram.

A solider was getting his sword sharpened. "Are you planning to go to Senji to fight?" asked the blacksmith.

"Why should I go to Senji to fight? Our king Krishnappa is an upright man, and when one is so upright, can trouble be far away? Someone will come and make trouble for him, I am sure."

♦

A flower seller's shop in Singavaram. "I want a beautiful garland. I don't care how much it costs."

"Please wait. I will have one ready for you in a few minutes. Are you taking it to the festival?"

"Yes, yes."

"Is it for the king? I will make a lovely garland."

The man looked around to make sure there was no one else there. He then lowered his voice and said, "Not for the king. It is for the queen. Haven't you heard? We are going to have a new queen. She is going to be crowned ruler of Singavaram. This garland is for her."

"This is news to me."

"The whole town is talking about this. How could you not have heard?"

Peria Pedhu's men were doing their job well.

♦

The procession began. The King's retinue moved towards the court hall. Krishnappa asked his queen, "Where is your father? I haven't seen him for the last two or three days. And no one has been allowed into his quarters."

"Maybe he is unwell. He would have been here otherwise."

Long live the King!

Long live the King who never swerves from the path of righteousness!

The shouts of the people rent the air. Flowers were showered on the King. Garlands were placed around his neck. King Krishnappa and his queen Chennamma basked in the adulation of the people.

No one noticed the young nagaswaram player slip into the palace.

Long live Raghunatha!

Long live King Krishnappa!

Suddenly, someone shouted, "Long live princess Thamarai!"

And several voices joined in.

Krishnappa was shocked. Chennamma turned pale.

"Long live our new queen! Long live the king's sense of justice!"

"What is happening?" asked Krishnappa calmly, concealing his emotions.

An old man came forward and said, "You must forgive us. You tried to keep your goodness concealed, because of your modesty. But how long can you keep your goodness hidden? We have come to know of what you have done. We know that you have found your brother's daughter and that you want her to be the queen."

"It is true that I found my brother's daughter. It is also true that I tried to bring her here. But she… the true heir…"

The king faltered.

And that was when a voice was heard which announced, "Here is the true heir!"

It was Peria Pedhu. He held Deivanayaki by the hand and brought her before Krishnappa.

FOURTEEN

An ant couldn't have moved more slowly than Kanchipurathan. A snake couldn't have slithered more silently. Kanchipurathan made an unobtrusive and quiet entry into the palace. There was no one in the palace. Everyone must have left for the festival. But occasionally, a guard or a servant would surface, and Kanchipurathan would then duck behind a pillar or hide in a corridor.

His face was scratched by plants. He was bruised by pillars he collided with. The twilight hours had helped him make his entry into the palace unobserved. But now the darkness was proving to be a disadvantage. Now that it was dark, fireworks were being let off, and they illumined even dark corners of the palace. Even an ant or fly would be visible in the glare of the fireworks.

Kanchipurathan quickened his stride, and walked through what seemed like endless corridors and halls.

Which was Raghunatha's room? Whom should he ask?

"Come here. Give us a hand! Help, please! Come on!"

The moment he heard voices, Kanchipurathan began to look for a place to hide. He was now in the palace garden. To his right was a pond with water lilies in it. In the middle of it was a fountain.

Kanchipurathan lay down, and rolled silently into the pond. All he could hear were the words, "Help!"

The pond was deep. He held his breath and stayed under water. Several seconds later, he thought he would come up for breath, and then duck again. He raised his head.

He could see someone standing on the edge of the pond. The man laughed. "So you think death is preferable to helping the cook!"

So this was a cook! But who had called out for help?

"I was having my bath," said Kanchipurathan.

"If Raghunatha had seen you, this would have been your last bath."

"Raghunatha? He..."

"There is no time to talk now. I need help. Give me a hand," said the cook, pointing to a huge vessel full of sambar.

So this was why he had been asking someone to give him a hand!

"I have to take this vessel there," said the cook, pointing to a place some distance away.

"Is it for a feast?"

"Yes. Today is the day when food is served to the poor people of the town. Everything else was ready a long time ago. The sambar took time." Kanchipurathan and the cook picked up the vessel and made their way towards the pavilion.

There was a jostling crowd outside the pavilion. Some of the cook's assistants were cleaning vessels.

"This way, this way," said the cook to Kanchipurathan. "Why are you pulling in that direction? That's where the sewer is."

Suddenly Kanchipurathan dropped the vessel, and tipped the vessel over. All the sambar emptied out! "You did that on purpose! Why did you do that?" shouted the cook.

Kanchipurathan picked up something from the spilt sambar and showed it to the cook. It was a cobra!

"It must have fallen into the boiling sambar. I noticed it when you asked me to give you a hand with the vessel," said Kanchipurathan.

The cook fell at his feet. "You have saved my life, and the lives of countless poor people. How can I ever repay you?"

"By showing me where I can find Raghunatha," replied Kanchipurathan, without hesitation.

"Please keep your distance from him. He is a wolf."

"And I am here to defang him."

"He is cunning. He is a trickster. He is always up to some trick or other. Even now…"

"Even now?"

"He hasn't come out of his quarters for the last few days. He doesn't allow anyone inside, not even the man who takes his food to him. Shouldn't he have accompanied the King and Queen to the festival? But he has not."

"Tell me how to get to his room."

"Do you see that verandah there? Outside the third door on your right, you will find guards in red colour uniform. Outside the room you will find a lamp covered by a red lampshade. Red is Raghunatha's favourite colour."

Good. And if there is anything that isn't red, I will turn it red by covering it with his blood, Kanchipurathan said to himself.

Kanchipurathan had no difficulty locating the room the cook had described.

He could see a guard outside the room. He stayed in the shadows and snapped his fingers. "Who is it?" asked the guard and came towards Kanchipurathan to explore. Kanchipurathan pounced on him, and knocked him out.

♦

Kanchipurathan quickly put on the guard's red uniform and just when he was done, Raghunatha emerged from his room. He slammed the door to his room. "Everyone will be waiting for me at the festival. Or else I would have..."

Kanchipurathan ground his teeth.

After Raghunatha had left, Kanchipurathan knocked on the door and called softly, "Anyone in there?"

No response. He found a ventilator. What if he threw something inside? It shouldn't be too heavy. It shouldn't be something that would make a noisy landing. What should he throw into the room? He tore a few silk curtains, rolled them into a ball and tried to fling them into the room. But the ball of cloth got stuck in the ventilator and didn't drop into the room. But something unexpected happened. One of the fireworks that had been set off, landed on the ventilator and the ball of silk caught fire, and the burning ball of silk fell into the room.

Kanchipurathan heard a woman scream!

◆

In the court hall, the sounds of celebration rent the air.

Deivanayaki did look regal. The moment the people saw her, they were convinced she was of royal birth.

They shouted with joy!

"Stop! Stop!" thundered Krishnappa. His eyes were red with anger. "If someone claims she is the heir to the throne, will you believe her at once? This woman here is an impostor!"

"If this is not the heir to the throne, if this is not Thamarai, then where is the real Thamarai? Can you tell us?" asked Peria Pedhu.

An old man said, "Your Majesty, when we heard that you had brought the Princess back, we all rejoiced…"

"Shut up!" shouted Krishnappa.

Peria Pedhu smiled. "My, my! The king loses his temper so easily!"

"I hate liars."

"So what will you do when you look into the mirror?" Pedhu gave him a contemptuous smile. "Let me make one thing clear. I have proof that she was sold in Srirangam and that I bought her. You can also see the lotus tattoo on her arm. The moment I saw it, I knew she was from a royal family. That is why I brought her up like a princess. I wasn't prepared to lose my adopted daughter. Not even if a throne was offered to her. That was why I didn't lay claim to the throne on her behalf. But recently, I learnt that you wanted to give up the throne and that the people were anxious to see their princess made queen. That is why I have brought her here. It's not as if this kingdom of Singavaram is going to mean much to her. She has lived a luxurious life. I have friends in the Company. It won't be difficult for my adopted daughter to ascend the throne of Singavaram. If the people of Singavaram say that they do not want to see Thamarai on the throne, we will leave."

Krishnappa addressed the people, "My dear friends! You do not know the truth. I know that you all have great regard for Thamarai. But this girl here is not Thamarai."

"If that is so, where is the real Thamarai?"

"Unfortunately, she slipped and fell into the moat and was killed by the crocodiles."

"No, Thamarai is not dead. She is alive and well in our palace," said a voice. It was Raghunatha!

FIFTEEN

Kanchipurathan could wait no longer, for he could tell that it was Thamarai who had screamed. "Thamarai, don't worry. It's me. I am here. I will save you," he said.

She was alive. The flames seemed to dance madly. The swirling flames looked like snakes searching desperately for prey.

From a distance came the sounds of revelry.

Kanchipurathan pushed against the door. The guard's uniform was a hindrance. So he shed it, and pushed with his bare shoulders. The brass decorations on the door tore into his flesh. The bells on the door jangled, and seemed to mock his efforts. Blood gushed from his many wounds, as if it wanted to be witness to his courage.

The door opened. But he could see nothing, because of the smoke.

"Thamarai, where are you?"

No reply.

"Thamarai, Thamarai," Kanchipurathan's breath came in gasps. He groped his way into the room. He stumbled over someone. "Thamarai?" He hugged her to his chest. Falling debirs blocked the door he had come through. He could no longer make his exit through that door. He found a staircase.

Fire, fire. Bring some sand. Fetch water!

He could hear agitated voices outside.

Kanchipurathan hesitated for a second. Here was help at hand.

But was it help that had come his way? No, it would only put his beloved Thamarai's life in danger.

He ran up the stairs to have a look. The stairs led to an open terrace. He ran up to the parapet wall and looked down. There was a thick bed of grass in the garden outside. He wouldn't get hurt if he landed on it.

He ran back, and tried to revive Thamarai. But it was no use. He was relieved to find that she had no burn injuries. He picked her up, ran up the stairs, went on to the terrace, and jumped on to the bed of grass. He saw a pond some distance away. All he had to do was to sprinkle some water on her face, and she would come out of the faint. But when he was scooping up water, he heard voices. "Here she is," said someone. Thamarai had been spotted. A crowd of people ran towards her. "Out of the way. Move. The king is here." So that was Krishnappa? And the woman beside him must be Chennamma. And the old man there must be Raghunatha, the rogue.

Thamarai had now come out of the faint. But she still felt dizzy. A maid held her, so that she wouldn't fall.

The king, queen and the others in the royal entourage moved, and behind them walked Thamarai.

Where were they going? And why?

Kanchipurathan followed discreetly.

The fire had been put out. But the acrid smell of smoke still hung in the air.

When Kanchipurathan melted into the crowd near the court hall, Raghunatha was saying, "Here she is—princess Thamarai. This is Thamarai."

"Proof?"

The challenging voice sounded familiar to Kanchipurathan. It couldn't be… But it was! It was Peria Pedhu, with his daughter Deivanayaki.

"Let me repeat. This girl called Deivanayaki, who grew up as my daughter, is the heir to the throne of Singavaram. Madasami, come here and tell the people what you know."

Madasami said, "We'd been to Srirangam to buy slaves. The slave merchant said that the king and queen of Singavaram had been thrown off by an elephant, but that the princess, despite being thrown off too, had escaped. He said that no one had noticed that the girl was alive. Upon coming to know that Thamarai was a princess, my master brought her up like a princess."

Kanchipurathan knew that Peria Pedhu would not take risks if the stakes were not high. The king of Singavaram and Raghunatha were both traitors. They had brought Thamarai here to kill her. Kanchipurathan thought he should offer his support to Pedhu, but he stopped when he heard Pedhu's words. "One of my slaves knew how much I loved my foster daughter. She was seriously ill recently, and physicians gave up hope. I was about to consume poison and end my life. Unfortunately, that slave isn't here to testify on my behalf. He is in Sumatra."

Kanchipurathan stepped back. Peria Pedhu was lying. But the question was, why was he lying?

Raghunatha shot a contemptuous smile at Madasami. "What proof can you offer to establish that this girl is Thamarai?"

"Good question!" the crowd approved of Raghuntha's query. The crowd was more impressed by Thamarai, who was simply attired, than by gaudily dressed Deivanayaki.

"I will answer you. What is the royal emblem of Singavaram? The lotus. Your flag bears the lotus symbol. The king's royal insignia – a lotus—can be seen on his ring. And what do you see here— tattooed on Thamarai's arm? A lotus."

"Yes. A lotus. A lotus." The crowd echoed.

Raghunatha gave a confident laugh.

"This man from Chennai is absolutely right. Here is the flag of Singavaram. You can see a picture of a lotus there. Here is the Queen's royal ring—yes that too has a lotus motif on it. True. But..." He paused for dramatic effect, and then continued. "But as you can see, it's not just a lotus that you find there, but also two leaves. Not just one leaf, but two." He then lifted Thamarai's arm. "Now look at this girl's hand. You can see a tattoo of a lotus flower and two leaves too. Have a look at the girl who has come from Chennai as a rival claimant to the throne. Do you see two leaves on her arm? Please have a look and tell me. I am shortsighted..."

"No, no. We see only one leaf on this girl's hand. Impostor. Cheat," the people shouted.

A general came forward with his sword drawn. "They must be punished..."

"No, no. Let the impostor and her father stay in our palace as our guests and witness the coronation of the real princess. Make arrangements for their stay," ordered Raghunatha.

Peria Pedhu's body shook with rage and shame. Deivanayaki had turned red with shame.

"I will come to the coronation. Not to witness it, but to claim my slave. You will find that this girl Thamarai is branded with the initials 'P.P.'. That is to indicate she is my slave. I will come as her master and take her back. She will always be my slave. Keep that in mind," said Pedhu.

The crowd was furious.

Shut up!

Cut out his tongue!

Brand him and make him a slave!

Suddenly, a bunch of gold coins was tossed before Pedhu. "Take them," said a citizen of Singavaram. "Take the money. But don't dare touch our princess."

"Yes, yes. Here's a coin from me too," said several voices, and more and more gold coins landed at

Pedhu's feet. "Pick them up and go," growled the people.

Deivanayaki was terrified. "Father, please let us go. Please."

Pedhu had no option but to leave. "You have the strength of numbers on your side today. So I am unable to oppose you. But I will return with the Company's cannons. Let me see whether you oppose me when I return."

His words were met with boos from the people.

Raghunatha addressed the people. "We had anticipated that there would be such problems. That is why we had spread the rumour that the princess had slipped into the moat and had been eaten by crocodiles. Now that there is no longer any danger to the Princess' life, we will soon have the coronation. Astrologers will soon fix a suitable date for the coronation."

Long live Raghunatha!

Long live the royal family of Singavaram!

Long live our princess!

Kanchipurathan, who stood watching the quick turn of events, bit his lip.

♦

Thamarai was on her bed.

"Do not be afraid. I've asked men to stand guard over your room," said Raghunatha.

What strange experiences she had had! She was happy. But where was he? Where was the one who had told her not to be afraid?

She had hundreds of questions, and only he could answer them.

A serving girl entered with a plate of fruits and some milk.

Thamarai said, "Please do not disturb me. I don't want anything to eat."

"Not even when *I* have brought the food?"

"Who is this?" Thamarai was shedding tears of joy.

The 'maid' moved her veil aside, and there was Kanchipurathan! "I was afraid that your new found status would keep you from recognising old friends," he said.

"Do not say that," she covered his lips with her slender fingers. "Whatever luxuries come my way, I will never forget that they were made possible only because of your sacrifices."

"You are going to be a queen. When you pass through the streets in your palanquin, I will be one of the many standing by cheering their queen."

Thamaari jumped up. "How can you say that? If you do not want me to be the queen, you just have to say so. I will come with you this minute."

"No, no, princess…"

"Do you have to address me formally?"

"What kind of a man is Raghunatha?"

"He is a very good man. He is the one who saved me from the king's cunning plan to eliminate me. Raghunatha hid me in his room for three days, without the knowledge of his daughter and son-in-law. 'Let them be under the impression that you are dead. At the right time, I will reveal that you are very much alive,' he said to me. And a lot has happened since…"

"Let me take leave of you…"

Thamarai gripped his hand and wouldn't let go. "Please do not leave me alone. I am gullible. I need your guidance, your protection."

(Kanchipurathan melted.)

"I know, I know. I understand," said Krishnappa to Raghunatha. Pointing to Chennamma, he said, "Your daughter may not have understood her father's motives. But I know you always keep our welfare in mind."

"Did you hear that, Chennamma?" said Raghunatha.

But Chennamma was not convinced. "I told you repeatedly that you were inviting trouble. I will not accept any explanations from either of you."

"What next?" asked Krishnappa.

"As we have announced before the people—we must have the coronation," said Raghunatha.

"What?" Krishnappa said agitatedly.

"See? See? What did I tell you?" Chennamma joined in.

Raghunatha smiled. "There are two ways to defeat your enemy. One is to get rid of him. The other is to keep him on your side. We failed in our attempt to get rid of her. So I am resorting to the second way."

Chennamma said furiously, "So are you suggesting that that wretched girl should become the ruler, and we should be her servants?"

"My child, let her be the queen. But she will be queen only in name. We will be the people who wield power. She will be a mere puppet."

Krishnappa gave a dejected laugh. "I am not sure it will be that way. I have a strong feeling that the strings of that puppet are not in your hands, but in someone else's...." He stopped, and ran to the window. "Who is it?" he called out.

"What is the matter?" asked Raghunatha.

"I had a feeling someone was peeping into the room."

SIXTEEN

"This one is no good. This looks good, but isn't valuable. Ah! This is lovely. These gems aren't well set. Have the gems reset."

The jeweller had displayed all the jewels he had brought. Krishnappa and Chennamma were seated on a carpet, and were inspecting the jewellery.

Raghunatha was reclining on a cot, and had a glass of wine in his hands. He looked at his reflection in the wine. His nerves were taut with excitement. He sighed. His face reflected his lust. The pictures on the walls took on an erotic hue in his imagination.

"Father, does this look good?"

"Wonderful! Wonderful!" Raghunatha took the gem studded necklace from his daughter, and said, "I like this very much. Let me keep it."

"I am blessed," said the jeweller.

Raghunatha put away the glass of wine and said, "You continue. I'll be back soon." When he left the room, his pace quickened.

"You may leave," Krishnappa said to the jeweller.

Chennamma, who was watching her father walk briskly, smiled. "Father is into his second childhood, I think. See how he craves jewels!"

"Correction. He isn't behaving like a child, but is behaving more like a young man."

"I don't understand."

Krishnappa walked up to the window, and rested his hands on the windowsill.

"Will you not explain to me?" asked Chennamma.

"What do you want to me to explain? Thamarai…"

"Father dealt with the situation so cleverly. Else we would have been in trouble."

"You just keep repeating that. But did you pause to think why he kept Thamarai hidden in his palace?"

"Father has already explained the reason for that. He had anticipated trouble. And his fears were not unfounded. We saw what happened, didn't we?"

"He used the sudden turn of events to justify what he had done. If it had been his plan to keep Thamarai hidden in his palace, why did he not take us into confidence? Why did he get a maid to dress up like Thamarai and take her to the moat? Why did he have to hoodwink us into thinking that was Thamarai?"

"I suppose he wanted to keep the fact that Thamarai was alive, secret. He did it for our own good."

"Of course. That girl is going to be crowned and you and I are going to end up being her servants. That too is something he has planned for our good," said Krishnappa sarcastically.

"You are always suspicious. Will a man wish his daughter and his son-in law ill? And what does father gain by doing all this?"

"Gain?" laughed Krishnappa, as he moved away from the window. "As I told you, he isn't into his second childhood, but into a second spell of youth. When your mother died twenty years ago, I asked him to marry someone suitable. But he didn't pay attention to me then. But he's now decided to remarry..."

"Never, never," cried Chennamma.

♦

"**H**ey, you! Come here"

Kanchipurathan, who was getting ready for work in Singavaram, stopped. His dhoti had been hitched up. He had a spade in his hands.

The turban and badge of the man who had hailed Kanchipurathan showed that he was an employee of the government. "Do you know how to read and write?" he asked.

"A little," said Kanchipurathan.

"Now read this and tell this old man what it says," said the man, handing to Kanchipurathan a palm leaf. An old man, tears in his eyes, stood beside him.

Kanchipurathan read the palm leaf. "This is the judgement of the Panchayat. It says that since you have not repaid a loan you took, all your possessions should be handed over to the creditor."

"All the old man's possessions have been handed over to this man here. The old man has been complaining to me. What can I do?"

The creditor seemed to be a reasonable man. "And what am I to do? This old man took a loan from me, for medical expenses. His son required treatment for some ailment. The treatment didn't help and his son died. It is four years since I lent him the money. How else will I get my money back?" he asked.

"What the creditor says sounds reasonable to me," said Kanchipurathan to the old man.

"Reasonable? Do you think I want land or anything else at this stage in my life? I am worried because when all my possessions were handed over to this man, clothes I was stitching for the royal family for the coronation have also been given to this man. And that's what worries me!"

The government employee was irritated by the old man's outburst. "If something that belongs to the palace has been given away, then go and give your excuses to the palace officials. I was asked to take away everything in your house, and I carried out my orders."

"Old man, how could you, the palace tailor, be so careless?" asked Kanchipurathan.

"This isn't the chief tailor. This man's the assistant of the chief tailor," explained the creditor.

"I have a suggestion," said Kanchipurathan to him. "If the old man doesn't hand over the clothes to the palace officials, then he will incur their wrath. Moreover, if there are any hitches in the coronation ceremony, then that will reflect badly on the people of Singavaram. So why don't you give back the clothes to this old man? I will repay his debt. The day after the coronation, meet me here. I will repay this man's loan."

"You? I don't even know who you are," laughed the creditor.

The crowd that had gathered said, pointing to Kanchipurathan, "He can be trusted. He helps out anyone who needs help."

The creditor wasn't convinced, and he said, "All right. But if this man is not here the day after the coronation, you will all be in deep trouble."

"Come on. Let's go," said Kanchipurathan to the old man, and they followed the creditor.

A maid's voice broke into Thamarai's dreams, "Princess, special clothes have to be made for the coronation. The palace tailor is here to take measurements."

Thamarai sat up. She put her feet on a footstool, and shot the tailor a sideways glance.

He had an unprepossessing appearance. Was this the tailor?

"Have you any experience in stitching?" she asked.

Pat came the reply, "It's my habit to take up professions I have no experience in. Didn't I even serve as your physician once?"

Thamarai asked the maid to stay outside the room. "Don't let anyone in," she told her.

The two of them could hardly wait for the door to close. They fell into each other's arms. When Kanchipurathan finally managed to extricate himself from the tight embrace he said, "The coronation is four days from now. And then..."

"And then?"

Kanchipurathan pointed to her hands that had encircled his waist, and said, "These hands that embrace me will be busy signing orders."

Thamarai laughed. "My first order will be to you."

"And what will that be?"

"That you should always be at my feet, serving me."

"I have my doubts whether the coronation will go through," said Kanchipurathan, his brows furrowing in worry.

"I have no doubt that it will go through. And once it's over, you will always be beside me. That's certain too."

"Let's see."

"Wait, where are you going?"

"I heard voices outside."

Outside the door, Raghunatha's voice could be heard, "You dog! How dare you stop me? Move aside."

The maid blocked his way. "Please, my Lord. The Queen has told me strictly not to let anyone in."

"She isn't yet the Queen," said Raghunatha.

"Maybe not. But she is my mistress."

Raghunatha ground his teeth angrily. "Who is inside?"

"The tailor. He is taking measurements, to make clothes for the coronation."

"Is he a young man or an old man?"

"A young man."

The next second, Raghunatha gripped her hand and dragged her away from the door, and called out to a guard. "This girl is to be tortured, until she tells the truth. Stick the tip of your sword under each of her fingernails, until she tells the truth."

When the guard stuck his sword under a fingernail the girl screamed in pain and said, "I'll tell you whatever I know. Please tell him to stop."

"All right," said Raghunatha, and asked the guard to leave.

"Now tell me, does he come here often?"

"Yes, my Lord. It appears as if they have known each other for a long time. He comes in some disguise or the other."

"Is the man who is inside the same man who comes in different disguises?"

"I think so."

Raghunatha paced the corridor for a few minutes, his hands clasped behind his back. "You go back to your place outside the door. You mustn't tell the princess about the enquiries I made. If you do, then the guard's sword will no longer be used just for torture. It will pierce your heart."

"My Lord, I will not breathe a word," said the maid.

Raghunatha took out the necklace he had kept hidden in the folds of his clothes. When he walked up to Thamarai's room, the door was wide open. "Are you comfortable here, my child?" he asked Thamarai.

"With you to look after me, how can I have anything to complain about?" Thamarai said.

Raghunatha was pleased. "The day of the coronation is drawing near. You need peace of mind and a lot of rest. You must not look worn out or worried. If you do, then that will give your enemies a chance to spin stories about your reluctance to ascend the throne."

"Nothing of the sort will happen. Don't worry."

"You are kind hearted," said Raghunatha, as he smoothened down her hair. "I am told you allow people into your room without exercising your discretion. Don't do that in future. Don't let anyone into your room."

Thamarai laughed. "A good ruler should be accessible to all her subjects."

"You are clever and adamant," said Raghunatha. His tone of voice reflected his anger. He showed her the necklace, and said, "See what I have brought for you."

"How lovely! But you saved my life! What is the need for any other gift?"

"Please wear it, my child." With great difficulty Raghunatha resisted the temptation to put it round her neck himself.

Thamarai wore it and looked at herself in the mirror.

"How beautiful it looks on you!" exclaimed Raghunatha.

Thamarai bowed before him and said, "I have not been fortunate enough to hear such words from my father. But God has been kind to me. I have heard you say words I would have been happy to hear my father say."

Had Raghunatha's face darkened? It was hard to tell.

"I have to go. Be careful. Don't let anyone into your room. I will also tell the guards to be vigilant."

After he left, Krishnappa and Chennamma, who had been hiding in the corridor, emerged. "Now do you believe me? Or do you still doubt me?" Krishnappa asked his wife.

"I can't believe that my father... at this age... at his age..."

Krishnappa laughed. "This is the right age. Women lose interest in such things as they age. But it's the exact opposite in the case of men. Come on, let's go."

♦

The resonance of Vedic mantras. The grandeur of musical instruments being played. Shouts and cheers from the people.

Long Live Queen Thamarai!

Let Singavaram's fame last forever!

The two day drill that Raghunatha and the ministers had given Thamarai had prepared her for the coronation. When she should stand, which direction she should face, when she should sit down, who should be greeted by her, whose salutations she should accept—Thamarai knew exactly what she had to do.

But she just went through the motions like an automaton. Where was 'he'? Was he somewhere in the crowd, watching her?

Her eyes searched the crowd. The priest of the royal family took the gem encrusted crown to Krishnappa and Chennamma, who blessed it. The army generals placed their swords and shields before the crown and prostrated before it.

The crown was anointed with turmeric water and milk and then handed over to Raghunatha. Thamarai rose from the throne, and bent before Raghunatha. He placed the crown on her head. There were tears in her eyes. Where was he? This kingdom was hers because of him.

A priest, who was there as the representative of the Company, asked the poet sent by Rani Mangamma, "What next?"

"The new Queen will give gifts to the poor."

Zulfikar Khan had come from Senji, where he had laid siege to the fort. He was engaged in conversation with the representative of King Aurangazeb.

There was a huge crowd of people waiting for gifts from the Queen. She placed clothes, coins, fruits in the outstretched hands.

Suddenly—

A rugged hand was stretched towards Thamarai, and a lotus petal was offered to her.

"It's you! What will I give you? How can I ever repay you?" Her eyes filled with tears.

Kanchipurathan stood smiling at her.

She pulled off her ruby ring and placed it in his palm.

Someone grabbed it from him.

Raghunatha!

He smiled and said to Thamarai, "I've found out who it was who saved you from the fire. You didn't tell me who rescued you. So I decided to find out myself and then reward him. Now I know who it was."

"Good."

Raghunatha held Kanchipurathan's hand and said, "Please come with me. I have made special arrangements for you."

SEVENTEEN

"It is the duty of every subject to protect the life of the Queen. To accept a gift for doing so, will only bring discredit to me," said Kanchipurathan.

But Raghunatha said, "I appreciate your humility. But we cannot fail in our duty to honour a brave man. Please come with me."

Kanchipurathan looked at Thamarai.

Thamarai smiled at him. "He is the eldest member of our family. No one disregards his words," she said.

"Your wish is my command," Kanchipurathan said.

"This way," said Raghunatha, and led him away.

"I am not used to such deferential treatment," said Kanchipurathan.

"You have to get accustomed to it," Raghunatha said.

"I meant deferential treatment from you."

Raghunatha's face darkened. But he controlled his anger and said, "Yes, that's true. But then, we meet such dutiful subjects only once in a while. We don't get many opportunities to honour people like you. Please come in. This is where I stay."

Kanchipurathan sat on a chair, and looked round the room.

Raghunatha brought him fruits and milk. "I had expected that you would come to the coronation, and I had asked my men to prepare another room for your stay. I don't know if it is ready."

Kanchipurathan peeled a red banana, and began to eat it. "Why do you have to make such preparations to receive a poor man?"

"Poor man? Do you think I haven't noticed? The Queen has a soft spot for you. There is no escape for you, my dear friend."

"You are very well informed," said Kanchipurathan.

Raghunatha called out to his servants. But no one responded. "Lazy men! If we have some celebrations for a day, they use that as an excuse to take leave for nine days."

He rang a silver bell. Still no one came.

"Let me go and fetch someone," said Kanchipurathan.

"No, no. Let me do that," Raghunatha said angrily, and left the room. He found a guard, who apologised, "Please forgive me, my Lord. I was tired and I fell asleep."

"Please do not scold him," said Kanchipurathan. "Please let him go."

"Go away. You have been spared because of the kindness of this gentleman," said Raghunatha to the guard. "Go to the room that has been allocated to this gentleman and see if everything is in place."

When the man left, Raghunatha struck up a conversation with Kanchipurathan. "One hears a lot about Chennai. I suppose there are no lazy people there. Am I right?"

"I do not know if there are no lazy people there. But I do know that there are none that are cruel. Even traitors are fewer in number."

"Really?" Raghunatha asked, and wanted to continue the conversation, but couldn't, because the guard came in running, and said, "Danger to the Queen!"

"Danger to Chennamma?" asked Raghunatha.

"No, danger to the new Queen."

"What are you saying? What has happened to Queen Thamarai?" asked Kanchipurathan.

The guard, who had come running to convey the news, was panting. "The Queen was giving gifts. An old man asked for an unusual gift."

"What did he ask for? That is why I keep saying that we should give up all these stupid customs," said Raghunatha.

"That old man's son is a prisoner in the underground prison. He wanted his son to be released."

"And I suppose the Queen agreed. Only those who have committed the most heinous crimes are imprisoned in the underground prison."

"The Queen took pity on the old man, and went in person to the underground prison. And there the Queen opened the door to one of the rooms. And because of some mechanical contrivance …"

"Mechanical contrivance?" asked Kanchipurathan impatiently.

"The door closed because of some mechanical contrivance and the Queen is trapped inside that room. The guards have been trying to break open the door, but they haven't been able to."

"Where is that prison? Take me there," said Kanchipurathan.

"I will attend to this. You don't have to bother," said Raghunatha. But Kanchipurathan paid no heed. Raghunatha took him to a place behind the palace. He said Kanchipurathan would have to go down the steps there. Kanchipurathan began his descent down the steps. A mighty push and Kanchipurathan rolled down the steps. A door above him closed. He was trapped in a prison cell.

Raghunatha came up, and tossed a coin to the guard, "That's for giving a convincing performance."

♦

Rituals. Customary practices of the royal family. Receiving gifts. Giving gifts. Thamarai was worn out. Every inch of her body ached and begged for rest. She was told that she had to keep smiling, even if she was tired. Her lips simply refused to co-operate. Wicked lips. They smiled of their own accord when 'he' was there. Now they simply refused to do what was asked of them. They needed to be punished, and the punishment would come from 'his' lips. Thamarai blushed at the thought of his lips meeting hers.

"You may leave now," the priest of the royal family gave her permission to leave.

She went to her quarters with her retinue of servants following her.

He should have waited for her here. But where was he? She asked one of her maids to go to Raghunatha's quarters and fetch Kanchipurathan.

The maid came back and told Thamarai that Kanchipurathan had left long ago. "Left? Go and ask Raghunatha where he is."

"The old man is irritable. He said he had a headache and that if I bothered him with questions, he would kill me."

"All right. Then I will go myself and ask him."

"Not necessary, Your Majesty," said a maid who had entered just then.

"Parimalam, what do you have to say?"

Parimalam signaled to the other maids to leave the room. Parimalam showed Thamarai a gold coin and whispered something in her ears. "Impossible. I refuse to believe this," said Thamarai.

She came out of her room, and hesitated for a second, and then went ahead.

♦

The city was beginning to sleep. The noise was slowly subsiding. A few fireworks still went off here and there, but most citizens had returned home.

Raghunatha got up from his bed. A cool breeze came in through the open window. He sighed. Loneliness oppressed him. That enemy. As long as he was alive, Raghunatha would know no peace. He went out, determination marking his stride.

He walked toward the prison. But when he reached the prison, he found the door to the prison open. Who was responsible? Raghunatha yelled. "Who gave you permission to open this door?"

"We were ordered to open it," said one of the prison guards.

"Who gave you the order?"

"The former king, and his consort, and the new Queen were all here. They read the royal declaration from the new Queen."

"Declaration? What declaration?"

"It was a royal declaration to free all prisoners. I thought you knew about this."

Raghunatha was furious. He turned back, like an injured tiger.

He didn't go back to his room, but stormed into Krishnappa's room.

Krishnappa and Chennamma were playing chess. "Chess? And I thought playing chess was sinful," said Raghunatha.

Chennamma said, "Not as sinful as chopping off people's heads."

"Please move a little. Won't you give me some space?" asked Raghunatha, as he sat on the edge of the bed.

"We feel we have conceded too much to you," replied Krishnappa and moved a little so that Raghunatha could sit on the bed.

Raghunatha smiled. "I will leave now. I do not want to intrude. Just tell me this. Why were you interested in setting free Thamarai's lover—Kanchipurathan?"

"And why were you so eager to imprison him?" Chennamma asked her father. "You haven't told me why you imprisoned him. Each of us has to look out for his or her own welfare."

"Is that so? Now what is your plan?"

"We will tell you when you need to be told," said Krishnappa.

"When that slave girl and her lover destroy this kingdom, you will regret your action."

"Don't worry. Haven't you been giving us your valuable advice all these years? In the same way, when the need arises, we will advise Thamarai," said Krishnappa.

Raghunatha then shed tears and said, "Even though you abuse me, I bear no ill will towards you. How can I be angry with my daughter and son-in-law? You will soon see whether Thamarai heeds your advice, or decides to do exactly as she pleases."

He wiped the tears from his eyes, and staggered out.

♦

Emperor Aurangazeb's footwear!

Aurangazeb's elephant was arriving!

There was excitement in the court hall.

The elephant looked like a hill that was swaying. It walked in, impressing everyone with its majestic gait, and its ornate decorations.

The Queen's face registered her surprise. Who were these people?

The minister ran up to her, and said, "These people have brought the Emperor's footwear from Delhi. We should honour it. That's the custom."

Thamarai's eyes widened in surprise. "That means..."

"You have to rise from your throne, and place the Emperor's footwear on your throne. You have to bow before it."

"Really?" Turning to the army general, she asked, "Do you think I must do that?"

The young general pulled out his sword, and ran up to the Queen and whispered something to her.

"All right. We will do as you say," she said.

The general asked the mahout to hand over the footwear to him. The mahout lowered one of the pair of sandals.

"Throw it near my feet," said Thamarai.

Deafening silence. The people surged forward.

"The footwear... must be placed on the throne, Your Majesty," said the minister. Fear had made his voice shrill.

"No, No." The voices of Krishnappa and Chennamma could be heard.

Thamarai put her left foot on the sandal that had been lowered.

A few voices could be heard saying, "Insult to the Delhi Emperor."

But most of the people shouted, "Long live the Queen's courage!"

"See how arrogant she is?" Raghunatha said to his daughter.

"That general—he is the one who has instigated her to do this," said Krishnappa.

"Of course, it is he who has instigated her. And do you know who he is?"

Krishnappa stared at the newly appointed general, and his eyes widened in wonder as recognition dawned on him.

The general was Kanchipurathan.

EIGHTEEN

Had a magician waved his magic wand? Was that why everyone in the court hall stood transfixed?

Emperor Aurangazeb's representative was completely taken aback. The elephant had toured the whole of India, and had been welcomed with honours everywhere. The Emperor's footwear had been treated like royalty in every kingdom the elephant had visited. No one would have dared to do what Thamarai had done now. Aurangazeb's representative drew his sword, and rushed towards Thamarai, but stopped short. "Your Majesty, if I were to punish you, then I would be insulting my emperor. But be sure of this— another representative of our emperor will soon meet you— on the battlefield. I will take leave of you now."

He put Aurangazeb's footwear on the back of the elephant. The men who had accompanied it filed out and the elephant followed.

The courtiers seemed to have come out of the spell. They began to talk in hushed tones.

Raghunatha pushed aside Krishnappa's restraining hand, and walked up to Thamarai, and whispered something to her.

"Is that so?" she asked. The lines of worry on her face could be clearly seen. "There is need for a secret meeting with my council of ministers. All of you may leave now. If any important decision is taken in the council of ministers, you will be informed tomorrow."

The courtiers left.

"Uncle, is he speaking the truth?" Thamarai asked her uncle Krishnappa.

"What did he say?"

"I told her the truth," said Raghunatha gleefully. "There has never been such an occasion in the history of Singavaram. No such opportunity to show our courage ever presented itself before. Senji is our neighbouring kingdom. Aurangazeb's general Zulfikar has laid siege to that kingdom. The representative who has been insulted will now go to Zulfikar. Zulfikar will divert his army to Singavaram. He will also send for more troops from Delhi. Will we not make preparations too? We may be a small kingdom, but we will fight to the last man, woman and child. We will all die the death of martyrs. Beside the hill of Singavaram, there will be a hill of dead bodies."

"No, no. That should never happen. Tell me how we can prevent that from happening," said Thamarai.

"I will tell you what you should do. Send some men to catch up with that elephant from Delhi. Let us apologise for what happened."

"Old man! An uncontrolled tongue is like a venomous snake!" Kanchipurathan said. "Mind your words. No one who has any self- respect will apologise for what happened."

"Is that so? Do slaves in Chennai have self-respect?"

"Stop. You are not only insulting the general, but my brother's daughter too," said Krishnappa.

"Your brother's daughter has ascended the throne to destroy the entire kingdom."

"Even so, it is far better to die because of my brother's daughter, than to be dishonoured by the Emperor of Delhi."

"Kanchipurathan is erring because he is young and…"

"These days, old men behave like young men! That being the case, why should I not be impelled by my youth?" asked Kanchipurathan.

"Let us talk of what we need to do," pleaded Thamarai.

"What we need to do is to apologise to the Emperor's representative. Why should we wait to be attacked by Zulfikar?"

Thamarai's eyes met Kanchipurathan's. He left at once.

◆

Knock, knock. "Hello!" Knock, knock.

"Who is it?" The old tailor put down his needle and thread, and opened the door.

"Good morning. This is Kanchipurathan. I am here to repay your debt."

"Come on in. That man who lent me money comes here every day and scolds me."

"How can he do that? I had told him I would meet him today."

Kanchipurathan opened the folds of his dhoti, and out rolled gold coins!

"Hey! Have you found employment?"

"Yes, I have. In the palace."

"Palace? What job is it?"

"They call me general."

"General?!" The creditor who had come to collect the money exclaimed in disbelief.

He had made up his mind not to go back empty handed and had therefore brought some people with him.

"Yes, yes— this is the new general."

"I heard he turned away the Emperor's representative."

"The Queen is fond of him. He is from Chennai."

The people outside were sharing information about Kanchipurathan.

"Take the money," Kanchipurathan said to the creditor.

He then went out into the street and shouted. "Come on, all the brave sons of Singavaram. Those who value self-respect, come here and listen to me. You have only one life to lose. Let it be lost in vanquishing the enemy. Die with fame! I can understand your fears. But Aurangazeb cannot defeat you. None can defeat you. All we need is self-confidence and grit."

A few men gathered round him. Someone asked, "Aren't there soldiers in our army? How can we who are unarmed fight?"

"Weapons are a necessity for the coward. Do brave men need chariots and elephants and horses? Our hands are our spears. Our legs are horses. Our chests are our armour. Our thoughts are our swords. What more do you want? Come on, friends."

Kanchipurathan didn't wait for a bigger crowd to gather. He walked on. He could tell that he was being followed. Each of the men behind him carried some weapon or the other— a stout stick, a dagger, a scythe, a spear!

A young man kept close to Kanchipurathan. "My name is Durai Velan. From now on I am going to be known by a different name."

"And what is your new name?"

"G.P.B— general's personal bodyguard!"

Kanchipurathan laughed. "We'll have the naming ceremony later. Now show me Zulfikar's army camp. Are all his tents close to Senji, or are they spread out?"

"All of them used to be close to Senji. But the siege has been on for a long time. Zulfikar has been unable to flush out Rajaram, the king of Senji. Zulfikar's men are tired. I have also heard that Zulfikar doesn't trust Emperor Aurangazeb's son and has imprisoned him. There are many fissures in his army. Each of the important leaders in the army has his own camp."

Kanchipurathan smiled. "That is good news for us."

Kanchipurathan's men were coming down the hill. The Sun was going down too.

Soon it was dark. They could see the flames in one or two of the tents in the enemy camp. "Shh!" Kanchipurathan warned his men. "Darkness and stealth will be our allies from now on. We have to creep silently to the first tent, and from there to the next…"

There were hundred men with him. But they moved silently, watching their steps.

Did the horses sense that there were strangers in their midst? They neighed. But before the enemy became alert, Kanchipurathan gave the order to his men to charge.

Zulfikar's men were asleep. Before they could wake up, Kanchipurathan's men had seized their weapons. There was another tent some distance from the rest. But…

One of Zulfikar's men had escaped, and was riding hell for leather towards his commander's tent to warn him.

"Careful! Hide!" Kanchipurathan shouted to his men. But…

Bang! Bang! The sound was deafening!

Durai Velan came running to Kanchipurathan. "They have been alerted. They are firing cannons at us."

"We'll be killed," Kanchipurathan heard his men shouting.

"Wait. Let us..." Kanchipurathan didn't complete his sentence. He had been hit on his leg. He lost consciousness, and Durai Velan kept him from falling down.

♦

When he came out of the faint, Kanchipuarathan saw that he was near Singavaram.

He didn't say a word to Durai Velan, the one who had saved his life. He limped around, looking for his men. "Don't worry," said Durai Velan. "Our men have escaped."

Kanchipurathan sighed and said, "I exposed unarmed men to danger."

"Do not blame yourself. They should consider themselves blessed because they got an opportunity to serve their country. Now hold on to me." Kanchipurathan held on to Durai Velan and limped up to a spring. They then rested under a jamun tree. Durai Velan gave the branches a shake and fruits dropped down on them. The two of them ate the fruits. Durai Velan said, "Discretion is more important than courage. We were not discreet. We thought sheer emotion would help us win a battle. And all we've got for our efforts are injuires..."

Durai Velan stopped talking, when he found that Kanchipurathan was not listening to him. "Look," said Kanchipurathan, pointing to a boy. The boy was about to eat his lunch. He had opened a vessel containing rice and some pickles, but he wasn't able to eat, for circling above his head were vultures! Any minute now, the birds would grab the vessel and fly off. But the boy wasn't as helpless as he looked. He was clever. He had a rope to which a stone was tied. He used one hand to swing the sling over his head, while he used the other to eat!

"Give me that rope. I will keep the birds away, so that you can eat in peace," Kanchipurathan said to the boy.

But Kanchipurathan didn't even have to swing the sling. The vultures flew away, when they found that the boy now had someone beside him.

The boy licked his fingers. He was enjoying the tart pickle. An idea struck Kanchipurathan. "Here is your rope," he said to the boy, and hastened to where Durai Velan was sitting. Durai Velan was surprised at Kanchipurathan's new found enthusiasm. "Your leg. Be careful. Don't put weight on that leg," he warned Kanchipurathan.

♦

"Long live the Queen's fame!" said the man, as he entered the royal court.

"Welcome, Nedumaran!" said Krishnappa. "This is the Deputy Chief of our army," he introduced the newcomer to Thamarai.

"Shouldn't you be fighting the enemy? Why are you here? Have you come to consult us?" asked Thamarai.

The Deputy Chief was taken aback. A shadow of doubt crossed his wrinkled face.

"I don't understand. Where did you expect me to be at this time?" he said.

Krishnappa was surprised. "Didn't the general consult you? Did he not take you with him?"

"No."

Raghunatha gave a contemptuous laugh, as he entered. "Haven't you heard the news?"

"This is not the time for your sarcasm," said Krishnappa.

"True, true. This is the time for running away from the battlefield."

"What!" Thamarai, Chennamma and Krishnappa exclaimed.

"Why should you be surprised? What does Kanchipurathan know about military strategy? He talks glibly. He is a lazy fellow who talks when he should act. And is it his fault if you assume he has hidden talents?"

"Stop," said Thamarai. "Whether he has any abilities or not is something the people should worry about.

That is none of your business. Tell us the news you were about to convey."

"I was going to tell you about how Singavaram has been humiliated. A battle is something that requires planning, strategy, clever spying and working out a suitable time to launch an attack. You don't pick up a motley crowd of villagers and lead them into battle. Shame. Shame."

"What are you saying…" Krishnappa ground his teeth.

"Give me a patient hearing. Kanchipurathan went off to fight Zulfikar, accompanied by some villagers he picked up in the market. Zulfikar beat them to a pulp. Those with self-respect gave up their lives. The shameless ones…"

"The shameless ones like you, indulge in gossip in the women's quarters, right?" interrupted a voice.

Thamarai ran up to Kanchipurathan, "You aren't hurt, are you?"

"I am not. And the country's reputation hasn't been hurt either."

"We have been told that you attacked Zulfikar Khan and that…" said Krishnappa.

"Yes, I was hasty, and for that I seek the Queen's forgiveness. But I now have a new plan, and I seek the co-operation of everyone."

"I await your orders," said the Deputy Chief.

"All right. Do we have elephants in our army? Strong ones?"

"Yes, we have an elephant force."

"I don't need an entire division. I just need three strong elephants. I also need three strong door chains, the kind used for the doors of the fort."

Krishnappa was confused. Thamarai was worried, and Raghunatha gave Kanchipurathan a mocking smile.

That night Kanchipurathan was given what he asked for, and he left Singavaram.

NINETEEN

Stars had begun to make their appearance in the twilight sky.

"Do you remember my instructions?" asked Kanchipurathan. Three elephants stood outside the armoury.

"Yes, I do," said the Deputy Chief of the army. "I have to leave with a small force—five hundred strong. I must approach Zulfikar's camp silently. At midnight, you will attack him from behind. I have to make use of the resulting confusion in his ranks to attack from the front."

"Right," said Kanchipurathan. "You must wait till I attack, and only then must you attack. Until then you must remain hidden. No one should know you are hidden there. You are not to tell anyone of our plans."

"As you command."

"Lift them, lift them"— fifteen soldiers heaved under the weight of iron chains. They heaped the chains before Kanchipurathan. "Mount the chains on the backs of the elephants— one for each elephant," Kanchipurathan ordered.

As the soldiers were engaged in carrying out his order, Kanchipurathan asked, "Can anyone show me the secret path that leads out of Singavaram?"

"There— he will show you the way," the Deputy Chief pointed to a dwarf.

"He grew up in the forest around Singavaram. He will lead you out through a secret passage that no one knows of. That path circles the Senji hill and fort. It will take you to the back of Zulfikar's camp."

Kanchipurathan followed the dwarf. The three elephants followed him— without a mahout. The dwarf led the way.

The Deputy Chief stood watching them make their way into the dense forest.

"I am sorry, my dear friend. I am sorry for you," said a voice. Startled, the deputy chief turned round to find Raghunatha there. "What a good soldier you are! And yet you have to take orders from a stranger."

The Deputy Chief laughed. "Well, that's the case in the palace too. There used to be great rulers. But now there is no trace of them."

Raghunatha's face darkened. "I don't mind if you make fun of me. Go ahead, and do it. I am an old man. How long am I going to be alive? But you are young. Shouldn't you rise to a great position?"

"I will."

"I am surprised that you entertain such hopes. When the old general retired, the Queen should have made you the head of the army. But she gave that post to a stranger, and that was when the last chapter of your military career was written."

"Please do not be disloyal to the royal family."

"Kanchipurathan sees you as a threat to him, and he has laid a trap for you. And you, like an unsuspecting deer that is trapped in a hunter's net, are going to fall prey to his plans. I just thought of that, and I felt sorry for you."

"And what proof do you have for what you say?"

"You will get your proof when you are defeated tomorrow night. Aurangazeb's forces will pounce on you and will massacre your small army. If you escape alive, you will not be able to live down the shame. It will be easy to deprive you of the post you now hold. And if you were to die on the battlefield, all the better for Kanchipurathan."

The deputy chief was confused, and Raghunatha pressed home his advantage.

"There is only way to make Kanchipurathan's plans come to naught."

"And what is that?"

"You mustn't go to the battle with your forces."

♦

"Aren't you a dear? Please eat this."

"Keee"— the parrot hopped inside its cage, refusing the fruit Chennamma was offering it.

Thamarai laughed, and put away what she was reading.

"This parrot has become very naughty. It refuses to eat the fruit I am giving it," complained Chennamma.

Thamarai said to the parrot, "You adamant girl! Is this right?" She took the fruit from Chennamma and kept it in the palm of her hand. "Come on. Take this."

The parrot pecked at the fruit in Thamarai's hand.

"Hey, gently. It hurts. Your beak is sharp. You are an ingrate. My mother here looked after you all these years, but you favour me over her. Is this fair?" said Thamarai to the bird.

Chennamma ran her hands through Thamarai's hair lovingly. "I am the newcomer, Thamarai. You belong to this family. I only married into this family. The whole country loves you because of your kindness. Not just this parrot — even the plants in the royal garden are going to obey you. They will bear flowers and fruits, when you command them to."

"Mother, don't equate me with God."

Thamarai looked out of the window and sighed.

"Don't worry, Thamarai. He will be back and he will be victorious in the battle," said Chennamma. Thamarai blushed. "My best wishes for the success of your romance," Chennamma whispered in her ears. But she sounded concerned. Thamarai asked, "Mother, is there something wrong? Why do you sound sad?"

"Thamarai, please don't worry."

"Is it possible to watch the battle from the watchtower?" asked Thamarai.

"No. The battlefield isn't so close to our fort. But we can see the highway, if you wish."

They held hands and walked out. When they got close to the watchtower, the guard saluted them.

"Watch out. The steps are in need of repair," warned Chennamma.

They went up, and looked out. The strong wind tore at Thamarai's hair. "Look— that is the road from Chennai," Chennamma pointed.

"Isn't that the road I came through?" Thamarai asked. "Look— there are four or five people dragging something."

Chennamma said, "They are coming from Chennai. But what is that they are dragging? I've never seen a vehicle like this before."

"Mother. I can't make out much from here. Why don't we go to the highway and have a look?"

"You are no longer a commoner. You are the Queen. Don't forget that."

"But I am bored. I stay cooped up in the palace all the time. I want to go out."

"Thamarai, what will the people say if they see you walking on the highway? Wait. I have an idea."

Thamarai's playfulness seemed to be infectious and Chennamma took Thamarai to her room.

"Wear these," she said and gave Thamarai the clothes of a sepoy. "These disguises belong to the King. They've come in handy now. Quick. Change into these clothes."

Thamarai changed into a sepoy's clothes, and so did Chennamma. They stuck on false moustaches. "Mother, your moustache isn't stuck on properly. Let me fix it," said Thamarai.

"And the bindi on your forehead hasn't been rubbed off completely. Let me rub it off," said Chennamma and proceeded to do so.

A secret message had been sent through a maid. Two horses waited near the rear entrance of the palace. They mounted the horses and were on their way.

♦

"Push. Push it."

"The path here is rugged. No amount of pushing is going to help."

"The company official has nothing to do. Ask him for help."

"He is a wicked man."

The company official, who was on horseback, couldn't understand the entire conversation, but he could understand parts of it. . "Are you finding it difficult to push it?"

"Yes. That's because the path is steep."

"All right. There are two men coming this way. Take their help," said the officer.

The two sepoys reined in their horses. One of them asked in a shrill feminine voice, "What is this?"

"You are dressed nattily. But you don't know what this is. Haven't you seen a cannon?"

"We have heard of cannons, but have never seen one."

The two sepoys inspected the cannon. "Why are you wasting time staring at it? Give us a hand," said the official, jumping down from horse.

The two sepoys and the officer pushed too. The sepoy with the shrill voice asked, "Where is this cannon going?"

"To Devanampettai, where the company has a fort."

"And with whom is the company going to fight?"

"There isn't going to be any battle. They are going to buy the land around the fort."

"And so?"

"This cannon will be mounted on the wall of the fort, and then fired. All the land up to where the cannon-ball lands will belong to the company. Those are the terms of the Senji King's sale."

"So that's what this cannon is for?"

"Yes. And if the company is to get a lot of land, then the ball must cover a long distance. That's why we have brought a special cannon from Chennai."

"Push, push. Come on." The white man was unaccustomed to hard labour in the heat. He was panting and sweating profusely. At last, after much effort, they crossed the uphill path.

"Thank you," said the company officer. "Where are you from?"

"Singavaram."

"Singavaram? It's a queen who rules there, right?"

"Yes."

The sepoys took leave of the official.

They watched until the cannon was out of sight. "Hmm. And if they only knew that it was the queen of Singavaram who pushed the cannon for them…" Thamarai laughed. "That officer from the company would have fainted."

Chennamma did not join in her laughter.

"Is something the matter?" asked Thamarai.

"Your uncle will be looking for us."

Thamarai hesitated. "Is this the way that our armies took?"

"No, no. That's a different path. Come on. Let's go."

At the entrance, two guards blocked their entry into the palace. "Move aside."

"Our orders are that no one is to be allowed inside."

"Whose orders?"

"Raghunatha's."

"We are not ordinary sepoys."

"Yes, of course. You are of royal blood. Singavaram blood," mocked Raghunatha. Behind him stood Krishnappa.

"Father this is not the time to play games," said Chennamma and took off her turban.

"Now, are you going to let us in, or not?" she asked the guards.

"Forgive us. We didn't know it was you," the guard apologised.

"I don't approve of what you did, Chennamma," said Krishnappa angrily.

"Don't kings go on an inspection of their capital? This was like that."

"Foolhardiness," Raghunatha ground his teeth. "You endangered the Queen's life. If you had not been my daughter, I would have thrown you in prison."

"And if you had not been my father, I would have cut off your head," said Chennamma.

"Did I endanger the Queen's life?" asked Raghunatha

"You did something worse. You betrayed the country."

Thamarai looked at her in shock. Krishnappa said, "Please be quiet, Chennamma."

"Before you accuse someone, you must have proof for the accusation, my daughter," said Raghunatha.

"Yes, I have proof," said Chennamma, and took out a palm leaf, with a message written on it. Raghunatha snatched it from her and hurled it down the hill. It rolled down and disappeared from view.

"What was that? What was written on it? To whom?" Krishnappa's eyes were red shot.

"That was nothing. Don't believe a word of what Chennamma says." Rgahunatha stuttered, and made a hasty exit.

Thamarai said, "I was with you all the time. Where did you pick up this palm leaf?"

"The officer of the company had this tucked in his belt. It slipped from his belt. I picked it up, when I saw the royal insignia of the Singavaram royal family. My father had written to the Company."

"Did you read it?"

"Yes, I did. I told the officer that I had to adjust my clothes. I went behind a tree and read it. The message to the company from my father was that he was ready to sell land in Singavaram, in the same way that the king of Senji had sold land in his kingdom. It was a request to the company to dethrone you and put him on the throne."

Krishnappa pulled his sword from its scabbard, but Thamarai stopped him. "Please don't hurt him. He is an old man. He has been foolish…"

"Do you want to spare him because he is my father? Please don't. Never forgive someone who plots against the country," said Chennamma.

"I don't think he will harm us. Leave him alone," said Thamarai.

"All right, I will spare his life this time, because you have pleaded on his behalf. But the next time, I will not spare his life," said Krishnappa.

Chennamma concurred with her husband. "It is dangerous to keep my father here with us."

Raghunatha, who had been outside the door listening to this conversation, was furious. He was also afraid. He couldn't think clearly. "So, it has come to this, has it? I am not going to give up. It will be a fight to the finish. Anyway, I've made plans to get rid of Kanchipurathan, and even if one of them should succeed, then it will be to my advantage."

His eyes gleamed like a snake's.

♦

For two days and one night, two men and three elephants walked tirelessly.

Dry leaves crumbled under their feet. Sometimes Kanchipurathan fell into ditches that he hadn't noticed.

"Will we soon be near Zulfikar's camp?" he asked the dwarf. But there was no reply. "Is your mouth stuffed with a *kozhukattai*?[3] Why aren't you answering me?" Kanchipurathan turned round. There was no trace of the dwarf. He heard a mocking laugh from somewhere. But where did it come from?

---

3   *Kozhukattai* - a small round sweetmeat

TWENTY

"Where are you?" called out Kanchipurathan. He cupped his hands and yelled. No response. The dwarf had tricked him, and had left him in the middle of the forest. How was he to find his way out?

Where were the stars that had peeped out from behind the clouds a few minutes ago? The streaks of lightning seemed like Mohinis ripping up the blue sky. The thunder sounded like the roar of thousands of lions.

And then it began to rain. For a few minutes the thick foliage of the trees sheltered Kanchipurathan and his three elephants. But soon the rain became heavier. Kanchipurathan shivered in the cold. The elephants trumpeted, and the forest seemed to shake from the sound.

Kanchipurathan saw an overhanging rock and took shelter under it. The elephants did not join him. They seemed to be enjoying the rain.

"We will all be able to escape. But I feel sorry for that dwarf," said Kanchipurathan loudly to the elephants.

The elephants flapped their ears, as if to ask, "Why?"

Kanchipurathan shot sideways glances to his left and right and continued, "That dwarf's wife and children are in danger. I have left instructions that if I don't reach Zulfikar's camp by tomorrow, then it should be assumed I've fallen prey to the dwarf's cunning. I have instructed my men to kill his wife and children..."

"Forgive me! Please forgive me!" the dwarf fell at Kanchipurathan's feet.

"Get up. If we reach Zulfikar's camp by tomorrow morning, then no harm will befall your family."

"Quick, get on to the back of an elephant. I should never have paid heed to that old man Raghunatha's words." the dwarf said.

Kanchipurathan smiled, and climbed on to the back of an elephant.

The dwarf cut down the low hanging branches of trees.

"This is the Vettavalam forest. This is the secret path that leads to Senji. It is called 'Satan's entrance'."

"Get down from the elephant," said Kanchipurathan, and he climbed down too.

"Push down the iron chains. Let each elephant pick up a chain in its trunk," he said to the dwarf.

"What happens after that?"

"Do as I say," growled Kanchipurathan. He was no longer in a playful mood. He looked stern.

♦

The rain came down in torrents. Fort, palace, forest and hill were all blanketed by rain.

Inside the Senji fort, administration was paralysed.

No one in the royal family could sleep. If they did, all they saw in their dreams was the figure of Zulfikar Khan.

In Rajagiri, in Kalyana Mahal, near the women's quarters, five pairs of worried eyes looked out through the windows. They could see the Vettavalam forest bathed in rain, illuminated by lightning.

"Can you see anyone approaching?" asked King Rajaram. His eyes and voice reflected his concern. Of his eight ministers, four were present in the room. But no one answered their king.

The Peshwa Neelamoreshwar sighed. "Your sister's husband sowed the seeds, and we are reaping the harvest. What can anyone do now? His generals looted Kanchipuram. Think of the countless people who were rendered homeless by Gopal Pandit and Vittal Pillai. How many people were driven out of Kanchipuram! We are paying for that sin."

The finance minister had his own worries to grapple with. "We had asked the Company for 100 barrels of gunpowder and 2000 cannon balls. Why haven't they replied to our request?"

"What did you expect?" asked the Foreign Affairs minister Mataki Sudadar. "Did we behave honestly with them? They say that we sold them the village of Manjakuppam and sold the same village to the Dutch too! We have only enemies wherever we look."

The King shouted angrily, "Have I no friends? Go and make enquiries near the Thiruvannamalai gate. That town is our link to the rest of the world. The people there will tell you that any minute reinforcements will arrive from my friend - the King of Thanjavur."

"The Thiruvannamalai gate isn't properly guarded. It could fall into enemy hands."

"I have sent a spy to find out what's happening in the enemy camp. Here he comes," said the Finance Minister.

A soldier entered, bowed before the king and said, "Zulfikar has imprisoned Aurangazeb's son Kam Baksh and his family. Zulfikar's father Azad Khan is terrified of what the Emperor will do when he finds out his son and his family have been imprisoned."

"Excellent!" exclaimed King Rajaram, with childlike enthusiasm, as if all the threats to his kingdom had vanished in a trice.

The spy continued, "There may be a lack of unity in the enemy ranks. But he seems to be strong otherwise. It is also being said that reinforcements will soon strengthen his hands."

"All right. You may go," said the Peshwa, resignation in his voice.

"Tell the women of the palace to be prepared to immolate themselves. We will make one last attack tonight," he said.

"Women immolating themselves? There is going to be no need for that. We will return victorious. No doubt about that," said the King.

"Why don't we send all the women to Thanjavur, through the Vettavalam forest? Will not Ekoji, the king of Thanjavur, take care of them?" asked the Foreign Affairs Minister.

"He will, if they reach Thanajvur alive," said a deputy general. "The Muslims are keeping an eye on all the important routes. If you want our women to be captured by the Muslims and to lose their honour at the hands of the Muslims, then send them out."

The King, who was reclining on his bed, punched the pillows. "Our expectations have been belied! If only everything had gone according to plan... Nimaji! Look there! Look at Satan's entrance. Is someone coming through the Vettavalam forest? Wait for lightning to illuminate the entrance. Look! Look!"

The four ministers looked out through the window.

"Is that a horse? No! It looks like an elephant!"

King Rajaram was delighted. "They are coming to help us."

"No, no. They are not coming to the fort through Satan's entrance," said the Peshwa. "Wait! Let me see where the elephants are headed, the next time there is a streak of lightning. Yes! The elephants are not coming towards the entrance to the fort. They are walking in the direction of Zulfikar's camp. Is it one elephant? Are there many? I can't tell."

"Why don't we go and have a look?" Rajaram said, with new found confidence.

His enthusiasm was infectious.

Are rains ever partial? They were causing damage in Zulfikar's camp too. The tents had been pitched months ago, and there were holes in them, through which the rain came in and drenched the soldiers. Their stock of groceries was ruined too. The pegs that held the tents had been loosened and the tents began to quake.

The Mughal generals were camped in tents some distance from each other. Each cluster of tents was surrounded by a wall.

Zulfikar was inside his tent. His eyes were cruel. His orange hued beard seemed to reflect his aggressiveness. His muscular body proclaimed that to him war was mere sport.

"Huzur! Everything's ruined!" one of his deputies came running in. "The white men and the Marathas had blocked the roads through which groceries would have been brought to us. But in spite of such hurdles, I had gathered groceries and stored them. Everything has been ruined by the rain. All the provisions are floating in the rain water!"

"Idiot!" Zulfikar rose from his bed. How tall he was! His head touched the top of the tent! "Food! That's all you can think of. If you had not thought about food all the time, Senji, this small pea sized kingdom would have been ours long ago. Get out!"

The deputy was silent. "I told you to get out! If it rains here, it will also be raining in Senji. The King of Senji too will face difficulties because of the rain. Now is the time to strike. Where are our men who man the cannons? Ask them to fire the cannons towards the Senji fort."

"Who will fire the cannons?" a voice outside the tent asked.

It was Zulfikar's father, Azad Khan.

"Why, what has happened to our men?" asked Zulfikar.

"Look! There they are, leaving your camp!"

A huge crowd of people was leaving the camp, their personal belongings bundled and tucked under their arms. "Stop! Where are you gong?" Zulfikar asked them. No one heeded his shouts. One of them answered," We are not prepared to die of hunger. If we go to Vandavasi, we will get food and shelter, and we will also be able to find employment."

"No, don't go. Just wait for a coupe of days," Zulfikar pleaded. "Syed Lazkar Khan is coming through Cuddapah, with money and weapons from the Emperor... Be patient."

"We are not prepared to believe you." The soldiers walked on.

"I was planning to conquer Singavaram, after destroying Senji. A new Queen has ascended the throne there. She insulted the Emperor, by refusing to receive his sandals with respect. I wanted to teach her a lesson."

Zulfikar's father said, "There is no use arguing with them."

Zulfikar said, "Did you hear what my father said? He says you are unfit to do anything but eat. Should you not prove him wrong? We set out with the intention of bringing all of Hindustan under the control of our Emperor Aurangazeb. Until we have achieved our goal, we must not return. Let us all take a pledge that we will achieve that goal!"

Some men hesitated. Zulfikar pressed home his advantage. "Think of all those territories we have conquered—Raichur, Kurnool, Nandyal, Cuddapah, Karamkonda. Did not our enemies lose in all these places? If they had not, would we have been able to set foot in Karnataka? Is this small Senji such a difficult proposition? Stop and turn back!"

Suddenly there was a change in the attitude of the soldiers. "Long live General Zulfikar Khan!" they shouted.

Azad Khan beamed with pride at his son's cleverness. "You are truly a leader of men."

But further conversation was ruled out, because Zulfikar saw two men running towards him. He was shocked, for they were the men he had placed in charge of the tent where Prince Kam Baksh was kept prisoner. And behind them were the men who had been guarding the Northern and Western entrances.

"Run, general. Run, if you value your life," they shouted.

"Why, what has happened?"

"Satan! Satan in the form of three elephants. And two Satans on the back of the elephants. They suddenly emerged from the Vettavalam forest and began to attack."

"Aren't you ashamed to be sacred of a few elephants?"

"No, they are no ordinary elephants. Each of them has an iron chain in its hands. They swish the chains fiercely."

"Idiots! We have men stationed on all sides of the fort. Tell our men to attack these elephants from behind. Quick!"

TWENTY ONE

The enemy forces resembled an ant hill crushed underfoot by cows! They were like a garden plundered by monkeys! Like a herd of deer caught in a deluge!

Break! Destroy! Scatter! Run!

Like cyclones, like earthquakes, like floods—the elephants caused destruction in the enemy camp. Kanchipurathan, perched on one of the elephants, enjoyed seeing the enemy forces flee! His heart swelled with pride at the success of his plan! As the elephants lashed out with iron chains at the enemy soldiers, they fell down, mortally wounded. Kanchipurathan was overjoyed.

"Do you see what is happening?" Kanchipurathan asked the dwarf.

"Wonderful!" the dwarf answered. "No one but you could have thought up such a wonderful plan!" He stood on the elephant's back and waved his hands in delight.

"Down, down. You'll be hurt," warned Kanchipurathan.

Spears and arrows came flying towards them. They would have torn into the dwarf, if he had not ducked. As Zulfikar's army retreated, Kanchipurathan's elephants advanced. Kanchipurathan lay down on the back of the elephant. "And where do you think I learnt this trick?" he asked the dwarf. "From a boy!"

"Really? When?"

"Swing the chain. That's it. Good!" Kanchipurathan encouraged his elephant and then answered the dwarf, "He was a very young boy. But a very smart boy. He used a sling to keep vultures at bay. And from him I learnt…"

"Victory is ours!" the dwarf clapped his hands, but suddenly he faltered, "Look. We are being attacked from behind!"

Kanchipurathan turned to find Zulfikar leading his forces towards him.

"And we are also being attacked from the front. The forces that ran away are back. We are caught between the two," shouted the dwarf.

"Don't be afraid," said Kanchipurathan. "We are not alone. The Deputy Chief of our army will be here soon." He looked in the direction of Singavaram. But there was no sign of the Singavaram forces.

The red light on top of the watch tower should have been lit by now. That was to be the indication that the Deputy had left Singavaram and was on his way. But there was no red light to be seen. Kanchipurathan had been betrayed. Why the Deputy Chief had betrayed him, wondered Kanchipurathan.

But there was no time to think about anything now.

He turned the dwarf's elephant in one direction and his elephant in another. The third elephant was stationed in such a way that he could direct it in whichever direction he needed to, later. He made his elephant and the dwarf's elephant swing the chains faster.

The rains had let up, and Zulfikar's cannons began to fire. Kanchipurathan and the dwarf would fall to cannon fire any minute now.

"Look! God has saved us. Here is an army to help us," shouted the dwarf.

"Our army, Deputy," said Kanchipurathan. But the next second he corrected himself. "No, this is not our army. That is the flag of Senji. It's the king of Senji with his army!"

Kanchipurathan could guess what had happened. When Rajaram knew Zulfikar's forces were being attacked, he had sent his forces out of the Senji fort, to lend a helping hand.

Fear—the fear that they were losing and the confusion resulting from the unexpected attack—had made Zulfikar's men mess up the cannons and the ammunition. The cannon balls had not hit any target, but lay scattered everywhere. The only result of all that firing was that they had exhausted all their ammunition.

When Rajaram's army and Kanchipurathan met each other, there was no enemy for them to tackle.

"Run! Run all of you!" said Kanchipurathan.

"All of you run to Chennai. I am told that the Company has a huge vat full of porridge for beggars.

Go and have your fill there," said the dwarf to Zulfikar's fleeing forces.

Kanchipurathan climbed down from the elephant. He saw the bodies that lay scattered round him. He heard wounded men screaming in pain. Vultures circled the scene of battle. The Sun was rising, and the extent of damage caused to the enemy was clear.

There were tears in Kanchipurathan's eyes.

"Such things are inevitable in any battle, my friend," said one of Rajaram's generals.

"If you had delayed even a second, we would have ended up like these men," said Kanchipurathan.

"And there would have been none to feel sorry for you."

Kanchipurathan wiped the tears from his eyes.

The three Maratha generals of Senji embraced Kanchipurathan, the man who had saved Senji.

"My role was only a small one," said Kanchipurathan.

"But it was timely, and therefore larger in magnitude than the Universe," said Nimaji Scindia. "You helped us when we needed help. Look. Those are the forces that Ramachandra, our representative in the North, has sent. Dhansingh Jadav and Santaji Ghorpode are arriving with 30 000 soldiers on horseback. The danger to Senji has passed."

A solider on horseback came out of the Senji fort. "The king wants to see the general who came all the way from Singavaram with elephants to save Senji," he said.

Kanchipurathan turned down the invitation, "There is no time for that. I have to return to Singavaram. Besides, I don't think I have done anything that deserves an audience with the king."

But Nagojimane said, "It is disrespectful to refuse the King's invitation. He will not detain you for long. Please come."

Kanchipurathan accompanied the Maratha generals. But his eyes scanned the Singavaram hill. Why wasn't the red light there? What had happened to the deputy?

♦

'You are like the sudden gift of sight to a man who has been blind all his life! You are an unexpected treasure.'—these are clichéd words of praise, my friend. And they are quite meaningless. Today you have saved Senji, and there can be no words to describe what you have done," said Rajaram, King of Senji.

Kalyana Mahal was full of all the important officials and generals. Soldiers who had been wounded in the battle had just administered some first aid to their wounds and hadn't fully dressed the wounds. They were there to celebrate the victory.

Kanchipurathan had never been the cynosure of all eyes, and he was embarrassed. He looked around to see if there was some way in which he could make himself inconspicuous.

The Peshwa gave a sword to the King, and as the crowd cheered, the King placed the sword in Kanchipurathan's hands and said, "Please accept this as a token of our gratitude."

Kanchipurathan accepted the honour with a smile. "I know some proverbs that would be apt here. There's one that says that it so happened that when a crow sat on a palm tree, a fruit dropped down, and the crow got the credit for knocking down the fruit! My arrival in the nick of time was like that. I tried to defeat the enemy of Singavaram and my efforts were childish. Actually, it was Senji's heroic defense that clinched victory. Anyway, this is an opportunity for Singavaram and Senji to be friends always!"

"Well said, my friend!" said Rajaram, the King of Senji. "I hear a lot about the new Queen of Singavaram. I am told she is beautiful and very intelligent too. My son, the Crown prince of Senji, is a good soldier, and is also well educated."

Kanchipurathan couldn't understand why the King was talking about his son, but the crowd could guess. They cheered loudly.

Rajaram continued, "The Singavaram royal family is of ancient lineage. It is a family with a formidable reputation. They have marital relations with many royal families. My sister, Ambika, will soon be there, to discuss a possible marriage. Please tell your Queen this. Today marks the beginning of a long and lasting relationship with Singavaram."

Kanchipurathan could not pay attention to anything that was being said. He made his excuses, and left.

♦

Kanchipurathan stopped the elephant at the foot of the Singavaram hill. A palanquin was waiting there for him. "Where is the Deputy Chief of the army? Is he ashamed of himself, for letting me down? Is he therefore hiding somewhere?" he asked.

The men waiting there for Kanchipurathan did not reply. They looked confused. One of them said, "The Queen has sent this palanquin for you. We have been asked to escort you with honours to Singavaram."

"I am grateful to the Queen for this honour. But I want an answer to my question. I would consider that a greater honour than anything else."

"We do not know."

Another of the men said, "Everyone is waiting to honour you. They have fixed an auspicious time for the ceremony. You will have to hurry, or we will be late."

Kanchipurathan mulled over what the man said, and then turned to the dwarf who was manning the other two elephants and said, "Come here and get into the palanquin."

"What?!" the men who had come there to escort him said in disbelief.

"This man has as much of a role in Singavaram's victory as I have. Tell the Queen that."

He then walked away. Where was the Deputy Chief of the army? That was the question that kept nagging him. Wherever he went, he received the same reply. No one had seen the Deputy. But in the armoury, he received a different reply. "The Deputy Chief of the army was here and said he was preparing for a battle. But after that, we never saw him. Maybe he is on some secret mission."

"Where is his house?"

"I know. I will show you the way," said one of the men working in the armoury.

♦

"The auspicious time I had fixed is slipping away," the royal family's priest fretted.

"He is a good soldier. But he doesn't show any respect for conventions," Krishnappa muttered.

Thamarai, who was seated on her throne, was worried. She turned to her aunt Chennamma and said, "Do you think some danger has befallen him on the way back home?"

"That he is blessed by the gods has been amply demonstrated on many occasions. Don't worry, Thamarai. He and danger are miles apart," Chennamma said.

"There is the palanquin," shouted the crowd.

"But where is the general? I see a dwarf inside the palanquin!" exclaimed Krishnappa.

The palanquin bearers said, "The general said he has some important work to take care of."

"What! How can he not come when the Queen has ordered him to? How can anything else be more important?" the people assembled in the palace said.

Chennamma whispered to Thamarai, "I think you are too lenient with him."

"The time is no longer auspicious for the ceremony. We will have to postpone it to tomorrow," said the priest. The people started to leave. But—

"Long live Singavaram!" said someone. It was Kanchipurathan! He bowed before Thamarai.

Thamarai beamed. She could see that he was injured but breathed a sigh of relief when she saw that none of the injuries was serious.

Krishnappa chided him affectionately, "The Queen was waiting to honour you. You shouldn't have come late."

"Please forgive me. It is important to receive honours at the appointed hour. I understand. But there isn't any particular time for a subject to complain to the Queen, is there?" asked Kanchipurathan.

"What is your complaint?"

"I want justice for this," said Kanchipurathan, and pulled out a mangalsutra.[4]

"A mangalsutra!" exclaimed Thamarai and Chennamma.

---

[4] *Mangalsutra- a sacred thread worn by married women*

TWENTY TWO

There was a mangalsutra[5] in Kanchipurathan's hands.

Krishnappa took it from him. "The locket has the claws of a tiger, indicating that it belongs to the wife of a brave warrior," he said.

"Not just a warrior. It belongs to the wife of the Deputy Chief of the army. Her husband has been killed. I seek justice for her," said Kanchipurathan.

"The Deputy Chief..." three voices exclaimed.

"Yes, he is dead. No, no. He has been killed. And he was not killed in battle, but was stabbed from behind," said Kanchipurathan.

"Who did it? And why?"

"I will answer the why first. I had ordered that a small force was to come to Senji under his command. Raghunatha advised him not to follow my orders. The Deputy Chief was confused. Should he obey my orders, or the orders of the old man who was related to the royal family? His wife made it clear to him that he must obey the chief of the army. He realised where his duty lay and set out for battle, when he was stabbed!"

"Who did it?"

---

5   *Mangalsutra- a sacred thread that married Hindu women wear. It is removed upon the husband's death.*

Kanchipurathan looked round. There were a few soldiers there. He dismissed them, and then said to Chennamma, "Your father."

"My father!"

"That great warrior's wife came to know that her husband had been killed by Raghunatha. But she didn't want to talk publicly about it when a war was on. So she kept silent. But she committed Suttee[6]. I gathered all the details by questioning her neighbours."

Krishnappa shouted, "Where is Raghunatha?"

Thamarai intervened and said, "Please be patient. Let us make further enquires and then…"

"No. Never. My father must not be forgiven for this. There was a time when we were his accomplices too. But he must realise that we are no longer plotting against the queen. My father had lustful thoughts about Thamarai. We thought it was a temporary aberration, and we forgave him. He killed a serving girl by pushing her into the moat. We forgave him for that too, on account of his old age. He imprisoned the General in the underground prison. We ignored his treachery. He bargained with the Company to sell off a portion of the kingdom. Although that was treason, we still did not punish him. But he should no longer be forgiven," said Chennamma. No one dared to speak a word against her.

---

6   *Suttee- the custom where a widow immolated herself on her husband's funeral pyre*

Krishnappa summoned a guard and ordered him to bring Raghunatha to the court hall.

The guard returned in a few minutes. "He isn't in his quarters. I was told that he left on horseback."

"What!"

A solider entered and handed a letter to Thamarai. "This was found on Raghunatha's bed, Your Majesty," he said.

Thamarai read the message, *"Don't think I am running away because of fear. I will be back soon, and with the Company's forces to help me. Raghunatha."*

♦

It was a beautiful night. Creepers swaying to the breeze, and stars in a clear blue sky. But Thamarai was in no mood to enjoy any of this. She looked sadly at Kanchipurathan who was there to take leave of her. "Do you have to go? Can't you go a few days later?"

Kanchipurathan smiled. "Your Majesty must forgive me. Actually I should have left yesterday. I cannot let a venomous snake have its way. I have to follow it and fight it. Raghunatha has gone to Chennai. And he has promised to bring the Company's forces here. I have to go, Your Majesty."

The next second, an arrow flew past Thamarai and embedded itself in a tree. Thamarai screamed. She had had a narrow escape.

"Who is it?" Kanchipurathan ran in the direction from which the arrow had been shot, but he could find no one there. He searched in the bushes and didn't leave an inch of space uncovered, but found no one.

Thamarai was pale with fear. "Your Majesty. We must go back to the palace. Someone is trying to kill you. He doesn't know that I am your shield, the idiot!"

When he took Thamarai to the palace, Kanchipurathan said, "I am going to delay my Chennai visit by a couple of days. I want to know if that arrow was an accident or if it was intended for you. I can't leave without finding out the mystery behind that arrow."

"I don't want you to be in danger because of me," said Thamarai.

Kanchipurathan waited for three days. There was no other such incident. So he decided to leave.

♦

Move! Make way for the general! He's off to Chennai. There was a crowd to see him off. An old lady pushed her way through the crowd. "I know him. Let me talk to him," she said.

Kanchipurathan recognised her voice. "Bring that old lady to me," he ordered.

The crowd parted and made way for her. The old lady ran up to Kanchipurathan. "How are you grandma?" Kanchipurathan asked. How could he forget this lady? She was the one who had made his entry into the palace possible. Her son was a nagaswaram player, and Kanchipurathan had taken his place at the palace.

"We are all fine, young man. My son is all right now," the old lady replied.

"I am glad to hear that, grandma. If you need some help, just come to the palace."

The old lady didn't reply. But it was clear that she didn't have any faith in Kanchipurathan's words.

"Why are you silent?" he asked. "Don't hesitate. Go on. Tell me what the matter is."

"Things don't move so fast in government circles." She looked round to make sure no one was within earshot. She then wiped the tears from her eyes and said, "We haven't been paid our dues for the last two years. Do you know how many times we have requested the palace accountant and the administrative officer to look into the matter?"

"You could have come to the palace and complained in person."

The old lady laughed. "Do you think I didn't come to the palace? Do you think those armed guards will let me in? They pushed me away. I begged them to let me in, but they wouldn't."

Kanchipurathan ground his teeth, He then said to the old lady, "Grandma. You go home. I will go to the palace and make sure you get what is due to you."

He picked up the bridle and gave it a twist.

But he didn't ride towards Chennai. He rode towards the palace.

♦

Thamarai had not recovered from the emotional farewell. She was emotionally spent. What was that? She heard someone riding towards the palace. Who was it who was riding so fast?

It couldn't be, but it was! It was he!

Her heart gave a leap. But the next minute a look of concern enveloped her face. Why was he returning?

"Why have you come back?" she asked Kanchipurathan.

"Thamarai," he began and checked himself. "Sorry. Your Majesty, forgive me."

"I wish you would make the mistake of calling by my name more often. These days you never address me by name. Do you know how happy I am that you called me Thamarai?"

Kanchipurathan did not respond, but said instead, "I am here to remind the Queen of her duties. A lotus is alive only when it is in mud. And a ruler commands respect as long as he or she is in touch with the common man. We are told that even God is respected only because He is easy to access."

"And do I not mingle freely with my people?"

"An old lady complained a while ago. She came here many times to complain to you, and was turned away by your guards."

"Really? I do not want to be out of touch with my people. I wish there was some way in which I could meet them periodically."

"There is a way, my dear," said Krishnappa, who had entered just then.

Chennamma was with him. "Your father—my elder brother—had an arrangement. Look through that window."

"I see an old pavilion. It's dilapidated and locked too."

"There is a bell there. Anyone who wanted to meet the king could go there and ring the bell. My brother would come out running to meet them, whatever time of day it was. And he would see that justice was done to them. It's a bell specially made and brought in from Madurai. It's made of bronze."

"Are you happy now?" Thamarai asked Kanchipurathan, with a smile.

Krishnappa clapped his hands and summoned the dwarf who had been peeping into the room. "Here is the General's friend. We will make arrangements to revive the practice…"

♦

The next day...

The pavilion with the bell had been opened. A huge crowd had gathered. Thamarai stood beneath the huge bell and said, "My dear people of Singavaram! I want to reduce the distance between you and me. From now on..."

The dwarf had been looking up at the bell and he screamed, "Your Majesty! Move! Danger! Danger!"

The next second—

The sound of wood breaking. The beam to which the bell was tied had broken, and the bell came crashing down.

The crowd was shocked into silence. What a catastrophe had been averted! If the Queen had delayed even a fraction of a second...

Kanchipurathan was the first to steady himself, "The time isn't propitious for us to revive the practice. We'll have to postpone it to another day. All of you leave, please."

The crowd began to disperse. The royal family and the ministers remained. Thamarai had not got over the shock, and she still quivered with fear.

Kanchipurathan turned to the dwarf and said, "You were the one who made arrangements. Why did you not check if the beam and rope were strong?"

"I did. Some traitors must have been at work after I checked them."

"Don't scold him. After all, he is the one who saved Thamarai's life," Krishnappa said.

Kanchipurathan was worried. "Raghunatha has left behind someone to harm Thamarai. I must find out who it is."

♦

A couple of days after the incident—outside Thamarai's room—

Kanchipurathan kept himself hidden, and waited. Yes, he could hear footsteps in the corridor.

Kanchipurathan moved slowly, and pounced on the man. He dragged him to the courtyard and looked at him in the moonlight.

"It's you!" he said in shock and disbelief.

TWENTY THREE

"**Y**ou! It's you!" Kanchipurathan pulled out his dagger, and would have plunged it in the man's heart.

"Forgive me, please. I shouldn't have done it." The dwarf fell at Kanchipurathan's feet!

"Get up!" said Kanchipurathan. "You have saved your life by falling at my feet. I trusted you. I thought you were my friend. Traitor!"

"No, I am not a traitor. I swear on God. Believe me," the dwarf cried. "I did all this because of my affection for you, because of my regard for the Queen."

"A likely story!"

"It's the truth. I know you and the Queen are in love with each other. But you were preparing to leave for Chennai. The Queen will be happy only if you are with her. And I will be happy too, if you and she are not separated. That is why I rigged up these things to frighten you into staying back…"

"You fool! You have ruined my plans!" Kanchipurathan studied the dwarf's face. It proclaimed his innocence.

"If I had had bad intentions, would I have saved the Queen in the nick of time every time a mishap was about to occur?" asked the dwarf.

"Get out of my sight! Idiot!" Kanchipurathan pushed him away. "I have wasted time because of you. Go away."

Kanchipurathan hurried to Thamarai's room. He explained what had happened. And then he set off for Chennai. But not in his uniform. He was dressed like a civilian.

Kanchipurathan decided to take the Vandavasi, Tirukazhukundram, Mahabalipuram route to Chennai.

A festival was being celebrated in Tirukazhukundram. It was getting hot, and Kanchipurathan made his way to a tamarind tree, under the shade of which a man was selling tender coconuts. Kanchipurathan picked up a few coconuts, shook them to check which of them was full of water. After he'd had chosen one and had had the tender coconut water, he handed the coconut back to the vendor, asking him to scoop out the pulp, when he heard someone shout, "This is unfair! Most unfair!"

"You old man! How dare you lie?" said a few other voices. Kanchipurathan hastened to see what the argument was about.

"What's happening?" he asked. He saw three sepoys trying to take away a horse. They were sepoys who worked for the Company. He could tell by the colour of their uniforms.

An old man was holding onto the bridle and refusing to let go. Tears flowed from his eyes. "I am a poor man. I reared this horse from the time it was a foal. I am selling it because I need the money."

One of the sepoys tugged at the old man's dhoti and said, "Well if it's your horse then prove it."

"I bought it years ago in Madurai. How can I produce any proof now?"

"Let him go," said Kanchipurathan to the sepoy and slapped his hand away from the old man's dhoti. "Tell me, brave man, will a thief sell a stolen horse in a bazaar?"

"This is a horse that belongs to the Company. Horses belonging to the Company get stolen very often in Chennai," said the three sepoys.

"I am not surprised. With idiots like you, one day even the Governor will disappear!"

The crowd laughed.

"Only a horse belonging to the Company will be of such good breed."

"Tell me old man, when you bought this horse in Madurai, did they tell you it came from Kathiawar?"

"I've been trying to recall that word. Now that you mention it, yes, the seller did say it was from Kathiawar."

"Idiots," Kanchipurathan said to the sepoys. "Look at the ears of this horse. The tips of the ears are like the tip of a mango. Only horses from Kathiawar have ears like these. Show me a Company horse with ears like these."

"Clever man! He's got a point," the crowd began to say.

The Company sepoys slipped away. And when the crowd found that the quarrel had fizzled out, it moved away.

"You saved my horse," the old man said.

"You can sell this horse now."

"Horse for sale! It's good breed!" the old man shouted.

"Old man, you don't seem to have any marketing skills. Let me show you how to do it," said Kanchipurathan to the old man. He then shouted, "Come and have a look at this horse. It's a rare breed. Have you heard of the verse in Seevakachintamani which says that there were horses that caused more damage in the enemy forces than even sharp arrows? Well, that verse was talking about horses of this breed. A verse in Puranaanooru says that there were horses that tore into the enemy forces like boats that tore through the waters of the ocean. That verse too was talking about this kind of horse." A crowd had now gathered round the horse.

Hundred rupees! One hundred and twenty! One hundred and seventy five!

The bids kept getting higher and higher!

Finally, the horse was sold for 200 rupees. Kanchipurathan handed the reins of the horse to the buyer, and gave the coins to the old man. "I will take leave of you now," he said to the old man.

"Please come to my house. Please," said the old man.

"I have no time. I have something very important to take care of," protested Kanchipurathan. But the old man insisted and finally Kanchipurathan had to yield.

♦

His hut was at the foot of a hill. It was dusk by the time Kanchipurathan and the old man reached the hut.

A young man was seated outside the hut. It was clear that he was impatient. "Father, you have kept me waiting for so long. I should never have paid heed to you. I am leaving now," he said.

"Please do not be angry, my son. This man here helped me sell the horse for a good price. Look, here's the money."

"All right. Spend it wisely."

"This is for you. I sold my horse, which was very dear to me, for your sake. Use the money to set up a business. Do whatever business you want to do. But please don't leave me alone. I am old and I do not want to be parted from my only son."

"So that's why you asked me to wait and went off with that horse? You cannot make me stay here. My friends are waiting for me. We have come from

Trichy and we have to go to Mysore. I just thought I would pay you a visit. In retrospect I think I shouldn't have done that. Let me go."

Kanchipurathan put his hands on the young man's shoulders and gently forced him to sit down. "Friend, please be patient. It's hard to find energetic young men like you these days. Now tell me, what exactly is this disagreement you have with your father? Tell me before you leave."

"My name is Senthil. My father wants me to stay in this village. But I don't want to."

Kanchipurathan smiled. It was like hearing an echo of his voice. He too had left Kanchipuram because he was bored with life there. "You said you were going to Mysore. Why are you going there?"

"The Mysore King Chikkadevaraya has built a dam across the Cauvery. How will Thanjavur and Trichy get water for irrigation, if the Cauvery is dammed? The crops there will wilt without water. A severe famine will be the ultimate consequence."

"So what do you propose to do?" murmured the old man.

"I am going to prove that Tamilians are brave people. Rani Mangamma of Trichy and the Thanjavur King indulge in useless discussions. I am going to prove that there are men of action in Tamil Nadu. A few of us are going to Mysore, to destroy that dam. Ours is a secret mission. Now tell me, isn't it important that I go to Mysore?"

Kanchipurathan didn't reply. How could he fault Senthil's motives?

He looked at the old man, and was moved by the look of concern on his face. "You are right, young man. There is nothing wrong with your motives. But you must consider your father's age. You have a duty to look after him in his old age."

"Duty! Don't talk to me about duty! There are so many able bodied men like you, who should have undertaken this task. But did they? Even you seem to have nothing better to do than to travel aimlessly."

"All right. I will go to Mysore instead of you. What do you have to say to that?" Kanchipurathan suggested.

"I... you..."

"Why do you hesitate? Tell me where your friends are."

"They are in the rest house near the temple. But you..."

The old man interrupted, "I don't want you to risk your life for my sake."

"Don't worry," Kanchipurathan said to the old man. "Senthil, stay with your father at least till I am back from Mysore. I must thank you for giving me an opportunity to serve the country."

It was dark when Kanchipurathan reached the pavilion. He could see many young men in the pavilion. "Who is there?" one of them asked.

"Senthil," replied Kanchipurathan.

"Get up. Get up." The man woke up everyone who was sleeping in the pavilion. He didn't speak loudly, but whispered. Kanchipurathan wasn't asleep. He was only pretending to be asleep. He opened his eyes slowly.

The men in the pavilion were all awake now. "Please go to the next room," the man whispered to them.

Kanchipurathan was amused! But he was also a little apprehensive. No one had noticed that it was he, not Senthil who had joined them. The sun would rise in a few hours. And they would discover that a stranger had joined their ranks. What would happen once they found an impostor in their midst?

"Hurry up," said the man who had woken them all up. Kanchipurathan went into the next room. "Has everyone got one?" asked someone.

What was it that everyone was supposed to receive? "I haven't got one," said Kanchipurathan.

"Here, take one."

Kanchipurathan stretched his hand in the direction from which the voice came. A false moustache, beard, wig, a long robe, a mud pot, and wooden footwear were placed in his outstretched hand. They were all supposed to disguise themselves as mendicants!

Kanchipurathan was excited. He put on the disguise. "Shh. Quiet, all of you." That must be the voice of the chief. "From now on we aren't soldiers. We are travelling mendicants. Only after we reach Chennai, will we be able to decide our next move. Until then, we must remain disguised. You mustn't engage in conversation. Just keep repeating the various names of God."

By the time they had all put on the disguise, and had come out, the sun was rising, and Kanchipurathan noticed that there were fifty men in the group. They were all more or less the same age as Kanchipurathan. None of them asked him any questions, and Kanchipurathan was glad they didn't.

It kept drizzling the whole day, and the path was muddy. They reached Poonamallee, and decided to spend the night there. It was raining heavily now. The chief said, "I can see a temple there. Let us stay there."

When the men entered the temple, hot pongal[7] was being served in the temple. Kanchipurathan looked round. There were many mendicants in the temple, but they were all real ones, not fakes like Kanchipurathan and his companions.

The wind howled. The trees swayed in the wind. A coconut tree was uprooted and came crashing.

"There is going to be a flood," said one of the men, licking his fingers.

The mendicant sitting next to him said, "This is nothing. You should come to Mysore."

"Are you from Mysore?"

"I was there till day before yesterday. It poured. The dam built by Chikkadevaraya broke. It was washed

---

7   *Pongal- rice and lentil preparation*

away by the flood. It is said that it will be impossible to build a dam across the Cauvery again."

Kanchipurathan looked at his companions. Had they not heard that the dam was broken? Or were they pretending not to have heard?

"Can I have some pickle, please?" Kanchipurathan asked the temple cook, and then moved to where the chief was seated. "Did you hear what that man said? The dam in Mysore has been washed away," whispered kanchipurathan.

"Yes, yes," said the chief. He didn't seem to be in the least concerned or interested.

Kanchipurathan became suspicious. "Wasn't it because of that dam that the rice fields of Thanjavur and Trichy didn't receive water for irrigation? Isn't that why Trichy and Thanjavur were facing a famine? I thought we were going there to break that dam."

"Don't be stupid. Why should we bother about those who die in a famine? Let them die. What is it to us? Let us attend to our work."

Kanchipurathan was shocked. These men had nothing to do with the breaking of the dam. He had joined the wrong group by mistake! How could it have happened? He didn't know.

He moved over and sat beside another man belonging to the group. "What is the name of this place?"

"Poonamallee."

"Poonamallee," Kanchipurathan repeated a few times. "My wife and children are a nuisance."

"Why what do they do?"

"When I return, they bother me with so many questions. They want to know the name of every village and town I passed through. I try to keep myself informed, so that I can answer their questions."

"So you're a henpecked husband!" teased the man.

"It's my fate. What was the name of that place we stayed in yesterday?"

"Chinna Chatram."

"Is there any other rest house there?"

"Yes, there is a bigger one to the right of the temple."

So he must have gone to the wrong rest house and joined the wrong group, Kanchipurathan realised. But further enquires became impossible, because someone in the temple told them to be quiet and let people sleep.

All was not lost. Kanchipurathan knew that he could slip away quietly. But he didn't want to. Where were these men going and why? He was curious and wanted to find out.

◆

They left Poonamallee early the next morning, and reached Vepery. The area bore a festive look. Festoons were suspended across the streets.

Plantain trees had been erected here and there. Mughal soldiers and soldiers from the Company were riding around on horseback.

Kanchipurathan did not have to ask anyone any questions. He picked up information from the conversation of his companions.

"The Company is celebrating the end of their troubles. Lingappa used to be in this area, and he would waylay all vehicles bound for the fort. He would either take away all the goods, or he would levy hefty taxes on the goods. Now the Company is rid of that nuisance. That's why the men of the Company are in a celebratory mood."

"How did they get rid of that nuisance?" Kanchipurathan asked.

"This man is an idiot. Have you heard of Zulfikar Khan—the General of the Emperor of Delhi? He looks so frightening, that you will faint if you were to see him face to face."

Kanchipurathan, with great difficulty, kept away from smiling. "I've heard of him. How does he come into the story now?"

"Poor man. He lost to the King of Senji, and he and his men had to come to Chennai. The men of the Company gave them shelter, and food. Out of gratitude, Zulfikar has ceded the villages of Vepery, Tondiarpet, Ezhumbur and Purasaiwakkam to the Company. The Company now has full rights over the area. That's what they are celebrating. Now do you understand, you idiot?"

"Yes, yes," said Kanchipurathan.

They could hear the galloping of horses. A cloud of dust rose up. The chief of Kanchipurathan's group said, "That must be an officer of the Company. Be quiet. We are supposed to meet him here."

The officer of the company and his interpreter arrived.

The interpreter asked, "The officer wants to know if you are the men going to Singavaram."

The officer gave the fifty men a glance and said something to the interpreter, who, again translated, "This is an operation that has to be kept secret. Are all the men reliable?"

"Yes," answered the chief.

Kanchipurathan's heart missed a beat, when Singavaram was mentioned.

It was clear to Kanchipurathan that Peria Pedhu and Raghunatha, together with the Company, had come up with a plot against Singavaram.

TWENTY FOUR

Chennai! Chennai again! The city that attracted the young! The city that sings paeans to modernity! The city that challenges one's resourcefulness! Kanchipurathan was entering the city that welcomes youth, honours cleverness, and rewards courage.

A city Kanchipurathan was familiar with. A city he had experience of.

Kanchipurathan's heart gave a leap and he felt a pleasant balmy breeze in his heart. Had he imbibed some magic elixir? He felt his spirits soar.

Memories—pleasant memories—memories of the time spent with Thamarai—excited him.

The mendicants were entering Chennai. "We have to spend a few days inside the fort. We are waiting for reinforcements from Calcutta," said the officer of the East India Company, who had met them in Vepery.

The roads they travelled through in Chennai were ones that kindled memories in Kanchipurathan.

This was the place where slaves were whipped. And there were the men with whips in their hands. If only they knew that Kanchipurathan, now in the guise of a mendicant, had once thrashed one of the supervisors—Kanchipurathan smiled.

Here was the street through which he and Thamarai had run, holding hands. That was the wall she had leant against, unable to move further. "Come on. We just have to cover a little more distance," he had urged her. He had put his hands round her shoulders. Even now the thought of his arms around Thamarai excited him.

Thamarai! Thamarai! We don't need the luxuries of a palace. You don't need the crown. Nor do I need the sword. Let us go back to what we used to be—you, a slave and me, a wanderer.

"Please stand in line."

A voice broke into his thoughts. He realised that they had entered the fort. The leader of the group of mendicants lined them up in a row.

Four chiefs of the Company's forces inspected them. One of them tugged Kanchipurathan's beard, and said, "Fix your beard securely."

Kanchipurathan smiled. This was the official who had once asked Kanchipurathan to shave his wife's head. He didn't recognise Kanchipurathan now.

Suddenly someone said, "You will all leave in three days. You don't have to keep your disguises until then. I will arrange for ordinary clothes to be given to you."

The men were relieved. They gladly shed their false beards and moustaches. But Kanchipurathan was taken aback. Senthil's friends would know the wrong man was in their midst. He looked around, not knowing what to do. "Wait a minute. Who said you could discard your disguises? You must keep your disguises. That way no one will suspect you. You can travel freely inside the city. Remain disguised," said another official of the Company.

The men muttered their disapproval. Kanchipurathan was the only one who was happy.

They were all housed in an old building next to a stable. The person who served them food was the same old cook who worked for the Company. But he too failed to recognise Kanchipurathan.

The men were tired after their long journey and they fell asleep. But Kanchipurathan couldn't sleep. He rolled over to the door, got up and slowly made his way out.

Where was Sivachidambaram? What would he be doing now?

Silence had enveloped the place. But one or two crickets, unable to sleep like Kanchipurathan, moaned. Kanchipurathan had not noticed a bucket near the well. He tripped over it, and was afraid there would be trouble for him soon. He was supposed to be spying for the Company, but here he was spying inside the Company's Fort.

Someone touched his shoulder. He turned round, but found no one there. On his shoulder was a chameleon. He pushed it down, and as it jumped off, the priest he had met in the beach turned up.

"Hello, young man! Haven't you seen all of the city yet?"

Kanchipurtathan tried to lull his suspicions.

"I think you have mistaken me for someone else."

"Maybe I have," said the priest. He picked up the chameleon, and rubbed it gently. "I am getting old. My eyesight is poor. So perhaps I mistook you for someone else."

Kanchipurathan heaved a sigh of relief, and tried to slip away.

"Wait. I may be old, but my Moses isn't. His eyesight is sharp. He has an excellent memory. He has a keen sense of smell. Even a dog of excellent breed stands no comparison with my Moses. So I have no doubt that you are my old friend Kanchipurathan."

Kanchipurathan was speechless. "I suppose you weren't able to look round the last time you came into the Fort. All right, explore the Fort. And if you proceed towards the North, you will see something that will make you happy."

The priest and his pet moved away. It took Kanchipurathan a few seconds to realise the significance of the priest's words.

He walked in the direction pointed by the priest, and there he found Sivachidambaram, in a solitary cell, pacing up and down like a tiger.

"Ayya!" he called softly. Was this Sivachidambaram? Was this the man whose eyes used to glow like fire? The last time Kanchipurathan had seen him, his skin had been shrivelled, due to lack of nutrition. Now his bones seemed to stick out.

"Long live freedom! Welcome, young man," Sivachidambaram said. He had recognised Kanchipurathan. "Just check if someone's coming."

"No, there is no one here."

Sivachidambaram untied a red leg wrap, from his knee. It was the kind of leg wrap that Sepoys who worked for the Company wore. Inside it was a map.

"Here, take this. It is a map of this fort."

But how was Kanchipurathan to conceal it? He couldn't wrap a red tape around his leg. He was dressed as a mendicant. How could he wear this leg wrap?

"Wrap it around your waist, and hide it with your dhoti," said Sivachidambaram.

Kanchipurathan concealed it as directed. "What should I do with this map?"

"Take it to Parangipettai, to the Dutch camp."

Kanchipurathan hesitated. Sivachidambaram smiled. "If you leave today, it will arouse suspicion. Leave tomorrow. Give the map to the Dutch. They will be able to handle the danger, the threat to Singavaram. Don't worry about your lover."

"Ayya... How did you know? I didn't..."

"Did you think you were my only informant? I can hear someone coming. You must go away now."

◆

The next afternoon. The Fort bell rang four times. Kanchipurathan, who had been playing a game of chess with an Armenian, said, "Let us continue later. I want to go for a swim in the sea."

He slipped away quite cleverly, but someone noticed him and called out, "Senthil!"

It was the leader of the group of mendicants. He said to the Company official, "This is Senthil. He can be trusted. Clever young man. Take him with you."

"Be prepared to leave," said the Englishman in Tamil and went in to fetch someone else.

"Am I not entitled to know where I am going?" Kanchipuarthan asked.

"Don't worry. It's a place only trustworthy men like you can enter—it's the Company's mint."

"What's happening there?"

"Gold coins come in from overseas, and are taken to the mint. There the goldsmiths affix seals on them. The Englishmen have made arrangements to oversee their work. Still, there are a lot of counterfeit coins doing the rounds. They want to find out how counterfeit coins replace good ones in the mint."

"I have something else I want to do," said Kanchipurathan.

The team leader lost his patience, "Senthil! You have become very lazy."

Kanchipurathan felt it was wise not to argue with him further.

♦

"What is that noise? What's happening there?" one of the Englishmen asked sternly.

The place, the slave quarters.

The two goldsmiths looked at each other. "Nothing to worry about," they said.

"All right. Quick. Get the work done." That was the other Englishman. The goldsmiths could see he was irritated. He was new to the city. He was new to the way of life in the city. He didn't know how to sit cross-legged like his colleague. He had been standing throughout. He rested his right leg on the pyol, and rested his elbow on the right leg. His face reflected his irritation.

The coins were heated, and the gold became pliant. One of the men pressed the Compay's seal on the gold coin, and the other struck it hard. An image of Lord Venkatesa of Tirupathi with His Consorts became clearly imprinted on the coin. A young goldsmith dropped the coins with seals affixed into a bucket of cold water. A constant sizzling sound could be heard in the mint, as the heated coins were dropped one after another into cold water.

The Englishman had a pair of weighing scales made of silver. He weighed each coin on the scales and then put it into a chest.

Kanchipurathan stood watching. His smile hid his seething fury. Talented goldsmiths had been reduced to the status of slaves. Hands that had fashioned exquisite jewellery were now given the task of pounding the Company emblem on coins!

Suddenly, there was the lash of a whip. The goldsmith's son screamed in pain. His back had been lashed by the Englishman's whip. The older goldsmith was helpless. He could only give his son a sympathetic look. The boy explained, "Father, the coin was hot, and so I blew my fingers after dropping the coin into the bucket of water. The Durai[8] thought I was trying to steal it." The boy sobbed.

There was no one to console him. Everyone was afraid of the English. But before the whip could descend again, Kanchipurathan stood shielding the boy, and glared at the Englishman.

Again, an unexplained sound from inside the house. "Let me go and check," said the goldsmith.

"No," said the Englishman.

"I am not taking anything with me. You can check."

"Why do you have to go?"

"My wife has gone into labour."

"I don't believe you. Let me come and have a look."

"Please, please listen to me, ayya. Men aren't allowed into the room. And you are a foreigner too."

"I cannot trust you." The Englishman moved towards the goldsmith's house, but was pulled back by Kanchipurathan. "If you step in, I will kill you. Mark my word, I will kill you. Our dignity is more important to us than anything else."

---

8   *Durai- term by which European men were referred to deferentially by Indians*

The two Englishman were shocked. "Are you this goldsmith's accomplice?" one of them asked.

"These men are not thieves. But you are not perceptive. You cannot judge character. You cannot tell if a man is honest or not."

An old woman came out of the goldsmith's house. "Please come in for a minute. The midwife wants to say something to you."

"Please let me go, ayya," begged the goldsmith.

"Rogue! Cheat!" the Englishman's face was red.

"Be patient. This is not the place where counterfeit coins are made. I know that for sure," said Kanchipurathan.

"Where do they come from then?"

"I'll find out soon, and let you know."

They heard the cries of a baby entering the world.

"See? And you refused to believe him!" Kanchipurathan said to the Englishmen.

"All right. Let's talk about your promise. You said you knew where the counterfeit coins came from."

"Here, have some sugar to celebrate the birth of the child," said Kanchipurathan to the Englishman and offered him the sugar that the old lady brought.

Five chests full of coins had been imprinted with the emblem, and Kanchipurathan put the chests in the coach.

♦

The coach passed through a dense grove. The branches of trees scraped against the roof of the coach. The wheels rolled on like the wheels of Fate. It was dusk, with night just a few hours away.

Kanchipurathan was seated beside the coachman, and kept dropping off. A mild snoring could be heard. The coachman checked to see if Kanchipurathan was really asleep. "Watch out! You may fall off," he said. But he didn't try to wake him up.

The Englishmen were on horseback, riding ahead of the coach.

The coachman showed signs of nervousness. He looked to his left and right, as if he was looking for something. Every now and then, he also looked at Kanchipurathan.

Kanchipurathan tried hard not to smile. But unbeknownst to the coachman, he was looking at him every few minutes. The coachman's nervousness was puzzling.

What was the coachman planning?

All it took was a fleeting moment. How it could be accomplished so quickly was a mystery. But Kanchipurathan was witness to what happened.

There were two tamarind trees, with overhanging branches. A man was perched on the branches. The coachman handed one of the chests to the man on the tree. Another man, also perched on the tree, handed a chest to the coachman, and this replaced the one that had been removed from the coach. It was clear now to Kanchipurathan, that this was how counterfeit coins entered circulation.

"Stop, please. I have stomach cramps," Kanchipurathan wailed suddenly.

The Englishmen were startled by the sudden wail, and the coachman stopped the coach. "What's the matter?" the Englishmen asked.

"I have stomach cramps. Let me get off the coach," said Kanchipurathan.

One of the officers of the Company said, "What kind of drama is this? Get back on the coach."

But the other Englishman was a shrewd man. When Kanchipurathan gave him a signal, he understood that something serious was afoot. He could see that Kanchipurathan's intention was to get off the vehicle under some pretext.

"All right. The Company cannot incur losses because of your aches and pains. You get down now. You can follow us when you are better," he said.

The coach sped away.

Kanchipurathan did not want to waste even a second. He ran back to the place where the chests had been changed. But he took care to move silently. And soon, on a beaten track he could see the two men, carrying the chest. There was a building in the distance. They seemed to be proceeding towards the building. Kanchipurathan followed them. But there must be some secret passage into the building, for the two men disappeared from sight. Kanchipurathan's head hit a window sill. The curtains swayed in the breeze. He put his hands on the sill, hoisted himself up, and jumped into the room. And there on a cot was Deivanayaki—Peria Pedhu's daughter!

TWENTY FIVE

Yes, this was indeed Peria Pedhu's mansion. He hadn't recognised it earlier, because of the darkness. Deivanayaki was fast asleep. Her head rested on her right hand. Her thick gold bangles were half hidden by her hair. Her pearl strand lay across her shoulder. Her voluptuous shoulders looked attractive in the light of the candle. The pleasant fragrance in the room didn't come from the incense sticks. It came from her.

Kanchipurathan tiptoed to the cot. There was no doubt about it. She was asleep. How lovely she was! And her beauty was going to waste! He sighed.

He could hear footsteps outside the room. Should he jump out through the window? He was now on the other side of the cot. He wouldn't have time to walk as far as the window. He could exit through the front door, but then he might cannon into whoever it was who was approaching. He peeped under the cot. The incense stick holder, with the smoking sticks, was under the cot. He might knock it over.

The thick curtain that covered the window seemed to be the only refuge. It was heavy. It could easily conceal two men.

No sooner had he made up his mind than he jumped behind the curtain. Two men entered the room. He knew both of them. One of them was Peria Pedhu, the man who had bought him at the beach. Kanchipurathan felt his back. He could feel the scar from Pedhu's branding. The other was the old man who had been chased out of Singavaram.

"Give it to me," said Pedhu.

Raghunatha hesitated. "Do you think that is the only way?"

"Yes, the only way and the surest way to succeed. Give it to me. Are you not willing to give it to me? Were you not speaking the truth when you said you would give it to me?"

"No, no. I have it here with me." Raghunatha took out a small box. "She will be unconscious for three days. Why don't we use this as the last resort?"

Pedhu bent down towards his daughter's cot. "She is asleep. When she wakes up, we will put our proposal before her. If she refuses, we will have to use what you have." He opened the jar of milk, and the tiny box that Pedhu gave him. He took out a powder from the box and added it to the milk, and stirred the milk. "I know how adamant she can be. That is why we have to resort to this method. How hard I have to try to make my daughter the ruler of Singavaram!"

Raghunatha laughed. "I've been waiting for you for three days. Your daughter made my stay here comfortable. I hadn't expected that you would agree to my plan so readily."

"Will anyone want to be paid to chew on sugarcane?" The two men were now near the window. There was a pleasant breeze blowing. If Raghunatha had extended his hand a wee bit, he would have been able to touch Kanchipurathan. They were that close to where Kanchipurathan was.

"I didn't know you would be coming," said Peria Pedhu. "There is an island called Bombay, to the North of the Maratha Kingdom. There is a Company official there, doing business. I heard that he had defied the Company, and was on his own. I was there to explore the possibility of entering into some sort of partnership with him."

"You are a lucky man. Whatever you touch turns to gold."

"But this time it turned to brass."

"Why? What happened?"

"The Company reined him in, and he couldn't stand up to them any longer. I too turned back, not wanting to do business with a coward."

"And upon your return you met this coward, I suppose," said Raghunatha, pointing to himself.

"Coward? You? I was witness to your courage, when I came to Singavaram. You spoke so bravely in the presence of thousands of people. When I came there to announce that my daughter was the Crown princess, you opposed me, and hounded us out of Singavaram. Raghunatha, even when I breathe my last, that is what I will recall. It is etched in my memory."

Raghunatha fell silent. "You haven't forgotten the unpleasant past."

"No, no. You are mistaken." Pedhu hastened to deny Raghunatha's observation.

Raghunatha continued, "I am an orphan. I have left my country and have come here. I have been rejected by my daughter and by my son-in-law, and have been driven out of Singavaram by them. Any human heart will ache for revenge in the circumstances. Listen to my heart beating. You can hear the word 'Revenge' with every beat."

"Your words are reassuring. What arrangements have you made in these three days?"

"I approached the Company. I met Governor Yale. He has agreed to help us with armed forces. He has also promised ammunition and weapons."

"Did he not ask you what you plan to do after killing Thamarai?"

"Of course he did. Did you think he wouldn't have? He must be a clever man. That is why the Company has sent him here."

They could hear Deivanayaki turning over in her bed.

"Shh." Pedhu put his finger on his lips and warned Raghunatha.

"I told the Governor that Pedhu's daughter Deivanayaki has already staked her claim to the throne of Singavaram. I assured him that once she is in power, the British flag will fly there, and the French and the Dutch will take to their heels."

"Will the Company's forces fight on our behalf?" asked Pedhu, twirling his moustache haughtily.

"Yes, yes. The Company's forces are going to Singavaram to instigate the people to revolt. A couple of days after they leave, we have to go to Singavaram too. I presume you will be able to get your daughter to agree to come with us."

Pedhu laughed. "She will not like our plans. She will refuse to come to Singavaram. But there's that medicinal powder, which we've added to the milk. Let her drink the milk. We'll carry her off to Singavaram. When she wakes up, she will find that she is already Queen of Singavaram. And once that happens, of what use will be her arguments?"

"Anyway, maybe you should try talking to her first."

"Let me see," said Pedhu. He looked at his sleeping daughter fondly. "When she was a month old, we went to Tiruchendur. A fortune teller had a look at her palm. My wife was a great believer in palmistry. I've never heard of anyone having the palm of a one month old baby examined by a palmist. But that is exactly what my wife did."

Raghunatha smiled. "And?"

"That fortune teller was a clever woman. She said, 'The lines on your daughter's palm indicate that she will be a Queen one day.' Needless to say she was amply rewarded by my wife. My wife was an innocent woman. She believed the palmist's prediction. She used to tell everyone that her daughter was destined to be a Queen one day. But she was not fortunate enough to be witness to it."

Pedhu said to his sleeping daughter, "Your mother's desire is going to become a reality soon, Deivanayaki. Once we get rid of Krishnappa, Chennamma and that wretched slave girl."

"Don't forget Kanchipurathan," said Raghunatha.

"Kanchipurathan?" Pedhu's face reflected his surprise. His anger too.

"Kanchipurathan is the name of a young man who turned up at Singavaram. He is that slave girl's lover. It was Rajaram, the King of Senji, who defeated Zulfikar Khan. Kanchipurathan just happened to be there. The foolish citizens of Singavaram believed that Kanchipurathan had played a major role in the defeat of Zulfikar Khan. And Kanchipurathan was bursting with pride. He is Thamarai's right hand man. If we get rid of him…"

"Kanchipurathan. He was shipped off to Sumatra as a slave. How did he turn up in Singavaram?"

"What?" exclaimed Raghunatha.

The two men must have spoken loudly, for Deivanayaki was awake now. She sat up in her bed.

Pedhu teased the wick of the lamp, so that it burnt brightly.

"Did I wake you up, Deivanayaki?"

Deivanayki rubbed her eyes. "Never mind, father. You wouldn't have come here at this hour, unless there was something important to convey to me. And you have come with a visitor from Singavaram."

Raghunatha smiled. "I was just telling your father that you took good care of me while he was away."

Deivanayaki walked around the room. "Is that all you told him?"

"What else should I have told him?"

"You didn't tell me why you were here in Chennai. I hoped you would at least have told my father."

"He's told me why he is here," said Pedhu. "Deivanayaki, are you not able to guess?"

"Guess what?"

"Your luck! Something you would never have dreamed of! Raghunatha is here because of you, my child. He is here to help us drive away that slave girl, and to put you on the throne of Singavaram."

Deivanayaki's face mirrored her anger and disgust. "I stopped dreaming a long time ago, father."

Pedhu gave Raghunatha a meaningful look.

"There will be no more dreams in your life. Everything will henceforth be real and joyful," said Raghunatha.

"Thank you very much. But whatever it is, let it happen here in the city of Chennai. Let the good fortune and the joy you speak of come to me inside my father's mansion."

"I never thought my daughter would be so naïve."

"Is naivete a synonym for discretion?" Deivanayaki asked.

"Deivanayaki, the last time we went to Singavaram, we hadn't made proper plans. This time our plans won't go wrong. Everything is in our favour. Raghunatha is also on our side. Come on, let's proceed. There is a Tamil proverb that says that those who strive will not suffer ignominy. Haven't you heard that proverb?"

"I have also heard a proverb that talks about a cat whose tongue was burned by hot milk," said Devianayaki. "Father, you and Raghunatha are men. You have faced many setbacks and disappointments in life. When life knocks you down, you may be hurt. But you pick yourself up and are ready to do battle again. That is because you are men. I am a woman, father, a woman!"

"And so?"

"A woman doesn't recover so easily from blows. She doesn't forget being shamed. When we went to Singavaram, we were insulted by the people. I will never forget their words. You might have forgotten. I haven't. I never will. I don't know how I kept myself from committing suicide. But if I were to face such shame again, I will kill myself. I have sworn to do so. So please excuse me, father."

"You speak cleverly, Deivanayki. But this time there will be no failure. Success will be ours," said Pedhu.

"Success is like a rainbow. It appears attractive only because it is at an inaccessible distance."

"It is your duty to accept the post of Queen, when it comes your way, for that would be an honour to your family."

"And if I were to fail, then my shame will also be that of my family's. Don't forget that."

"There is honour in being a Queen."

"I don't find it attractive. Many people have been ruined by their ambitions."

"Don't you want to be seated on a throne?"

"Not if that throne happens to be the mouth of a volcano."

"What about power?"

"I have never liked intoxicants, father."

"What about ministers who will obey you?"

"I can find any number of sycophants here."

"Your subjects will bow before you."

"It is also possible that I will lose my head."

"Silk garments?"

"I have many already."

"Jewels?"

"I am tired of jewels."

"Royal processions?"

"An invitation to danger."

Pedhu sighed.

"It is very late, my child. Go to bed. We will continue this conversation tomorrow morning."

When he and Raghunatha reached the doorway, Pedhu said, "Drink the milk before you go to bed."

"All right, father."

Deivanayaki could hear their receding footsteps.

But she did not go to bed.

She picked up the jug of milk and poured out the contents through the window. She then moved aside the curtain and said, "You may come out now."

TWENTY SIX

Kanchipurathan was taken aback to find that Deivanayaki knew of his presence, and was even more surprised by her sangfroid.

She must have seen him take refuge behind the curtain. So she had known right from the beginning that he was there!

"Come out, Kanchipurathan. There is no one here to brand you again. Nor is there anyone here to whip you. No one here to drag you away to join the other slaves. Come out."

Kanchipurathan's amazement grew. Not only did Deivanayaki know someone was hiding behind the curtain; she even knew who it was.

Kanchipurathan emerged from hiding and said, "I think you are mistaken…"

"A while ago, you bent down to check if I was asleep, and then you turned away to hide behind the curtain. I saw the branding on your back—P.P—I suppose that is a spelling error?"

Kanchipurathan laughed. "A daughter who is as smart as her father," he said.

"But ignorant with regard to one subject."

"And what is that?"

"Geography."

"Why do you think so?"

"I thought Sumatra was some distance away from here. I didn't know that Sumatra was behind the curtains in my bedroom. Kanchipurathan, if there is anyone who is smarter than my father and me, that is you."

"Thank you. But I too am deficient in one respect."

"And what might that be?"

"I used to believe that if a person's eyes were closed, that person was asleep. But I now realise that sometimes a person who is sleeping may still be able to sense what is going on around her."

"What cheek!" laughed Deivanayaki.

"Something I caught from you."

"You are ready with repartees."

"I also know that both of us have the same goal."

Deivanayaki observed Kanchipurathan. The rays of the moon filtering through the window, threw her beauty into relief. Her clothes were in disarray, but this failed to stir desire in Kanchipurathan.

Deivanayaki leaned against the window sill. She gave a long, sibilant sigh. "Did you say you and I have the same goal?"

"Isn't that true? You are determined never to go to Singavaram. And I am determined to see that you never enter Singavaram."

"Singavaram!" she said bitterly. "Do not mention that name to me again." There was anger in her voice now. "You were also responsible for my being shamed there."

"I only did my duty."

"Why don't you say that was your offering to your lover?"

"Very well, and why not? Let us call it an offering to my lover."

For a second, Deivanayaki's face turned dark with anger. "When I think of you and Singavaram, I lose my temper. In fact, I don't know why I have not handed you over to my father. That's something I cannot understand."

"And when I think of the fact that you are the daughter of the man who owns the most slaves in Tamil Nadu, I ache to strangle you to death. Why I haven't done it remains a mystery to me."

Deivanayaki laughed out loud. "If we begin to argue, we will go on and on. Let us admit it. We need each other's help."

"I don't know what help you want from me. But there is someone to help me all the time," said Kanchipurathan, pointing upwards.

"I bow before you, oh representative of God," teased Deivanayaki. "I'll tell you what I want. I want that old man who has come from Singavaram to be shamed."

"I can see that although the wound has healed, you still bear the scar."

"Perhaps. Raghunatha was responsible for my being insulted. My father has forgiven him. But I have not.

Nor am I going to co-operate with them in their plans."

"Is that why you have given up sleep, and are wide awake at night?"

"Yes, there is something I want you to do…" But she did not complete the sentence. "Someone's coming. Hide." Kanchipurathan went back to his hiding place. She picked up the jug of milk, lay back against the pillows, and acted like one drugged.

Peria Pedhu entered the room. Raghunatha waited outside. "Deivanayaki. Are you all right?" Pedhu asked her.

Deivanayaki spoke with a slur, and pretended that she was unable to continue. She gestured with her hands, trying to convey something to her father. But her hands refused to co-operate. "Father. I feel faint. Faint. I don't want to get up. I want to be in bed for days. As soon as I had the milk…. Do you think the servants have added a sedative to the milk?"

"Not at all. How can such things happen in my house?" Pedhu tucked a bed sheet around her. "You are tired. You need to rest."

He stood there for a few minutes, to make sure his daughter was asleep. He then joined Raghunatha. "See? She will not wake up for another three days," said Raghunatha. "And when she wakes up, she will be the Queen of Singavaram."

Their footsteps grew faint, and Deivanayaki sat up. "Queen of Singavaram!" she spat out angrily.

Kanchipurathan came out of his hiding place. "I have an idea. I know what you must do," he said.

"And what is that?"

"You must keep up the pretence, for three days. I will work to destroy Raghunatha's plans, and you will do the same from here."

"But on one condition. My enemy is Raghunatha. But you have included my father too in your list of enemies. I will be glad if Raghunatha's plans come to nought. But my father must remain unharmed."

"I promise that your father will not be harmed."

"My strength is my capacity to playact. And what's yours? And don't say God is your strength. Do you have money?"

"No. I am a modern Kuchela."

"The Puranic Kuchela did not participate in battles. Nor did he involve himself in plotting. So he didn't need money. But you are cast in a different mould. And let me tell you, nothing works as money does."

"Who says it doesn't? Open up your treasure chest, and fill my hands with money," said Kanchipurathan, and stretched out his hands.

"Wait," said Deivanayaki, and went out. She returned a few minutes later, and gave him a handful of gold coins.

Kanchipurathan bit a few of them, tapped them and said, "They are genuine."

"What else did you expect? That there would be counterfeit coins here?"

"Yes, chestfuls."

"That is a lie!"

"No. I am not lying. Counterfeit coins are being manufactured here."

"Kanchipurathan, mind your words. My father is an owner of slaves. He is heartless. Say anything you want of him. But one who manufactures counterfeit coins? Certainly not."

"Half good, half bad does not define anyone in this world. A man who is capable of doing something wrong, is quite capable of other wicked things too."

"That may be true. But the coins in circulation in these parts are the coins of the Company. My father wouldn't dare do anything against the Company. I can vouch for that."

"I saw with my own eyes," began Kanchipurathan, but did not complete what he wanted to say. He could see that Deivanayaki was furious. "I could be wrong. Will you do me a favour?"

"What is it?"

"Can you show me where Raghunatha is staying?"

"Come with me," said Deivanayaki, and peeped out into the corridor, to make sure there was no one there. She opened the door leading to the garden. She walked into the garden, and pointed to a building some distance away. "Do you see the lights there? That's where Raghunatha is staying."

Kanchipurathan pursed his lips in anger. He picked up a twig and broke into two.

"We'll meet in Singavaram," he said and took leave of Deivanayaki.

♦

"Have you put them away safely?"

"Yes, master."

"I hope no one knows about it."

"Not a soul."

"What about him?" The man's hand pointed to Peria Pedhui's mansion.

The men laughed. "Do you think we will breathe a word to him?"

Kanchipurathan was hiding in a tree, and listening to the conversation taking place in the room. He could see the men in the room too. The man reclining in bed and questioning the men was Raghunatha. The men who answered him placed before him a chest of counterfeit coins and took away a chest full of real coins.

"Here, take this," said Raghunatha, and gave each of the men a bagful of coins.

Kanchipurathan understood what Raghunatha was up to and why. He was collecting coins minted by the Company. The Company's coins were legal currency everywhere. If Pedhu and the Company were to back out in the last minute and refuse to help him, he had to make sure he had enough money to buy arms and to hire men. So he was replacing good coins with counterfeit ones.

But where had he stashed away the good coins? Kanchipurathan climbed down from the tree. The mansion in which Raghunatha had been housed had many rooms, but no guards. Most of the rooms were locked. He walked around the house, and came to the cowshed. He tripped over an old lady who was asleep outside the cowshed. "Watch where you are going, young man," she said.

Kanchipurathan recognised her. "Grandma, don't you remember me? I used to be a slave here. I even gave you my money once."

"Yes, of course. I do remember you. But why are you dressed like a renunciate? You are such a handsome man."

"I will explain later." Kanchipurathan led the old lady away from the cowshed, and whispered something to her.

A few seconds later...

The old lady screamed, "Help! Fire!"

TWENTY SEVEN

"Fire! Fire!"

The old lady's screams shattered the stillness of the night. Hurried footsteps could be heard.

"Where? Where is the fire?"

Many people came running- from Raghunatha's mansion, from Pedhu's mansion, from the highway. They all had torches in their hands.

Kanchipurathan smiled to himself. He scratched his back with a twig. The men looked at each other. "Who shouted that there was a fire?"

"I think it must have been that old lady there."

Raghunatha came there too. Tension was writ large on his face. "What is happening here?" asked Pedhu.

For a minute Kanchipurathan was afraid. What if Deivanayaki should come there too? What if she forgot that she was supposed to be in a drugged state?

But he had underestimated Devianayaki's cleverness. Despite all the commotion, she did not come out.

"This is the woman who shouted that there was a fire," the crowd brought the bold woman to Pedhu.

"Master, forgive me. I have disturbed you all," said the old woman, and fell at Pedhu's feet.

"Tie her up and whip her!" said Raghunatha.

"Hey, old woman. Stop blabbering and answer the master," said a guard.

Tears rolled down her cheeks. "I had a dream that my house had caught fire. I was frightened. That was why I screamed."

The guards were amused. Just a dream? They would have laughed out loud, but didn't, because of the presence of their master.

"You wretched old woman! Did you wake us all up because of a dream? Is there no place for you to sleep in the whole of this city? Go and find some other place to sleep," said Pedhu.

"That is the problem with old people," pacified Raghunatha.

"I don't mind being disturbed. I am upset because she has disturbed you—my guest."

"All right. In that case, let me forgive her," said Raghunatha, and smiled at her to show she had been forgiven. "Old woman, you go back to sleep now."

The crowd dispersed. The old woman lay down to sleep in the cowshed.

Raghunatha returned to the place where he was staying. The lamps had been put out, and the mansion was dark.

But Kanchipurathan was still perched on the tree. What was he waiting for?

Suddenly there was a look of radiance on his face. He was right—what he had anticipated was about to happen.

Raghunatha tiptoed out of the mansion. He looked around, to ensure that there was no one around.

He walked towards the fence. He stood near the abandoned well. Kanchipurathan was still on the tree, from where he could see Raghunatha.

Raghunatha moved a huge stone this way and that, as if to make sure it was properly placed, and then returned to his lodgings. As he passed under the tree, Kanchipurathan noticed the look of relief and satisfaction on Raghunatha's face.

As soon as Raghunatha had entered his lodgings, Kanchipuarathan slid down the tree.

He went to the cowshed, and whispered his thanks to the old lady.

"I am obliged to you. The money you gave me went a long way in meeting my granddaughter's wedding expenses," the old lady said.

"Do you know what I thought, when I watched you talk to Pedhu? I thought Chennai had beaten Kanchipuram."

"What do you mean?"

"I am from Kanchipuram. I used to think that no other city had talented artistes like the ones in Kanchipuram. But you have proved me wrong. I have met two great actresses here, in one night."

"I can't understand a word of what you are saying. I don't know why you wanted to me shout 'Fire', and why you wanted a crowd to gather here."

"I conducted a small psychological experiment. When there is danger, observe the people who gather. Every one of them will want to be sure that what is dear to them is safe. There is an old man here, who has some gold stashed away. I wanted to know where he had hidden the loot. That is why I asked you to shout. I wanted a crowd to gather here. Thanks for your help, grandma. You can go back to sleep now."

Kanchipurathan was in a hurry, but he wanted to make sure the old lady was comfortable. He took her to the stable, spread a sheet over to her, to keep her warm and took leave of her.

"Be careful. Someone or the other is always itching to do you harm," the old lady said.

Kanchipurathan twirled the stick in his hand, and said, "See how well armed I am. No one can harm me."

The old lady chuckled.

Kanchipurathan hurried towards the stone that Raghunatha had checked.

♦

There was nothing about that stone that would have aroused suspicion. Kanchipurathan tried to move it. He gave it a shake. He tapped it. It sounded hollow. With some effort, he gave it a heave, and it rolled aside. There were steps leading to a passage underground. He slowly descended the steps. It was almost dawn now. He could hear a slithering noise. That could come only if there were snakes there. He looked round. There were four or five iron chests flush against the wall, and around them were scorpions and crabs.

Kanchipurathan had had experience of Raghunatha's cunning. But could he get these creatures to obey him?

Kanchipurathan moved forward, and as he did, the creatures moved towards him. He was sure the chests contained the gold coins that Raghunatha had collected. But he had to open the chests to be doubly sure. And yet, how was he to do that, with all these poisonous creatures swarming all over the place?

He swished the little twig in his hand, and the creatures beat a hasty retreat.

"Cowards!" Kanchipurathan laughed. He moved towards the chests, but the creatures were back. He picked up his twig and brandished it menacingly, and they retreated again. Again he moved closer to the chests and again they came back. Again he wielded his twig and again they ran away. Kanchipurathan looked at the twig he had brought with him. And now the mystery cleared up. It was from a tree that served as an antidote to poison. The creatures could smell it and that was why they had retreated.

He opened the chests, and put his hands in. Gold coins! It was clear now that he had been right. Raghunatha was hoarding gold coins. And the idiots employed by the Company trusted Raghunatha!

◆

The sun was up, and a jamun fruit fell on Kanchipurathan. He looked up. It was Deivanayaki at the window of her room. "So is this the mark of a good man—to go away without taking leave? Have you found the evidence?"

"Yes," said Kanchipurathan and pointed to a small bundle in his hands. "But the culprit is not your father. It is Raghunatha."

"Oh, so it is the distinguished visitor! So what are you going to do about it?" she asked.

"I am going to show it to the Governor of the Company. And we need to do no more. They will take care of Raghunatha."

"It is not so easy," cautioned Deivanayaki. "What are you going to do next?"

"You will be annoyed if I tell you."

"Why?"

"Because I will have to mention the name of someone you don't like."

"Who is it?"

"Sivachidambaram. Don't you remember? You once told me to lop off his arms and his legs. The very same Sivachidambaram. I am going to help him in the plan he's chalked out against the Company. He's given me a task."

"Sivachidmabaram planning against the Company? Impossible. He's a coward."

"I cannot tolerate criticism of Sivachidambaram," said Kanchipurathan, and jumped into Deivanayaki's room through the window. "Look at this," he said and gave her a silk cloth that had something written on it.

"What is this?" she asked.

"Read it. It's proof that Sivachidambaram is not a coward."

As she read, Deivanayaki's eyes widened in wonder. "Is he such a brave man?" she asked in amazement. Her lips quivered.

TWENTY EIGHT

"Why are you surprised? Sivachidambaram has always been a revolutionary. If a list of those who fought to rid Bharat of foreigners is prepared someday, Sivachidamabaram's name is sure to be on that list."

Deivanayaki was silent. "What does he plan to do with this?" she asked, pointing to the silk cloth Kanchipurathan had given her.

"He wants me to give it to the Dutch. This gives one an idea of where the fort can be breached and where it is strong."

"I never thought he would be so brave," she said, and paced up and down the room.

"Intelligent people will not judge people by their appearance," said Kanchipurathan.

"I didn't judge him by his appearance. I disliked him because of his cowardice." Deivanayaki stopped. "I have a request. It's a request my father made to you."

"Your father asked me to rescue Sivachidambaram from the clutches of the Company."

"That is what I want you to do."

"Is that a request? Or an order?"

"Neither. It's a deal. You do what I want, and I will help you foil my father's plans regarding Singavaram."

"I am not in the least interested in your new found love for Sivachidambaram. But I will agree to your condition, because of my love for Thamarai," said Kanchipurathan and jumped out through the window.

It was beginning to drizzle.

♦

"I want to meet the Governor."

"Are you mad? Go away."

"It's very important."

"Whatever it is, you cannot meet him. Do you think the Governor will talk to a beggar like you?"

"Please. Allow me to talk to the Governor. If he decides to punish you for letting me in, then I promise I will take the punishment and see that you are spared."

"You get out of the way now. The Governor will soon be here. This is the time when he goes on a tour of the city. He doesn't like to see anyone standing near the coach."

"Is this the coach in which he will tour the city?"

"Yes. There he is. Out of the way." The coachman pushed Kanchipurathan out of the way.

Yale—the Governor of Chennai, the representative of the King of England, the President of the Company—walked twirling a walking stick. He was attired in white, with gold medals adorning him. He was surrounded by men on horseback. Yale got into the coach, and the coach took off.

"Stop. Stop the coach," shouted Kanchipurathan.

The coachman reined in the horses.

"Who is that man?" asked Yale.

"A mad man," replied the coachman.

Kanchipurathan ran up to the Governor and said, "A linchpin has fallen out. The coachman didn't notice it." He showed the Governor the linchpin.

"Excellent," said the Governor, patting Kanchipurathan with his walking stick.

"He's lying! He must have removed the linchpin!" the coachman wanted to say. But he thought better of it. Who would trust an old coachman, when a dashing young man, who was also a glib talker had a different story to tell?

"I have a request. I want to speak to you in private for a few moments," said Kanchipurathan.

The interpreter explained what Kanchipurathan had said.

"Mr. Robert!" called out the Governor. "Find out what this man has to say." Robert was the man who had taken Kanchipurathan to the mint.

"What is it?" he asked Kanchipurathan.

Kanchipurathan opened the bundle and showed him the gold coins. "These are the Company's coins. Gold coins."

"There is a place where chests of gold coins are stashed away. And counterfeit coins are put in circulation, instead of the Company's coins."

"Where are the coins kept? Who is doing it?"

"Raghunatha. In Peria Pedhu's mansion."

"Peria Pedhu and Raghunatha?" Robert was stunned.

"No, Peria Pedhu has nothing to do with it. He doesn't even know of it. It is Raghunatha's doing."

Robert laughed. "Raghunatha is close to the Company. He has asked us for help. And we plan to help him. This is just a ploy to keep us away from helping him."

"No, it is not. Raghunatha is the one…"

"Shut up!"

"Go away," said the interpreter to Kanchipurathan. "The white man is angry."

"Let him go to hell! He won't listen to those who speak the truth," muttered Kanchipurathan.

How right Deivanayaki had been! She had warned him that it was unlikely that the Company officials would believe his story.

All he could do was to go to Singavaram and warn Thamarai. But before he went to Singavaram, there was something else he had to do. He had to convey Deivanayaki's message to Sivachidambaram. Kanchipurathan decided to wait until dark.

♦

The wind howled. Doors slammed shut.

"I am glad to hear that Deivanayaki has changed," Sivachidambaram's voice betrayed no emotion.

"Deivanayaki too must be happy," said Kanchipurathan.

"And what can I do about that?"

"In order that she should be happy, you must come out of this prison and marry her. You can continue to be a revolutionary, even after marriage."

Sivachidambaram laughed. He ran his hand over the grey hairs on his chin. "Young man. My heydays are behind me. Deivanayaki is young. Does an old man like me have the strength to make her happy? You have brought this love letter to the wrong person. Besides, I may be hanged. And what will happen to Deivanayaki then?"

"I have the confidence that you will live a happy long life. The lucky woman who weds you will not be unhappy," said Kanchipurathan.

"It is wrong to marry two wives."

"Two wives?"

"Yes. I am already wedded to the revolutionary cause. If I were to marry Deivanayaki, there will be a lot of tension between Deivanayaki and my long standing wife!"

"You mustn't say such things. Haven't you heard Thiruvalluvar's praise for the life of a householder?"

"Don't waste your time, young man," said Sivachidambaram. "If you are hesitant to give that drawing of mine to the Dutch, then give it back to me. I will find someone else to do it."

"You think I am a coward, don't' you? You think I am afraid to do what you want me to do, and that is why I am backing out."

"I haven't thought of you as a coward. But if you continue to argue with me, then that is the conclusion I will have to come to."

"I promise. After I escort you to Deivanayaki, I will meet the Dutch. Trust me."

"In other words, unless I agree to come with you, you will not do what I want you to."

"You will not refuse to come with me."

"I refuse to come with you."

"Forgive me."

In the flash of a second, Kanchipurathan picked up the stout stick in the corner of the room, and the stick descended on the back of Sivachidambaram's neck.

Sivachidambaram fell down in pain.

"I am sorry. I had no other option." Kanchipurathan examined Sivachidambaram's neck. As he had anticipated, the blow had caused only a minor injury. But there was the danger that Sivachidambaram might regain consciousness, and begin to object. So Kanchipurathan tied his hands, and gagged him.

The wind continued to howl.

Kanchipurathan came out. The wind was so strong that he was afraid it would knock him down. He had to check out the different paths he could take.

♦

Suddenly, there was a great deal of commotion. Agitated voices could be heard. The roar of the ocean didn't seem distant. It seemed as if the ocean was close by.

"Come on, all of you. Wake up the sepoys," shouted an officer of the Company. "Wake up those travelling mendicants too. Bring them here!"

Kanchipurathan ran in the direction of the voices. He couldn't believe his eyes. Waves were dashing against the entrance to the fort!

Someone gave Kanchipurathan a rap on his shoulders. "Go on! What are you staring at?"

As Kanchipurathan drew closer to the voices, he could see that the sea water had entered the Fort. Using sandbags, sepoys were trying to block the entry of sea water. But Kanchipurathan could hear portions of the wall breaking and crashing down.

A drum was being sounded inside the town.

An officer shouted to his interpreter," Tell them to strike the drum in every street. Weavers, carpenters, washermen, peons—everyone should help. No able bodied man is to stay away."

Kanchipurathan also began to lift sacks of sand to block the entry of the water. He then realised that Sivachidambaram's drawing was getting wet, as he waded through knee deep water. Slowly, he gave the officer the slip. He shoved the silk cloth with the drawing into a cannon that was unguarded, and then went back to help.

"Hurry. Lift that sack," a supervisor whipped a boy. The boy was too puny to lift the sack.

"Leave him alone. I will carry the sacks he is supposed to," said Kanchipurathan, and proceeded to do so. With two of his own sacks to carry, he tucked the boy's sacks under his arms, and hurried to halt the intrusion of sea water into the Fort.

The supervisor complained to the officer, "This man is a troublemaker."

The officer had already made Kanchipurathan's acquaintance at the mint. He smiled and said, "Don't complain about him. He is a clever man, capable of doing a lot of things."

Kanchipurathan whispered to the boy, "Will you help me?"

"I will give up my life for you," said the boy.

Kanchipurathan laughed. "I just saved your life. Will I ask you to lose your life for me? There is a small hut some distance from here. There is a frail man there. Just check if he is safe. No one should see you going there. Will you do it?"

"Sure. Right away," said the boy, and ran off.

Kanchipurathan continued to block the entry of water with sacks of sand. The boy returned, "There is no one in that hut," said the boy. Sea water has entered the hut."

"Are you sure there is no one there?"

"Go and have a look yourself, if you don't trust me."

Kanchipurathan ran to the hut. The boy had spoken the truth. There was no one in the hut.

"Are you looking for Ayya?"

Kanchipurathan turned round in surprise, and found the cook's assistant there. Kanchipurathan breathed easy. This man knew Sivachidambaram. Kanchipurathan recalled Sivachidambaram telling him, that if he could not meet the Dutch, there were others wiling to do so. So Sivachidambaram clearly had many supporters in the Fort.

"I had left him here," Kanchipurathan said.

"I have sent him to Peria Pedhu's mansion. It looked like the sea water was going to enter the hut, and it has, as you can see. Ayya was in a faint. I sent him to Pedhu's mansion with a proper escort," said the cook's assistant.

"I am grateful to you," said Kanchipurathan.

Every minute was precious. He could delay no further. Thamarai was in danger. He had to go to her.

He retrieved the drawing from the cannon, and began to walk towards Thiruvallikeni.

"I suppose your mission in Chennai had been accomplished!" Kanchipurathan was startled by the voice and turned to find that it was the priest with his pet chameleon.

"I think so," replied Kanchipurathan.

"Success and failure are two sides of a coin. You have seen only success so far."

What was the priest trying to convey? A shadow of worry crossed Kanchipurathan's face, but he soon recovered.

He saw a Muslim trying to shoe a horse, and offered his help.

"You've come at the right moment. Come and give me a hand," the old man said.

◆

Around the same time, Robert was asking his sepoy some questions.

"What did that man do?"

"He came looking for Sivachidambaram. I answered as you had told me to. He went away believing that I had spoken the truth."

"And what about the drawing he hid in the cannon?"

"I have it here," said the sepoy and handed it to Robert.

"You may go," said Robert to the sepoy.

Robert then said to another official of the Company, "I knew that he was Peria Pedhu's slave. I saw Pedhu's initials on his back. I have made arrangements to have him watched."

"Is it with regard to the counterfeit coins in circulation?"

"That's a different matter," replied Robert durai.

TWENTY NINE

"Patience, Mr. Peria Pedhu. Patience, Mr. Raghunatha," Yale said picking his teeth with a toothpick made of ivory.

Governor Yale's room—the morning sun beat in through the open window. The peon outside kept pulling the punkah[9]. The Governor had just finished his breakfast and the man from the kitchen was carefully removing the dishes.

Three other Englishman stood some distance away from the Governor.

"We decided that my daughter would have to be taken away by force to Singavaram. So we've drugged her," said Pedhu.

"We will have to leave before the effect of the drug wears off," said Raghunatha. "Its effect is only for three days."

"But this is only the first day, isn't it?" asked Yale, spitting out some food particle he had managed to dislodge with the tooth pick. "We'll get weapons from Calcutta today. At least fifty men will be at your disposal..."

"But how will that be enough?" asked Raghunatha.

"Anything more than that is inadvisable. If we were to engage openly in a war with Singavaram, we will need at least 300 or 400 soldiers. We will incur the

---

9   *Punkah- cloth fan suspended from the ceiling. It was moved backwards and forwards by pulling a rope.*

displeasure of the Tanjore and Senji kings. We will incur the displeasure of the people. My way of doing it is the best. Let Raghunatha show me the places of strategic importance in Singavaram. My men will capture them overnight. Putting Peria Pedhu's daughter on the throne will be as natural as the sun rising in the East...Yes, who is it?"

A messenger who had been waiting outside was summoned in. He handed a palm leaf manuscript to the Govenror.

"Kasi Veeranna died this morning," announced Yale.

Everyone except Raghunatha was familiar with the name. Veeranna had been Pedhu's friend and competitor in business.

"He's done business with us, hasn't he? So he must be given Company honours. See to it," said Yale to one of his officers.

The officer left, only to be back soon. "There is a complication regarding Kasi Veeranna's funeral rites," said the officer.

"What is it?"

"His family says he should be cremated because he was a Hindu. But some Muslims claim that he was a Muslim and that his body should, therefore, be handed over to them."

"How strange!" remarked Yale. "Is this true, Mr. Peria Pedhu?"

"There was an air of mystery about Kasi Veeranna. There are many stories about him. But some years ago, I bought some slaves from him. They should be able to tell us something about him."

"Please find out. I authorise you to resolve this issue. I will pass an order that everyone should abide by your decision."

"And what about..." Raghunatha began.

"Please come this afternoon. But remember, you must give me a list of the places of strategic importance in Singavaram. I will plan how to take over those places."

He began to ply the toothpick again.

♦

"Don't tell me you don't know," said Pedhu sternly. "Eight years ago, we took ten slaves from Kasi Veeranna, in lieu of 200 rupees that he owed me. If you haven't kept track of this, what kind of an accountant are you? I am told the Delhi Sultan is looking for men to join his army. Why don't you make an application? Just look at yourself! How prosperous you look! You have looked after yourself very well. I can see that."

"You mustn't be angry with me, master," said the accountant. "We do have accounts that point to the purchase of slaves from Kasi Veeranna. But there is no record of the names of the slaves. But your daughter should know the names."

"Why didn't you tell me Deivanayaki knew the names?" Pedhu looked at Raghunatha, who appeared to be steeped in thought. "Why don't you take some rest, while I go and make enquiries about the slaves?" he said to Raghunatha.

"No, no. I want to come too. I want to watch the fun," said Raghunatha.

"Fun?"

"Yes, of course. It should be amusing to watch a father talk to his daughter who is in a drugged sleep."

"Oh dear, I forgot that she was asleep. In fact I have instructed my men to make sure no one disturbs her. Anyway, let's go and have a look."

The two men found that there was no change in Deivanayaki's state. Her eyes were still closed. Her breathing was steady. But her lips moved, indicating that she was muttering in her sleep.

"Sivachidambaram! Sivachidambaram! I...You..."

"Sivachidambaram?!" Pedhu exclaimed in amazement.

"Who is that?"

"A relative of mine. Wait. Let me listen to her."

"Father will not harm you. I am sure. The only problem is that I feel embarrassed about talking to my father about this. But we will soon be together. Sivachidambaram." Deivanayaki moaned a couple of times, and then turned over on her side and slept with her knees drawn up.

The past flashed before Pedhu's eyes. He recalled the handsome boy who had accompanied him in ships, boats, palanquins and on horseback. He recalled his sister's words, "Take care of my son." He recalled how Deivanayaki and Sivachidambaram used to play together.

He recalled the handsome young man who had said to him, "Do you expect me to take care of your slave trade? Never."

"Where is he now?" asked Raghunatha.

"In the fort. He is a prisoner. He was naïve. He raised slogans about revolution and independence. When someone as powerful as Lingappa has been rendered powerless, what can Sivachidambaram do? He was captured and imprisoned."

"Your daughter seems to be pining for him."

"That is what surprises me. She used to hate him. How did she suddenly change her mind and fall in love with him? If only I had known…" Pedhu sighed.

"Why don't you try to rescue him?"

"That revolutionary?! It is dangerous to admit I know him. That is why I haven't told anyone in the Company that he is related to me."

"Why should anyone in the Company know? Let us rescue him secretly. All the slogans and revolutionary plans will end the moment he is married to the Queen of Singavaram."

Peria Pedhu smiled. "Raghunatha, do you think that is possible?"

"It's up to us to make it possible."

Peria Pedhu looked at his daughter, and said, "My child, your dream will soon be reality."

A few minutes after the two men left, Deivanayaki sat up on the bed. A pigeon that she had reared flew in through the open window. She picked up some grains and held out her palm. She ran her hand gently over the pigeon's wings, as it pecked the grains in her outstretched palm. "Do you know what happened? I managed to convey it to my father. I am talking about my love for … As if you don't know him!"

◆

Everyone fell silent when Peria Pedhu entered the room. Kasi Veeranna's body was kept in the front hall. The old man about whom a number of stories had been doing the rounds now lay silent. The garland that Governor Yale had sent had been placed on Veeranna's body. The shawl from the Governor lay at his feet. His wives and children were in the adjacent room and their wailing could be heard across the road.

Some elders from the Muslim community welcomed Peria Pedhu. "Did you get the order from the Company?" he asked the Muslims.

"Yes, we did," they said. "We will abide by your decision."

An old man explained, "Veeranna ran away from this city when he was a young lad. He returned some years later. He lived in Thiruvalikkeni. He was a prosperous businessman, and called himself Hasan Khan. He built a mosque near Royapuram. But his business failed after some years. And he ran away again, and wasn't heard of for fifteen years. He then came back to the city. Only a few old men like me know the whole story. I could recognise him."

"Did you talk to him about this?"

"I did. He admitted to me that he was Hasan Khan, and that he was pretending to be a Hindu, to reap some advantages."

Peria Pedhu knew that Kasi Veeranna had been a very clever man. If saying he was a Muslim would have brought him any advantages, he would not have hesitated to say he was a Muslim.

"You wait here," he said, and went in with Raghunatha.

He looked at Kasi Veeranna. He could see that his ears had been pierced as a child. He looked behind his ears. He could see the conch and discus symbols of Lord Vishnu branded behind Veeranna's ears. There was no doubt at all—Kasi Veeranna had been a Hindu. He must have lied that he was a Muslim.

Peria Pedhu rose to deliver his judgement. A businessman called Venkatadri whispered to him,

"Please let your verdict be that he is a Hindu. I will help you in whatever way I can."

Pedhu smiled. Here was a man offering him a bribe to speak the truth! "I have seen you somewhere," he said to Venkatadri.

"You must have seen me in the fort. I have been given the contract to repair the damage caused when sea water entered the fort.

"The fort? That means many of your men must be inside the fort."

"Yes, of course."

Pedhu signalled to Raghunatha to stay and told all the others to leave. He then told Venkatadri what he wanted. "It won't be easy, but I will do it," promised Venkatadri.

Pedhu came out and said to the Muslims, "I am sorry to have to tell you that Veeranna was indeed a Hindu."

The Muslims were disappointed, but they magnanimously agreed to abide by the verdict, and dispersed.

◆

Among all the workers inside the fort, three were wearing blue turbans. They were the ones Pedhu had been asked to contact.

One of them was carting out broken stones. Pedhu summoned him. "Have you discovered where Sivachidambaram is?"

"We are looking for him. You must not be seen talking to us."

"Why not?"

"There are rumours that the Company's lawyer—Isaiah Cooley, has discovered our plans and has told the Governor about it."

"Has Kasi Veeranna been cremated?"

"Yes."

"Then there is nothing more to the matter. You carry out the task assigned to you without any fear."

"We are afraid for you."

Pedhu laughed. "Does the Company have the guts?"

"Peria Pedhu! Come! Quick! I've been looking for you," said Raghunatha.

"What is the matter? You sound pleased, as if you have captured the Singavaram fort."

"I *am* pleased. Once you have seen the lightning and heard the thunder, will you still continue to wonder whether it will rain? The ship from Calcutta has arrived. Trunks of weapons! Chests full of gunpowder. The officials of the Company are waiting for us. And you are here, talking to..." Raghunatha then lowered his voice and asked, "Any news about your nephew?"

"Efforts are underway to find him. If the weapons have arrived, we will have to leave tonight."

There was a bustling crowd outside the Governor's office. The coolies were bringing in huge chests. Leave them here. Move that chest. Why is this chest wet? One chest seems to be missing. There were many orders and commands to the coolies. But the Governor was not to be seen. Gresham—the man in charge of the cannons, was inspecting what looked like a ball. William Fraser was looking for a target to fire a gun. The storekeeper John Cheney was breaking open a chest. Many interpreters and sepoys stood around watching.

"See? I told you the ship would be here soon, but you didn't believe me. All these are new weapons," said Gresham proudly.

Peria Pedhu had never seen such weapons. He stared at them in amazement. "Can we leave for Singavaram now?" he asked.

"What's to stop us?" smiled Fraser. "It is easy to handle these weapons, isn't it?" he asked Gresham.

"Yes, yes," assured Gresham. "Do you know what this is?" he asked Pedhu.

"Are you making fun of me?" asked Pedhu.

"What about you, Raghunatha? Do you know what this is?"

"Never seen anything like this before."

"It's a ball filled with gunpowder. You don't need a rifle or a cannon to use this. All you have to do is to fling it. It will explode where it lands."

"We have only read about such weapons in our Puranas[10]," said Pedhu.

"Here, take one of these, Pedhu, and throw it," said Gresham, and held out a ball to Pedhu.

"Why waste it?" said Pedhu.

"Never mind. Should we not check the quality of what we have?"

Pedhu took the ball. He was apprehensive. He looked at the huge open space ahead of them. "Where shall I throw it?" he asked Gresham.

"So you've progressed to the stage of asking for a target!" laughed Gresham. He then said "Cheney, aren't we going to tear down that hut there?"

"Yes," said Cheney and Fraser.

Pedhu flung the ball at the hut. It landed on the hut and exploded. The hut was flattened.

"What do you think of it?" asked Gresham.

"It's great! And what aim!" marvelled Raghunatha.

Two sepoys came running towards them. "In the hut..."

"What about the hut?"

---

10   Puranas- Hindu religious texts

"We had left a prisoner there."

"What?!" Gresham exclaimed angrily.

"The sea water came in so suddenly, that we couldn't think of anywhere else to hide him."

"Should you not have told us about it?" The Englishmen laughed. "A prisoner in the hut? Let us go and see for ourselves." They proceeded towards the hut. Pedhu stood immobile, as if he had been nailed to the ground. He had turned pale. Raghunatha held his hands.

Even as Pedhu followed the Englishmen, the sepoys had dragged out a charred body from inside the hut.

"This is the prisoner. His name was Sivachidambaram," they announced.

"Ahhh," shouted Pedhu.

"Do you know this man? Why did you cry out?" asked Gresham. Cheney and Fraser stared at Pedhu.

Pedhu fought back the tears, and said, "This man? No, I don't know him."

The Englishmen looked at each other meaningfully.

THIRTY

She stood on her toes and tried to reach the fruit. The veins stood out on her stretched neck. Her waist seemed even more slender. But she couldn't reach the fruit.

"Hello! Shall I pluck a fruit for you?" Kanchipurathan jumped down from the tree.

"It's you!" Thamarai had moved a few steps back in fear.

"Were you taken aback? So what do you want? Are you going to say that you would far rather have me than a fruit?"

"Keep your distance," she said to Kanchipurathan, who moved close to her.

"Are you that angry with me?"

"Can't you see I have a sacred thread round my wrist?"

"What is it for?"

"There is to be a three day Vinayaka puja in the palace starting from tomorrow. Every year Saivite mendicants are served food in the Siva temple. Until the puja is over..."

"Mendicants... Saivite mendicants..."

Thamarai's face turned red with anger. "You've been away for so long. You have offered no explanations for your absence. Is this the time to be thinking about mendicants?"

"Forgive me, Your Majesty. When you said mendicants…" He saw Krishnappa and Chennamma approaching, and greeted them.

"So, our General is back, in time for the Vinayaka puja!" exclaimed Krishnappa. "Was your mission successful?"

"Yes. But I have a request."

"What is it?"

"Let the mendicants be served food in the palace instead of in the temple."

♦

The mendicants entered the dining hall of the palace.

A servant approached Kanchipurathan. "We've brought all the mendicants who have come from other towns to the palace. They are very happy," he said.

'Of course, their happiness is understandable. They had planned to enter the palace clandestinely, and if they are escorted in with honours, naturally, they are bound to be happy,' Kanchipurathan thought. "All right. Tonight, make sure the mendicants are served a great feast," he said to the servant, and winked at him.

"As you command."

Kanchipurathan went back to the entrance, with the sprightliness of a mischievous child.

A group of villagers was at the entrance, and were being refused entry by the guards. "Master, we have brought grains, pulses, and vegetables as offerings for the Vinayaka puja. We were told there are mendicants who are going to be served food. We'd like to help in the kitchen. But the guards won't let us in," said an old man.

Kanchipurathan snatched the spears of the guards and flung them away. "Idiots! This palace was built with the sweat and toil of these men. It is their hard work that makes life at the palace so comfortable."

He then said to the villagers, "Come in, friends. Come in."

The villagers poured into the palace.

♦

Thud! Slap! "Let me go!" "Please stop!"

Thwack! Slap!

"Ooh! It's unbearable. Let me go!"

Thamarai, who was engaged in a game of dice, looked up. "What is that? What's going on in the dining hall?"

Kanchipurathan smiled. "A feast is being served, Your Majesty."

Thamarai turned her head in the direction of the dining hall and listened. "Oh my God! Let us go, please. We'll run away. Please stop!" the cries from the dining hall continued.

Krishnappa ran in, "Thamarai! What injustice! Outrageous!"

"Uncle, what is the matter?" Thamarai asked.

Chennamma stood there wringing her hands. "Thamarai, is Singavaram under our control? Or is it under the control of a demon?"

"What is the matter?" Thamarai repeated. As if in answer to her question, came a loud cry from the dining hall. "Stop beating us! It hurts. Oooh."

"Did you hear that? The mendicants who are supposed to be feasting are being beaten up."

"Why? Why?" Thamarai's agitation was evident.

"If we tell them food is not going to be served, they will go way. But to invite them in and then to treat them this way is atrocious. It will bring dishonour to our family," said Chennamma. "The General owes us an explanation."

"Oooooh. It hurts," the cries continued.

"Let us stop that first," said Thamarai.

Kanchipurathan stood arms akimbo, blocking her way. "I never thought you would be so heartless," Thamarai said.

"Have you all finished speaking? The mendicants are receiving what they came here to give us."

"What are you saying, General?"

"Come with me, and you will understand."

The three of them followed Kanchipurathan. As they drew close to the dining hall, the cries grew louder.

"Stop," commanded Thamarai. The men froze, whips in hand. Villagers who had brought vegetables and grains stood there confused. The mendicants came running up to Thamarai. "Your Majesty, save us." They fell at her feet. "We were told that we would be served a feast here. But what we have received are whiplashes. How can you permit such atrocities in your kingdom?"

"Stop your playacting," thundered Kanchipurathan. "The Queen does not know why you are here. But I know." He dragged a mendicant from the crowd and ordered a soldier to search his bag. The soldier turned out the mendicant's bag, but found nothing inside but a small begging bowl, a rosary for his prayer and some palm leaf manuscripts. Kanchipurathan was taken aback. He then pointed to another mendicant and had his bag searched, but his bag too contained the same things. The bags of all the mendicants were searched, one after another, and Kanchipurathan found no incriminating evidence. Kanchipurathan stood before the mendicants and looked at every one of them. None of them had been part of the group he had seen in Tirukazhukundram. Kanchipurathan apologised profusely to the mendicants. "Never mind," they said. "We've received many gifts at the palace. Something went wrong this time."

Kanchipurathan was ashamed. "That was their plan. They should have been here today. What happened?" he muttered to himself.

"General, will you not tell us what happened?" asked Krishnappa.

When Kanchipurathan explained Raghunatha's military plans, the three of them were shocked.

"We should never have let my father escape. That was our biggest mistake," said Chennamma.

Some men peeped in. "Those are the villagers who've come here with vegetables and grains, to participate in the puja," said Krishnappa.

"Shall we tell them to leave?" asked Thamarai.

"No, no," said Kanchipurathan. "Raghunatha will try to execute his plan. If not today, then tomorrow. I will arrest only the fake mendicants."

"But what about those villagers?" asked Chennamma.

Kanchipuarthan said loudly, "All of you stay on in the palace. You can eat the food prepared for the mendicants. I will ask the man in charge of palace administration to provide you with mattresses. You may sleep in the palace."

The villagers expressed their gratitude.

The palace servants dispersed.

Krishnappa and Chennamma left the two young people alone.

Kanchipurathan was resting his hand on the window sill, and was looking out at the well-lit city. Thamarai asked, "Are you tired?"

"Only an incompetent man offers tiredness as an excuse. I want to ensure that we are vigilant tomorrow. I was thinking of what I have to do."

"Think as much as you want to. It's only when you do dangerous things, that my heart misses a beat."

"Don't worry. The last scene in my dramas is always comic. You have been witness to that, haven't you?"

"You tell me you are not tired. But you sound bitter. I don't want you to leave me. If you are with me, I feel as if I am protected by a thousand strong elephant force."

"I am sorry, Your Majesty. I must take leave of you now. I am awaiting news from Deivanayaki. When and how she will send word to me is something I don't know. It is best that I wait for her near the entrance to the city."

Thamarai reluctantly let him go. But an inexplicable fear kept nagging at her.

♦

There was a small channel across the rivulet.

Kanchipurathan's feet were in the water, but his eyes scanned the road. A few ducks brushed against his feet and made him feel ticklish. He shooed them away. He could see a bullock cart on the highway.

He could see a torch being waved from inside the cart. He was certain that someone in the cart was bringing him a message. Or it could be Deivanayaki herself in the cart. He got up, but a duck tugged at his feet. "Let me go," he said to the bird, and ruffled its feathers. He could feel a string on its neck, and found that tied to a string around its neck was a palm leaf manuscript. Kanchipurathan began to read the manuscript, "To the West of the rivulet is a blue colour palace. Knock thrice on the back door."

He ran in the direction indicated in the manuscript. Found the palace. Knocked thrice on the door. The door opened. A lady covered in a shawl emerged and said, "There's been a change in plans. My father and Raghunatha will be here shortly. And all three of us will leave at once."

"But what about the mendicants?"

"Apparently, the Mysore Nayak kings have already tried that trick. So everyone is careful when it comes to trusting mendicants. So they've decided to send the men in another disguise."

"What disguise is that?"

"I understand that there is a Vinayaka puja going on in the place, and that people bring offerings to the puja. So it was decided to send in spies in the guise of villagers and cooks. They are to carry rice and vegetables with them. Why? What is the matter? Why do you look so shocked?"

"It is too late. Too late!" Kanchipurathan fretted. "I have already allowed them into the palace."

He could see the palace in the distance. The palace that he wanted to guard, the woman he wanted to protect—were both in enemy hands now!

The one who was supposed to protect them—Kanchipurathan, stood petrified outside the palace!

THIRTY ONE

The night was silent except for the noise of the babbling brook. How many people would the brook have seen over the years! How many scenes would it have been witness to! It had a lot to talk about. How could it be silent? A palanquin halted outside the blue palace. The silhouettes of two men could be seen. It was easy to make out that the two men were Pedhu and Raghunatha.

"Careful. Bring her out. She mustn't wake up."

The men went in, and carried out Deivanayaki, and placed her gently in the palanquin. The two old men walked in front of the palanquin, and they made their way towards a Vinayaka temple. Raghunatha opened the door to the temple. "Give me a hand," said Raghunatha to the men, and proceeded to move the Vinayaka idol. When the idol was moved aside, an underground passage was revealed. Raghunatha peered into the passage and put his foot in. He could feel the steps. "This passage leads to the elephant pavilion," said Raghunatha. He summoned the palanquin bearers with a clap of his hands.

♦

The lights in the palace were put out one after another.

The three people in the room had no idea that they were sitting on a volcano that could erupt at any moment.

"Let's talk for some time. I am not able to go to sleep," said Thamarai.

"I too can't sleep until the General brings us word about what my father's further plans are," said Chennamma.

Krishnappa smiled.

"Why are you smiling? I am ashamed of my father's conduct? Do you have to make fun of me?"

"I am not making fun of you. I thought of Thamarai and that brought a smile to my face."

"Why? What have I done?" asked Thamarai.

Krishnappa laughed, "Just as there are gods that govern the wind, fire and water, there is a god who drives away sleep. He[11] is armed with a bow and arrow. He is torturing you, isn't he?"

Thamarai blushed.

Chennamma began to tease Thamarai too. "He may be a great archer. But he stands no comparison with our General. He will run away the moment he sees our General."

"And will Thamarai be able to sleep, if he is driven away?" asked Krishnappa.

---

11 *The reference is to Kamadeva, the god of love, who is armed with a bow and arrows*

"That's enough. Please stop. You seem to be in a playful mood. But I feel uneasy."

"Foolish girl!" Chennamma ran her hand affectionately over Thamarai's hair. "What is there to fear? My father's men who were supposed to come in the guise of mendicants did not turn up. So the danger to us is past. The General has gone to find out what my father is planning to do. He will definitely foil my father's plans."

Krishnappa saw someone outside the room. "Who is it?" he asked. It was one of the villagers. "What is that you have in your hands?" asked Krishnappa.

"It's nothing. It's just an iron ball," replied the villager.

"What is it for?"

"You must forgive me. I told my son not to do anything without permission from the royal family. But he didn't pay heed to me."

"What did he do?"

"He plucked almonds from the tree in the palace garden. He wants me to break the shell for him. That's why I am taking this iron ball."

Krishnappa took the ball from him and examined it. "What a strange thing to use to crack open the shell of almonds!" he exclaimed. "I've never seen anything like this in the palace."

There were three or four men trying to hold back a woman from entering the room.

"What is going on there?" asked Krishnappa.

One of the men said, "This woman is from our village. She is a good dancer..."

"Why don't we ask her to dance here?" said Thamarai.

The village woman ran in and fell at Thamarai's feet. "Your Majesty, that's what I've been wanting to do. But these men refused to put in a word for me."

"Go on. Dance," said Thamarai.

The village woman picked up a pot of milk, and twirled and twisted with the pot in hand. As she danced, she poured the milk in cups, and handed it to the three members of the royal family. They sipped the milk, and sat back to enjoy the dance. Slowly, they began to lose consciousness, and when they had passed out, the dancer stopped. A few "villagers" came in. A man who appeared to be their leader commanded, "Quick. Take them to their rooms... Raghunatha will be here to give us further instructions."

♦

"Deivanayaki! Deivanayaki!" The palanquin had been placed behind the elephant pavilion. Pedhu bent down, and stuck his head into the palanquin. He whispered to the sleeping girl. There was no response from the girl.

Raghunatha looked up at the sky. He was able to guess the time.

He paced up and down like a caged tiger. "Peria Pedhu, today is the day when I will avenge myself on those who insulted me. They exiled me from this country. But their fate is sealed."

"Be patient, Raghunatha. Let's not celebrate too soon. The palace will fall silent only a few hours before daybreak. Only then will our men be able to capture the palace. Let's take a stroll. Let's walk up to the lily pond."

"Is it all right to leave the palanquin unguarded?"

"Why not? The palace is full of our men. Should we not trust them?"

"They are men sent by the Company. And it was officers of the Company who killed your nephew Sivachidambaram."

"Let us not think of that tragedy. I don't want Deivanayaki to know of it."

"How long can you keep her from knowing?"

"Let her become Queen of Singavaram. I will inform her then, at the appropriate time. She will be shocked initially, but will get over it soon."

Raghunatha sat on the bank of the pond. "Pedhu, you are clever when it comes to business. But you are not worldly wise."

"Why do you say so?"

"If you were wise, you wouldn't have spoken so lightly of matters of the heart. I think you do not have much experience when it comes to romance."

"Am I to take it that you have a lot of experience in the matter?"

Raghunatha was silent. He sighed deeply. Could it be that somewhere in the midst of the lilies, he could see the face of Thamarai?

♦

The elephant pavilion. A figure emerged from the pavilion, and looked around.

It was covered from head to toe in a saree. It walked in the dark. There was no one to stop it. It kept close to the palace wall.

It entered a room. Looked for something. Not finding whatever it was that it was looking for, it went into another room. And then a third room. Its face brightened. "Your Majesty!" it whispered in the ears of the sleeping lady. There was no response. The figure held a herb near Thamarai's nostrils. Her body contorted in discomfort; she tossed and turned. The figure held her head firmly, so that she couldn't move her head. With the other hand it pressed the herb to Thamarai's nostrils. Slowly, Thamarai began to come out of her faint. When the battle between wakefulness and sleep was almost over, Thamarai opened her mouth to let out a scream, but the figure put its hand over her mouth and stopped her.

Thamarai rubbed her eyes. "I...I..." her speech was slurred.

"You are safe, Your Majesty. That dancer had laced your milk with a drug."

"But, who are you?"

"What a question! Will a peacock ask the rain bearing clouds such a question? Will bees put such a question to flowers?" The figure shed the sari that covered its head and face.

"It's you!"

"Shh!" Kanchipurathan out his finger on her lips and silenced her. "You are not on a throne now, Your Majesty. You are seated on a volcano."

"What?"

"Yes. I have been foolish. This palace has fallen into enemy hands." Kanchipurathan covered himself with the sari again. "Before dawn, you, Krishnappa, and Chennamma will be arrested. The enemies are inside the palace in the guise of villagers. When dawn breaks, Singavaram's history will change, through a silent, bloodless revolution. That is the plan of our enemies. Raghunatha and Peria Pedhu have already entered the palace complex. They are going to be at the head of the enemy forces."

Thamarai was terrified. "How can you describe all this so calmly?"

"I can not only do it calmly, but I can also do it smiling," said Kanchipurathan. "And do you know why? Because they are staging a drama, where the heroine is missing. The person they are planning to put on the throne is missing. Now isn't that cause for amusement?"

"Why? Deivanayaki...?"

"She is on our side, Your Majesty. I will tell you what brought about a change of heart in her case. She is safe in a mansion outside the city. I took her place. I wore her sari. I lay down in the palanquin she was supposed to occupy. Raghunatha brought me through all the secret passages that are known only to him. Pedhu and Raghunatha think that Deivanayaki is in the palanquin which has been left near the elephant pavilion."

"What are you going to do now?"

Kanchipurathan showed Thamarai a herb. "A physician gave me this herb when I was on my way to Singavaram from Chennai. I am going to use this herb to revive Chennamma and Krishnappa. Then they have to revive the ministers, generals, the guards of the armoury—roughly thirty people."

"Are we running short of time?"

"I am racing against time. You lie down on your bed." Kanchipurathan tiptoed to the door and opened it. A hand gripped him. "Got you! I've been looking for you since evening."

Kanchipurathan was shocked.

THIRTY TWO

Kanchipurathan tried to shake off the hand that gripped him, but he couldn't. The man held on to his hand tightly. His breath smelt of liquor. His eyes were blood shot. He seemed to be in a libidinous mood.

"You beauty! Don't try to give me the slip!" said the man.

Thamarai smiled at Kanchipurathan. She tried to keep from laughing out loud.

The drunkard said, "A while ago, you danced, and what a dance it was—with all those twists and turns! I decided then that you should be mine."

The man had mistaken Kanchipurathan for the girl who had laced the milk with a sedative.

"Dear One! Why would I want to be separated from you? Come on, let us make the most of the night," said Kanchipurathan to the man, and put his hand over his shoulders. Kanchipurathan led the man towards a dark corner of the garden.

Thamarai was too shocked to protest, but Kanchipurathan returned after a few minutes. "He's been despatched to the land of joy," laughed Kanchipurathan. "Come on, Your Majesty," he said, and led her towards the elephant pavilion.

There was danger all around them. It was like walking through a path strewn with thorns, like dancing on the tips of swords. They were surrounded by enemies on all sides. They walked quietly and carefully, and reached the palanquin on the banks of the lily pond.

"What should I do?" asked Thamarai.

"Fortuately, there isn't much difference in height and build between you and Deivanayaki..." Kanchipurathan whispered in her ears. "You'll have to pretend to be Deivanayakai for a day."

"What happens afterwards?"

"Raghunatha plans to announce before the council of ministers that Deivanayaki is the queen. He is going to do it day after tomorrow. Till then, don't let anyone see your face. Don't speak more than necessary. We will expose Raghunatha before the council of ministers. Peria Pedhu's plans will come to naught."

"And you?"

"Deivanayaki is waiting for news from me. I also have to keep my promise to Sivachidambaram." Kanchipurathan felt his waist. The palm leaf manuscript was safe. "Don't worry. Once I have carried out these tasks, I will come to the palace."

Tears welled up in Thamarai's eyes.

They could hear footsteps. "Quick! Come on, quick!" Kanchipurathan pushed Thamarai into the palanquin. He told her to pretend that she was unconscious. He covered her with a sheet.

There was a bathroom adjacent to Thamarai's bedroom. The man who had accosted

Kanchipurathan lay there, trussed up. He had passed out, and Kanchipurathan stripped off the man's clothes and donned them. Kanchipurathan discovered that the man had Raghunatha's ring, bearing the royal insignia. Kanchipurathan gave a wry smile. This was the man Raghunatha had put his trust in!

Kanchipurathan tied up the man again, gagged him and went out. He locked the door to the room. He walked towards the treasury. One of Raghunatha's spies was on guard at the entrance. When he saw Raghunatha's ring, he let Kanchipurathan in.

The treasury officer was fast asleep. Kanchipurathan shook him awake.

"It's you!" the official exclaimed.

"Shh! Listen to me." Kanchipurathan whispered to him…

The official could not bring himself to believe Kanchipurathan's story. But he couldn't completely disbelieve it either.

"As long as I am alive, I will not let any harm befall the Queen. I will die protecting her," the officer in charge of the treasury said.

"What I expect of you now is discretion."

"And so…?"

"Have you seen what a tiger does before it attacks a victim? It springs on the victim suddenly, having been in hiding till then. I want you to pretend that you are obeying Raghunatha. A few hours before dawn, Raghunatha plans to kidnap all the important palace officials and also the Queen. You and the other officials must agree to that plan."

"Isn't that what a coward would do?"

"No, that is what a clever man would do. Let us give Raghunatha the idea that his plan has been successful. However, the Queen will never be in his clutches. His downfall will begin the moment he makes his announcement."

"Forgive me for saying this. But your plan seems to be a circuitous way of defeating him."

"Sometimes, such plans become necessary. There are many more people I have to revive. I implore you to adhere to my plan."

"I will do as you say," agreed the treasury officer.

Kanchipurathan then went off to make some more visits, and wherever he went, it was Raghunatha's ring that helped him gain entry.

♦

The Sun was rising. The sky was bathed in crimson.

Kanchipurathan's walk betrayed his tiredness. But his spirit remained strong. His eyes were dull with worry and exertion. But it was clear that he was proud to have done his duty.

When he entered the blue coloured mansion, there was enthusiasm in his voice. "Deivanayaki! Tomorrow same time, the last scene of this drama!"

When he explained his plans to Deivanayaki, she became agitated.

"Have you forgotten your promise to me?" she asked.

"You are worried about your father, aren't you? Don't worry about him. He will remain unharmed."

Deivanayaki sighed. "If only my father didn't try to make money through crooked means…"

"Is there an honest way to become rich?" laughed Kanchipurathan. "Let us leave this place. I know of a place in the city, where you can stay."

"And where are you going after you leave me there?"

"Talk of fickle minded women! You have forgotten Sivachidambaram!"

Deivanayaki blushed. "Yes. Please complete the task he has assigned to you. When I return to Chennai, I want him to be waiting for me, no longer a prisoner, but a free man."

They left the blue colour mansion.

"Grandma!" Kanchipurathan knocked on the door of a house.

"Who is it?" An old lady opened the door.

"It's me," said Kanchipurathan. "I've brought a lady to learn how to play the nagaswaram from your son. But she will be a student just for a day."

"Your ways are always puzzling," she said to Kanchipurathan. "Anyway, do come in," she said to Deivanayaki, and shut the door.

♦

Time, noon

Place, The flagpole in the Dutch Fort.

Standing beneath the flagpole was a Dutchman, who was clearly in a bad mood. Standing near him were thirty sepoys, who didn't know what they could do to calm him down.

The Dutchman looked up at the tip of the flagpole, and this led to a renewal of his anger. "It's hardly seventy feet high. And there is no one here who is capable of climbing that. It's an insult to our country. Just look at that flag. It's all twisted! What a dishonour to my country! And there is none among you who is brave enough to climb that pole to fix the flag!"

"It's because of the rains that..." the men said hesitantly.

"Can I help?" The sepoys turned when they heard a new voice.

The man looked like a villager. "Who are you? Where are you from?" asked the Dutchman.

"I come from a town which has seen many flags fly. When I was a child, sliding down flagpoles was my favourite pastime. If you permit me..."

"Go ahead."

The man began shinning up the pole. Even a monkey couldn't have climbed up so quickly. Holding on to the pole with one hand, he unfurled the twisted flag. The Dutch flag was flying once again majestically.

He came down.

"Very good! What's your name?" asked the Dutchman.

"Kanchipurathan."

"Come with me," said the Dutchman, and led the way. On the way, Kanchipurathan explained the reason for his visit. Kanchipurathan was taken to a higher official of the Dutch East India Company. The official listened as the other Dutchman explained Kanchipurathan's mission.

"So Sivachidambaram sent you here!"

"Yes," said Kanchipurathan, and untied the silk cloth which he had tied to his dhoti. And when he opened it, he was shocked. "But, this isn't what Sivachidambaram gave me. This silk cloth has nothing on it! Where is the one he gave me?"

The Dutch official laughed. "You underestimated the intelligence of the Englishmen. You can never anticipate their moves."

"And I suppose you can," said Kanchipurathan.

"Of course we can. We are all the same race, aren't we?" He got up from his chair, and tapped Kanchipurathan on his shoulder. "You don't know what happened to Sivachidambaram, do you?"

"What happened to him?"

"The British had him killed. They got Peria Pedhu to kill him!" The Dutchman started to tell Kanchipurathan about Sivachidmabaram's end at Pedhu's hands.

♦

Around the same time, in Singavaram—

Tom-tom-tom

Drum beats.

People gathered round to hear the announcement the drummer was going to make. The drummer read from a palm leaf manuscript,

"An important message from the palace. Listen, all of you. There have been some important changes in the administration. All of you are to come to the palace hall tomorrow. The Queen orders you all to come."

He started striking the drum again, and moved on to another street.

"Changes in the administration? Has Queen Thamarai abdicated in favour of someone else?"

"But the drummer said that the Queen had ordered us to come there. How could she have abdicated then?"

"What if he meant someone else when he said Queen? Maybe that girl from Chennai has come with more proof to establish her claim to the throne."

Everyone had his or her own theories about what might have happened.

"Did you hear that?" Raghunatha asked Peria Pedhu. "You were afraid the people would not accept your daughter as the Queen. Now are you convinced?"

"Yes," Peria Pedhu beamed.

There was a roll of thunder and a few drops of rain fell on the ground.

"Let us take shelter on that pyol," said Raghunatha, pointing to the pyol of a small house.

"We must return to the palace soon," said Peria Pedhu. He noticed Raghunatha's face darkening.

"Peria Pedhu! Where is your daughter?" asked Raghunatha. His voice betrayed his anger.

"Why, in the palace, of course."

"If you think we are now in the palace, then what you say must be true!"

"What are you saying?"

"Just look through the window. There is your daughter," said Raghunatha.

Peria Pedhu looked into the house. "My daughter…"

"Yes, your daughter. So tell me now. For how long have father and daughter been planning to shame me publicly?" asked Raghunatha.

Peria Pedhu clutched Raghunatha's hand and said, "Believe me, my friend. My daughter has deceived me too."

"Again and again, someone spoils my well laid plans. But I am not going to be defeated this time." Raghunatha ground his teeth angrily.

"I am not going to let our plans fail. You go back to the palace, where I think Thamarai has taken Deivanayaki's place. Leave me to deal with my daughter."

"Can I trust you? I hope you will not go away to Chennai," said Raghunatha.

"Do you think I am a coward? I will bring Deivanayaki to the palace before midnight," swore Peria Pedhu.

♦

The next morning. We've heard people talk of a sea of humanity. If one wanted to know what the phrase meant, one should have been in Singavaram. There was a thronging multitude of people.

On the dais were three thrones. The people wondered what Peria Pedhu and Raghunatha were doing there.

The jostling crowd had a lot of questions and doubts. "Wasn't it Raghunatha who chased away that man from Chennai? But he is with him now. What is the meaning of this?"

"We heard that after our general drove away the Delhi Sultan's army, he drove out Raghunatha too. But now that man's back."

"Stop pushing. If there was space in front, would we not have moved?"

"I am a visitor to Singavaram. I was told that something important was going to be announced. I was curious. That is why I am here," said Kanchipurathan, who was disguised as a North Indian fakir.

"Shh! Raghunatha is rising from his seat. He is gong to say something. Let us hear what he has to say."

Raghunatha raised his hand to signal to the people to be silent. "My dear countrymen! A few months ago, when Peria Pedhu, a merchant from Chennai, said his foster daughter was the heir to the Singavaram throne, I did not believe him. But I had my doubts about Thamarai. So I went to Chennai and Srirangam and initiated enquiries. And my enquiries revealed that Thamarai was the impostor. So I have imprisoned her, and my daughter and son-in-law, who supported her. This girl Deivanayaki you see before you, will be crowned Queen at an auspicious time. None of the ministers has objected to this arrangement. I trust you too will approve."

"No, we object!" a voice rang out from the crowd. The man to whom the voice belonged walked up to the dais. "Peria Pedhu! Should you not ask your daughter if she is willing to be the Queen?"

"Oh, it's you—Kanchipurathan!"

"Why is your daughter's face averted? Ask her if she is willing to be Queen."

"Certainly!"

"Ask her to discard her veil. Let us see her face. Let her speak to us."

"Certainly, young man. Come here," said Raghunatha to the girl, and removed her veil.

Deivanayaki!

Defeat again for Kanchipurathan!

THIRTY THREE

But the dejection lasted for just a few seconds.

His confidence bounced back, and chased away his fears and doubts. Kanchipurathan smiled. Raghunatha was cocky, because Deivanayaki was his captive. Just you wait, Raghunatha! There cannot be a more naïve person than you. Wait until you hear Deivanayaki speak. Keep your eyes peeled! Watch out! Deivanayaki is digging a pit for you. Take care! You might be seriously injured when you fall into that pit!

Deivanayaki addressed the people.

"My dear subjects!"

Kanchipurathan was taken aback.

"It is my good fortune to serve you..."

What was Deivanayaki saying?

"I thank God for giving me the opportunity to serve you. I am glad to be your Queen."

Kanchipurathan was furious. But he knew that discretion was what was needed.

The people who had assembled there were shocked too.

"Isn't this the woman who was chased away once before?"

"Yes, she is the woman from Chennai."

"Whose support does she have?"

"Raghunatha is behind this plot."

"Shh. Raghunatha is going to address us."

Raghunatha adjusted his garments, the gold threads of which glittered. "People of Singavaram! Our former General is bent on confusing you. I know you want to kill him, and not allow him to utter words of treachery. But your magnanimity has got the better of you and that is why he is alive. He won't thank you for it, but I will."

Kanchipurathan laughed out loud. "All the people here are my friends. I know that they will not spare those who sow seeds of dissension in the country... Am I right, my friends?" Kanchipurathan turned to face the people, but he felt betrayed. Why did they not respond enthusiastically? Why was it, that except for one or two men, the rest were silent? And even the few who seemed to agree with him, only gave tentative nods.

Raghunatha laughed contemptuously.

"Listen to me, you slave from Chennai, who goes by the name of Kanchipurathan. The people of Singavaram are delighted to meet their new Queen. They do not have the time to even chase vagabonds like you. Do you know what is happening near the northern gate of the fort?" asked Raghunatha.

"What is happening there?"

"Go and have a look. No, no. Stay here. Let someone else go and have a look. You—the physician—you go to the northern gate and come back and tell this slave what's going on there. Let the others know too of what's going on there."

The physician and a few other men ran towards the northern gate. They came back and said, "Come on all of you. Everyone's getting gifts there. Men get a dhoti and a gold coin. Women are given sarees. Long live the Queen Deivanayaki!"

"Long live the Queen!"

The people pushed each other as they ran towards the gate. "Stop pushing. Wait for your turn. Long live the generous Queen."

The guards had a tough time trying to regulate the crowd. "There is enough for anyone. You don't have to rush," they said.

Kanchipurathan's face flushed with embarrassment.

"Wait. Stop." But nothing he said could stop the people. "Stop. Is it right that you should take a bribe and endorse treason? Is it right that you lend support to such injustice?" But it was of no avail. The crowd kept surging towards the northern gate of the fort.

He looked at Deivanayaki, but her eyes expressed her inability to do anything about the situation.

He looked again at the people who were making their way to the place where gifts were being given. He saw a familiar face. "Old man, stop. Do you remember me? I helped you recover your property. Do you remember?"

"Of course. How can I forget you?"

"Then please do not take these gifts. Please don't be shameless enough to take a bribe."

"Young man, did you think I would take what is offered? I have no intention of accepting their gifts."

Kanchipurathan heaved a sigh of relief. He recognised a lady in the crowd, and said, "Grandma. I left a girl under your care. How could you be so careless, and let her get away?"

The old lady wiped the tears from her eyes. "They came with soldiers. They threatened all of us, and my son and the others there could do nothing. Don't you know that we depend on the royal family for our livelihood? How can we incur their displeasure? What is the name of that man—Chinna Pedhu? Peria Pedhu? He said something to Deivanayaki, and she began to weep. She then left with him. And anyway, if she is the Queen, how can you..."

"Do you believe that story, grandma?" Kanchipurathan asked angrily. He could see the people queuing up for their gifts, and there was the old man who had sworn that he would never accept the gifts. Kanchipurathan felt let down, but he didn't let his emotions get the better of him. He had to find out where Thamarai was. Where was she?

◆

The pavilion was empty. There were two guards near the throne. Peria Pedhu stood there like a statue. Deivanayaki looked helpless. "Excellent. The

Queen has crossed the first hurdle. And as for the rest…"

"Stop," shouted Deivanayaki. "You have got what you wanted. Why do you continue to do this?" her hand pointed to a guard, the tip of whose sword was touching Peria Pedhu's back. "Tell that man to move away."

"Go away," ordered Raghunatha. The guard put his sword into its sheath and stepped aside.

Peria Pedhu relaxed, and gave a pathetic smile.

"Remember, Queen. I might have ordered my man not to put a sword to your father's back any more. But I have not relaxed my vigil. I will keep an eye on you. I make my plans carefully. But you slip away the moment an opportunity presents itself. And your father says, 'My daughter has always been a pampered child. Don't force her to do what she doesn't want to do.' Do you think I am a fool? If you spoil my plans your father will pay with his life. Keep that in mind," said Raghunatha.

Peria Pedhu followed Deivanayaki. Raghunatha stopped him and said, "Wait. There is a separate room for you, my friend. The days of hatching plots have ended. Didn't you know that?"

"Don't worry, father. I will take care of myself," said Deivanayki, with tears in her eyes.

The two men waited till she disappeared from view. They then gave each other a hug! "Raghunatha! What a great plan that was!" Peria Pedhu remarked.

"Shh. We don't want your daughter to hear us. We don't want our clever acting to go to waste, do we?"

"Raghunatha, now she will do exactly what we want her to do, won't she?"

"Of course, she will. Will a loving daughter not want to save her father's life? Will she not be prepared to make sacrifices for the sake of her father?"

They celebrated their victory with a drink.

♦

Someone tapped Kanchipurathan on his shoulder.

Kanchipurathan, who had been watching the crowd waiting to collect their gifts, turned round. Who was this tall man with a beard and moustache?

"Yes?" Kanchipurathan said. The man said nothing in reply, but signaled to Kanchipurathan to follow him.

"Where do you want me to come?" asked Kanchipurathan.

The man pointed to the hill.

"Who is there?"

The man looked round fearfully, and then put his hand on his head to indicate that someone of the royal family was there. "The Queen?" asked Kanchipurathan.

The man nodded, and tugged at Kanchipurathan's dhoti.

The tall man led the way, and Kanchipurathan followed. The path up the hill was thorny. The tall man pointed to something on the ground. "What is it?" asked Kanchipurathan, and looked down. He looked down a precipitous slope. Something warned Kanchipurathan. It must have been his intuition. He stepped aside in a trice, and the next second—

Two screams were heard. One of them was the voice of the tall man, as he went hurtling down the slope. The other was the scream of Kanchipurathan who had had a miraculous escape. "Oh God! The traitor has survived, and the loyal servant is dead. Is this fair?" said a voice from behind a bush.

Kanchipurathan looked at the man who emerged from behind the bush. It was the man who was in charge of the palace treasury. "Are you surprised at how I escaped?" the man asked Kanchipurathan. "You are an outsider, and so you did not hesitate to plot against the royal family. But did you think that someone who had served the family all his life would turn traitor too?"

"Are you calling me a traitor?" Kanchipurathan asked.

"What else do you expect me say? You wanted Raghunatha's plans to succeed. That is why you told all the palace officials to pay heed to Raghunatha's men. But I escaped and that is how I could see how treacherous you had been."

"You are wrong, my friend. My plans went wrong, because some unexpected things happened."

"That's the usual excuse you peddle."

"You made such secret plans to bump me off. You could so easily have found out what happened at the palace. Why did you not do that? If you had bothered to find out what had happened, you would have realised that I was the only one opposing Raghunatha."

"Now which scene is this, in the drama that you have enacted?"

Kanchipurathan gnashed his teeth. "All right, my friend. I will prove my loyalty to the crown in just eight days. I will put Thamarai back on the throne. If I do not do that, I will come back here, unarmed. I swear on my mother, I will be here. You can push me down into that abyss, and accomplish what that poor dumb man failed to do. Let my bones shatter to pieces. "

Kanchipurathan descended the hill.

♦

Many people were still waiting in line to receive their gifts. Kanchipurathan joined the queue.

His darling Thamarai was imprisoned somewhere in the palace. But where?

"Keep moving. There are others waiting behind you," the man behind Kanchipurathan pushed him.

Kanchipurathan took the dhoti and the coin. "Check your gifts," the guard distributing dhotis said to him. Kanchipurathan did not respond. "Hey, you. I'm talking to you. Check your gifts now, and see if everything is all right. There is no point going all the way to Kanchipuram and then coming back here to complain that we gave you a shop-soiled dhoti."

Kanchipurathan was shocked. Kanchipuram—his town! Why was it mentioned? Who was it who was giving him a message? He looked up, and saw the dwarf.

What was the dwarf trying to say? He had asked Kanchipurathan to check the dhoti. Was there a message hidden in the dhoti? Kanchipurathan moved away and opened the dhoti, and a palm leaf scroll dropped out. He read it, 'Thamarai, Krishnappa and Chennamma have been imprisoned in the underground prison. The prison is heavily guarded.'

THIRTY FOUR

Thamarai in the underground prison!

Kanchipurathan was shocked.

That was a terrible place to be in. He knew what it was like. He'd been there and experienced the horror of that prison. How could they have put Thamarai there? It was like casting a bunch of flowers in the sun, like dumping gold in the mire.

Kanchipurathan was in a state of panic now. How did the dwarf know that Thamarai was there? What else did he know?

Kanchipurathan wanted to meet him again. But there was still a long line of people waiting for their gifts.

Kanchipurathan joined the queue, but when his turn came, he noticed that the dwarf was no longer there. One of the two men there laughed and said, "Now isn't this our former General? Has he become so poor that he has to wait in line twice for doles?"

Kanchipurathan answered patiently, "Has the treasury become empty under the new dispensation? Can you not give a person two dhotis?" He placed the dhoti and coin he had received earlier before them. "Please give these to Raghunatha, with my compliments."

"Wait. Wait," the men called after him, as Kanchipurathan walked away.

"General, General..."

Kanchipurathan turned round to see who it was.

"General. No one but you can help me."

Who was this woman?

"Do you remember the man who was your Deputy General? He was killed by Raghunatha. I am his mother."

"My respects to you. I had asked the Queen to help your family," Kanchipurathan said.

"Come with me," the woman said, and led Kanchipurathan out of the city.

She took him to a field outside the city. Five or six men were busy harvesting the crop. There was a cart on the road. The bulls had been untied and were grazing. Kanchipurathan asked the old woman, "Is this your land? And who are these people harvesting the crop in your land? Are they doing it without your permission?"

"Any army that passes by helps itself to crops in the fields on the way. Last year some men took away our crops, and they were the Sultan's men. Now these men say they are from Mysore. Two days ago, an army went past. It was heading towards Salem and Coimbatore, to lay siege to those towns. These men here said they are responsible for providing food to that army. I don't care who they are. But how can they help themselves to what belongs to me? This has become a country where there is no protection for the common man."

Kanchipurathan looked round and, pointing to a building some distance away, he asked, "What's there in that building?"

"There was a time when it was used."

"And now?"

"It is a granary. But who has a surplus of grains? Who has enough grains to be stored under lock and key? I don't think a lock for that building is necessary at all."

Kanchipurathan thought for a while.

"Please help me. We will have no food, if these men take away our grains."

"Don't worry. I will help you," assured Kanchipurathan.

He tied his towel round his head like a turban. He tightened his dhoti. Humming a folk song, he walked towards the men from Mysore. He sat on a rock and said, "Quick, before Ramaiah comes. He deserves to lose his crop. But he might be here any minute now. He is sure to bring armed men. He is a wicked man. Quick. Finish your work before he arrives."

"Mind your business," snarled one of the men, who was piling up shaves of grains.

"Who is Ramaiah?" asked another.

"Haven't you heard of Ramaiah? He is the village chief. He is a ruthless man. If the villagers find out that some men from Mysore have been harvesting crops from his land clandestinely, I think they will serve you a feast."

The men laughed.

"But I am sorry for you, because you have not looked in that building," said Kanchipurathan pointing to the granary.

"What is there in that building?"

"I pity you. Here you are working yourselves to the bones, while there are sacks full of rice grains in that building. All you have to do is take your cart there, and load the sacks on to your cart and be on your way."

"We wish we had known that."

"Come on. I will show you the way to the granary."

He led them to the granary. As each of them entered, he said, "it is dark inside. But you can feel your way round."

"We can't find any sacks here."

"That is because it is dark inside. Keep looking." When all the men were inside the granary, Kanchipurathan slammed the door shut, and bolted it.

"The door is old, but it is strong," laughed Kanchipurathan.

"Let us out," the men shouted and banged on the door.

"My friends. Keep looking for the grains. If you do not find it in this life, you may find it in your next."

Kanchipurathan came out of the building, and stopped when he noticed a smaller door. He pushed it, and it opened. There was a narrow passage and Kanchipurathan made his way into the passage. He groped in the dark, and found two stones. He rubbed them, and with the spark he lit a dry leaf and looked round in the light. On the wall was an inscription. It said, '*Way to the underground prison.*'

Kanchipurathan put out the light. He moved slowly ahead. Suddenly, his head took a knock, and he realised he had come to the end of the passage. There was a huge boulder blocking the passage. The prison was on the other side of the boulder. But how was he going to move it? He struck the stones again, and found another inscription. '*There is no secret passage that Raghunatha does not know.*'

Raghunatha must have made a survey of all secret passages when Krishnappa was in power, and blocked all of them.

Kanchipurathan sat down disappointed. A cool breeze blew in. Wait a minute. Breeze—now where did that come from? Kanchipurathan began to check. There was a small gap between the boulder and the wall of the passage, and the breeze came in through that gap. But it wasn't big enough for him to put his hand in and try to move the rock. But he could hear voices on the other side.

"You may be a clever businessman, Peria Pedhu. But as far as politics is concerned, I am the clever one."

That was Raghunatha's voice. Could that be the garden outside the underground prison? The two men seemed to be walking as they conversed.

Peria Pedhu's reply could be heard, "You are right. Still, he worked for me. I know what tricks he is capable of."

Kanchipurathan smiled. They were talking about him. He listened carefully.

"All right, and since you know him better, what do you think we should do?"

"He must be killed."

"No, he mustn't. We mustn't make him a martyr. If we kill him, then people will start talking of him as a hero. Killing him and turning him into a martyr would be like arming an enemy."

"Still…"

"Please leave this to me. I know how to get rid of my enemies. I know when, where, and how to get rid of them."

"What conceit!" thought Kanchipurathan. He went back to the village and met the mother of the slain Deputy General. "I have locked up those men. But what you must do is this—get someone to harvest your crops as soon as possible, and store them safely," he told her.

♦

The city had gone to sleep.

Kanchipurathan lay down on the floor of a rest house. But just as he was about to drift off to sleep, he heard a chain moving. He looked up. He could see a man with his legs and hands in chains, with two guards sleeping beside him. The prisoner moaned in pain. Kanchipurathan noticed that he had a thick beard. "Drat. Can't you stop moving your hands and legs? We can't sleep with all that noise. We will take you to Raghunatha in the morning. You've been jailed twice. Maybe this time you will be sent to the underground prison. Or maybe you will be beheaded. Can't you stay still till then?"

"Forgive me," said the prisoner. Kanchipurathan looked at the prisoner and his eyes dilated in surprise. He waited till the guards went back to sleep, and then slowly crawled towards the prisoner. He tapped the prisoner gently on the shoulder and indicated that he should follow him. The prisoner pointed to his chains. Kanchipurathan lifted the chains, so that they made no noise, and the two men slowly made their way to the back of the rest house. Kanchiupurathan lifted the prisoner, and carried him to a rock some distance away. He set him down on the rock.

"Why have they put you in chains?"

"I opposed Raghunatha once before. I was happy thinking we were rid of him for good. But he came back. I was telling some men that I had no intention of paying tax to him. These men overheard me, and arrested me."

"For a minute, I hesitated, wondering if I was rescuing a good man, or whether I was helping a fugitive from justice. I am glad I have rescued a man who is on the right side." He proceeded to break the locks on the chains, with a stone. "Now listen to me. I am going to take your place," said Kanchipurathan.

"Please don't. Raghunatha is a wicked man."

"Let me deal with him." Kanchipurathan continued to work on the chains, until they gave way.

♦

The old man was being taken into the palace. "Let me go. Please. I can't take this anymore."

"As if you can't walk after having slept through the night at the rest house. Move." The two soldiers pushed the old man at Raghunatha's feet.

Raghunatha lifted the man's bearded chin, and looked at him. Recognition dawned. "Oh, it's you. I know this old man. He is a very good man. Peria Pedhu knows him well. This man is branded with the initials P.P."

Kanchipurathan cursed himself. He had forgotten all about the branded initials.

"He is a very good man. He doesn't deserve to live here in our country. Please escort him to the border and let him leave our country."

Suddenly there was a commotion outside the palace. Peria Pedhu came running in. "Raghunatha! I have some good news for you. Come and have a look. Do you see those men there? They have brought gifts from the king of Senji."

"Gifts from Senji? What for?" Raghunatha asked angrily.

"They have come here to seek the hand of Deivanayaki in marriage, to propose that she marry the Crown Prince of Senji..."

Raghunatha followed Pedhu, and the soldiers too left the room, and Kanchipurathan used the opportunity to make good his escape.

THIRTY FIVE

"Amma, amma," Thamarai moaned.

Of what use was crying for the mother, who had nurtured the child in her womb, but had fallen prey to the evil plans of those around her? "Don't cry, dear Thamarai," consoled Chennamma.

"No, let her cry. You and I mended our ways. We are remorseful for our deeds; we are ashamed of our wickedness. But none of this is going to bring down the government your father has put in place. Maybe the righteous tears of the one who has been wronged might have some dharmic effect. Let her shed tears," said Krishnappa.

Their hands and legs were tied. The rough rocky walls hurt their backs. The doors had spikes in them. The floor was damp and stank. Rows of ants were making their way across the floor. Hell was, perhaps, like this dank, dark prison.

"Water, please give me some water," begged Thamarai.

A guard stuck his hand through the bars, and he held out a glass of water to Thamarai. But he didn't take it close to her lips. And Thamarai, with her hands tied, couldn't take the glass in her hands.

"She is the Queen of the country. Give her some water. If things were to go her way, she could well be on the throne soon, and then she will reward you," said Krishnappa to the guard.

But the other guard knocked off the glass from the man's hands, and laughed cruelly. "You idiot! Do you think she is going to escape and reward you? If Raghunatha comes to know of this, he will have you killed. Did you think of that?" he asked, and pushed the kind hearted guard into the corridor.

The guard who had tried to offer Thamarai water fell at the feet of the second guard, and begged for forgiveness. "I got carried away. I will not make the same mistake again. Please do not tell Raghunatha about my foolishness."

"I am not a traitor like you. I won't tell him about your foolishness. Go away. Let me not see you here again." The man who had offered water to Thamarai was gone like lightning.

The second guard was called Kartikeyan. He tiptoed to the corridor and looked out. When he returned to the prison, he was smiling.

He fell at Krishnappa's feet and said, "Forgive me, Your Majesty. My family has served the royal family for generations. But I had to pretend that I was against you. Forgive me for being disrespectful…"

Krishnappa was moved. "I am glad there is someone here who cares about us."

Kartikeyan looked around fearfully and said to Thamarai, "Your Majesty, if you want to escape, I can help you."

He pulled out a bunch of keys and unlocked the chains that tied the three of them. He then pulled out a pouch containing chunam. He scooped some chunam, and applied a little bit on each of the rocks. Finally, the chunam applied on one of the rocks turned red. "Yes, this is it," he said triumphantly. He shook the rock gently. It moved. He tugged at it, and many rocks next to it moved too, revealing a secret passage.

"I was king for so many years. I never knew of such passages," exclaimed Krishnappa.

"Follow me," said Kartikeyan, and stepped into the passage.

The three prisoners followed him.

"Great, Kartikeya. You have done well," said a voice.

A group of soldiers surrounded the prisoners.

"How treacherous!" said Krishnappa to Kartikeya, who stood there grinning.

"Treachery? How can you talk of treachery, Krishnappa?" asked the chief of the guards, a man with a sickle shaped moustache. "This is a test. Do you understand, Kartikeya?"

"No, I do not," said Kartikeya.

"I wanted to check if these prisoners were resigned to their fate, or whether, given an opportunity, they would escape. They have proved that they haven't lost the will to live. So now when they lose their lives, it is going to be a greater punishment, isn't it?" he laughed.

"Stop, you rogue," shouted Krishnappa, only to be slapped hard.

"Uncle, please let them do what they want. We've been through so much. Let's face whatever it is they have in store for us," cried Thamarai.

"If a person tries to escape from an ordinary prison, he is sent to the underground prison. If he tries to escape from the underground prison, the punishment is severe. Now, look at where I am pointing," said the chief of guards. "Look at that place, while you can still see. Do you know what those red hot iron rods are used for? Have a look, while you still have eyes to see."

The prisoners stood transfixed with horror, for the man with the sickle shaped moustache was pointing to a heated iron rod.

"Now do you know what your punishment is? Those iron rods are going to be used to put out your eyes. I love the smell that comes out when a hot iron rod meets flesh."

Thamarai and Chennamma hugged each other in fright.

"But you have been treated kindly despite all your treachery, and for that you must thank our king Raghunatha..."

"I don't want to hear that man's name," snarled Krishnappa.

"Our magnanimous king Raghunatha has decided to give you one last chance to save yourselves. It is enough if one of you agrees to have his or her eyes blinded, and it is enough if that person stays in the underground prison. The other two can walk out of prison. Now make up your minds about which of you is going to lose his or her eyes."

"I'll be the one to have my eyes blinded," three voices cried out in unison.

"I am the one who deserves to be punished. If I had not killed my brother, none of this would have happened. So I will be the one to lose my eyes. The two of you must leave this prison," said Krishnappa.

"You are dearer to me than my eyes, my dear husband. How can I let you languish in prison, blinded? Isn't it my father who is behind all this? I should be the one to lose my eyes, for having allowed him to stay with us. You and Thamarai must leave. And you must get her married to her lover Kanchipurathan," said Chennamma.

"I am moved by the love you have shown this orphan. And now you are even prepared to lose your eyes for my sake. How can I let you both suffer on my account? Uncle, just as waves characterise the sea, suffering has always characterised my life. I was destined to be a slave, how could I have aspired for the throne? The moment I entered your palace, I brought sorrow to all of you. I am the one who should be punished," said Thamarai.

"That's enough. Reserve your lectures for a better audience, perhaps at the Vishnu temple. I am sure there are enough people who have nothing better to do and who will come to listen to you," said the jail warden, and asked a man with shaggy hair to bring the heated rod. The man asked the chief of guards,

"Is the rod hot enough?" But to his surprise, the rod was snatched from his hands by the jail warden. "It's hot enough not just for them, but also for you, the man who has come to rescue the prisoners," he said.

Even as Krishnappa, Chennamma and Thamarai stood shocked not knowing what to make of this latest twist, jail guards surrounded the man. "It's you!" exclaimed Thamarai, even as Kanchipurathan tried to shake off the grip of the jail guards!

THIRTY SIX

A salver heaped with rubies! Pedhu picked up a handful and let them slip through his fingers. Another tray had bunches of flowers. He smelt them. "What fragrance!" he remarked. Another salver was heaped with fruits. He picked up a few and gave them to those around him. Another plate had silk garments. He picked them up, held them against himself, to check which of them suited him.

How pleased Pedhu was! His joy was reflected in every movement of his. The men from Senji looked at him contemptuously. This did not escape Raghunatha's notice. "Pedhu, control yourself. Don't go overboard. Let them not think you have never seen such things before," Ragahunatha whispered in Pedhu's ears.

One of the soldiers from Senji came forward, and said, "Jai Bhavani! Long live the Maratha Empire! Long live the royal family of Singavaram! King Rajaram of Senji, who is from Chatrapati Sivaji's lineage, sends his compliments to the Queen of Singavaram. He sends his regards to her parents and to the elders of her family."

Peria Pedhu gave them a huge smile. His eyes sparkled with joy. But Raghunatha exhibited no such emotion. In a voice that gave away nothing, he enquired, "What brings you here?"

Peria Pedhu interjected, "I told you why they are here..."

"Let them state the purpose of their visit," Raghunatha said.

The men from Senji laid the gifts at Raghunatha's feet. The chief of the group of soldiers raised his sword, and said, "The kingdoms of Senji and Singavaram share a common border. Just as they are close geographically, we want a close relationship with the Singavaram royal family. Just as the quality of mercy should be combined with valour, just as fragrance and flowers are inseparable, so too should there be ties between the two kingdoms. Our King Rajaram believes that this will be beneficial to both kingdoms."

"True, true," Raghunatha said. "But how does your King propose to achieve this? Does your King expect our Queen to cede our land to you?"

"No, no," intervened Pedhu. Why was Raghunatha, a cunning man, now talking like one lacking in intelligence? Raghunatha quelled him with a baleful glare. Pedhu subsided into silence.

"Go on, what does your King want?" Raghunatha asked the messengers from Senji.

"Can there be a stronger bond than marriage? Our King hopes that marriage will bring together the people of the two nations. He wants our Prince to marry the Queen of Singavaram I am here to convey his desire to you," said one of the men from Senji.

Pedhu gave Raghunatha a triumphant smile. But Raghunatha showed no sign of enthusiasm. "I see," he said.

The man from Senji said, "We don't usually go to a kingdom seeking the hand of a princess."

"Neither do we usually give away our daughters to every potential suitor who approaches us," replied Raghunatha. "Your King has shown foresight in proposing this marriage. But..."

"What is the need for ifs and buts" asked Pedhu impatiently.

Raghunatha ignored him and continued, "Although it is true that Bharat is one country, still there are cultural differences between us. Your king is from the North. Your language, culture, and practices are different from ours. Although for now it seems to make sense to go ahead with this Tamil-Marathi marriage, who knows what repercussions it will have in future?"

The man from Senji did not relish Raghunatha's reply. "What is your decision in this matter?" he asked.

"I am unable to make up my mind now. Tell your King to be patient for some time. Let us think of the pros and cons of this alliance. If we are convinced that this marriage will have more advantages than disadvantages, then I will myself talk to your King."

"Let us leave," said the Senji messenger to his men angrily.

But Raghunatha was unfazed. "Pedhu, please honour our guests before they leave."

"Honour?" the messenger laughed bitterly. "You have made it quite clear how you honour your guests." But Raghunatha had left.

Pedhu was furious. But he put on a calm façade, and patted the messenger's shoulder gently and said, "Just ignore that old man's words. I am not going to reject your offer as that old man did."

"What can you do? Everyone says his word is law in Singavaram," said the messenger.

"That may be true. But I pay no heed to him." Pedhu summoned a servant and told him to prepare rooms for the messengers to stay in. "Please believe me. I am the father of the Queen, whose hand you have sought in marriage on behalf of your prince. As her father, I have the right to decide about this marriage. Raghunatha has no right to impose his decision on me. Nor does he have the power to do so."

Having housed the messengers in their rooms, Pedhu went out into the garden. "Father," called out Deivanayaki. Why did his usually chirpy daughter look so dull? Why did she look so tire and dejected? Pedhu said to her, "Deivanayaki, is it right that you should be so sad and listless? You are the Queen of this country. Should you not look more radiant?"

"I would be happier if I were on a bed of thorns, father. Why did you agree to Raghunatha's plans? I would never have agreed, if not for Raghunatha's threat that he would kill you."

"Threat to my life?" Pedhu laughed, forgetting for a minute that he had to keep up the playacting.

"Yes, isn't that what Raghunatha said? He said that if I refused to be Queen, he would kill you. That is why I am patient. But I find it increasingly difficult to put up with all this."

"Be patient for a few more days, my child."

"I have a suggestion. Find Kanchipurathan. He is the only one who can put Raghunatha in his place."

"So you have concluded that I am useless?"

"No. But even a courageous warrior does wear an armour, doesn't he? I am simply suggesting that you seek Kanchipurathan's help. I have a suggestion. Send a messenger to Chennai, without Raghunatha's knowledge."

"And?"

"Send word to the Company Governor. Ask him to ensure that that gentleman should be on our side."

"Which gentleman are you taking about?"

"Sivachidamabaram."

"Sivachaidamabaram?" Pedhu turned pale with fear.

"Do you think he won't come? He will, father. Ask him to forgive us for the way we treated him. He is very clever and brave. He will come to help us."

"He is... He is..."

"He is not a coward as you imagine him to be. I used to think he was a coward. But I was wrong. He is capable of doing the most daring things."

"He will come. I have no doubt about that." Hard-hearted Pedhu melted when he thought of his daughter's hopes and of how hurt she would be if she knew the truth. How was he going to tell her that Sivachidambaram was dead? That he had a hand in the killing of Sivachidmabaram? Even as he struggled with his emotions, Raghunatha arrived and said, "I am sorry to interrupt what must have been a private conversation between father and daughter. Go ahead. Let me not stand in the way. I am sure there is a lot that you need to discuss in private."

"Plotting is not something we do," spat out Deivanayaki, angrily.

"The Queen seems to be angry."

"Who cares for this title of Queen? It won't take me a second to throw it away. I am waiting for a suitable opportunity."

Raghunatha laughed. "The daughter's anger matches her father's."

"I am sorry. I am not in the mood for conversation with anyone," muttered Pedhu.

Raghunatha said, "Pedhu! You do not know of the danger inherent in the Senji proposal. You look only at the advantages. But there are many dangers in accepting that proposal."

"For example?"

"The victory of the Senji king against Zulfikar is temporary. Do you know who rules Bharat from

Kashmir to Kanyakumari? Aurangazeb. Do you think we can survive if we incur his displeasure? That fool in Senji has sealed his own fate. Should we also make the same mistake?"

"Oh, so that is the reason for your lukewarm response to that proposal. I thought there was another reason."

"And what might that be?"

"I thought if the two kingdoms were joined by matrimonial ties, your authority would be undermined and, that was the reason for your objections."

Raghunatha was livid. "My friend, sometimes a drama may soon turn into reality. Till now you have only been pretending that your life is under threat, and you have been doing that to convince your daughter. Just make sure that you do not annoy me so much that the threat becomes real. It won't take me a second to imprison both you and your daughter, and not even an ant in the kingdom will know where you are. I do not want to go to such an extent. But do not force my hand."

Pedhu was unperturbed. "Tomorrow, I will send word through the messengers that I accept the proposal of the King of Senji. I haven't sent the messengers away. I have housed them in the rest house."

"Have you, now? Let us go and have a look."

Pedhu followed him to the rest house. The doors were wide open and there was no one there.

THIRTY SEVEN

"Where are the men from Senji?" asked Peria Pedhu angrily.

"They were men with self-respect. So they went back," replied Raghunatha.

"What did you say to them?"

"Me? What did I say? Nothing. I came to know that you had decided to house them here for the night. I came here and sent for the cooks. And in the presence of your guests, I told the cooks what they had to cook for dinner. And then I asked the chief of the messengers from Senji a question."

"And what was that?"

"I told him that in Singavaram, we add a dash of salt to all our dishes. I asked him if they added salt to what they ate in Senji. The man took off with the rest of the messengers."

"Raghunatha!" Peria Pedhu shook Raghunatha by his shoulders. "Do you realise what a foolish thing you have done? A messenger from a King should be treated with the same respect as the King himself. Every kingdom is duty bound to respect the messenger of a King. A kingdom, where messengers are not honoured, is a country that is ruled by the devil!"

Raghunatha gave him a mocking smile.

Peria Pedhu kicked the sand in anger.

Place, Senji palace. The pavilion on top of the hill known as Rajagiri.

Seven of the eight ministers were there. King Rajaram was seated on his throne.

Peshwa Neela Moreshwar, said, "I am not in favour of this alliance. I feel you should not have sent those messengers to Singavaram. We are such a large kingdom. How can our Prince marry the Princess of a small kingdom?"

The Foreign Minister said, "This kingdom owes its origin to the Maratha Empire. We could have found a suitable alliance for the Prince from among Marathas."

"Have you all finished speaking?" asked the King. "Unfortunately our Prime Minister isn't here. He is the one who used to tell me about the good qualities of Thamarai, the Princess of Singavaram."

"Thamarai? So you don't know what has happened in Singavaram!" the Peshwa laughed. "Raghunatha has dethroned her. He's put a commoner from Chennai on the throne. Our spies told me this. I thought you already knew this."

"I didn't know. If I had known, I would never have sent the Prince there," said the King.

"The Prince? Did you send the Prince as a messenger?" all the ministers exclaimed in one voice.

"Yes, I did. He wanted to see that Princess. I told him he wasn't to reveal his identity, but could go as an ordinary messenger."

"It was a very wrong thing to do," the Peshwa said, even as the sound of a horse's hooves were heard.

The Prince had returned and he stormed in.

"I've been insulted!" he shouted. His eyes were red shot. He was covered with dust because of the ride. His shoulders quivered in anger. "A small kingdom, and look at their arrogance!" he said. "Goddess Bhavani is our protector and Chatrapathi Sivaji is our role model. And this small kingdom of Singavaram has dared to mock us. Should we not do something about this?"

He paused and looked at the ministers. Usually the ministers kept their calm. But now they seemed agitated too. What could be the reason?

The Peshwa's words threw light on the situation. "We were just telling your father that he should not have sent you. Please sit down and tell us what happened."

"This is not the time to sit down and relax," said the young Prince, with all the impetuosity and haste of youth. "And old man there asked me if I added salt to my food. I want to cut off his head and pickle it."

It was now the turn of the ministers to be furious. "Did he say that? We were just telling your father that Singavaram is too small a kingdom for us to have anything to do with them. How dare they treat you so!" said Minister Mataji Sudadar.

The Peshwa said, "We have taught Zulfikar a lesson. Now it is time to teach the ruler of Singavaram a lesson."

"What are you suggesting?" asked the King, hesitantly.

"Not a suggestion, Your Majesty. It's a plan. We want action," said the Foreign Minister.

"And I want action now, at once," said the Prince.

"All right. And we need a very small army to quell the forces of Singavaram. But..."

"What is your objection?" the ministers asked.

"Kanchipurathan. My dear friend Kanchipurathan. What if he should head the Singavaram army?"

"Don't worry, Your Majesty. Kanchipurathan was close to Thamarai. Do you think Raghunatha would have spared his life?"

"Has he killed Kanchipurathan?"

"No, he hasn't. But perhaps death would have been preferable to the state he has been reduced to. Kanchipurathan was stripped of all power and no one knows where he is now."

"In that case, it is all right. We must not spare those who have treated our friend so badly. I can forgive an insult to myself, but not an insult to my friend. Proceed to Singavaram. Let our cannons break open the walls of their fort. Raze the palace to the ground. Let future generations see the ruins and tell themselves that this was the place where a traitor lived. Kill that traitor!"

But there was a dissenting voice. The Finance Minister said, "I fully agree that the wicked shouldn't be spared. But what about all the innocent people in the palace? Why should they be killed? I am also told that there is an underground prison near the palace. We might end up destroying that too. There might be good people in that prison…"

"What a kind hearted man you are!" mocked Rajaram. "You are the Finance Minister. Now if you told me how much this adventure will cost us, then I would appreciate you. But why are you moralising?"

"Let us not waste time arguing," interrupted the Peshwa. "Shall I ask the General to make arrangements for our departure?"

"Go ahead," said the King.

♦

Was it a ripe red fruit? Was it a drop of blood? Or had a piece of the red evening sky perhaps broken and dropped to the ground? Inch by inch, red hot iron rods moved towards the four pairs of eyes. The four prisoners stood transfixed with fear. Kanchipurathan held Thamarai's shaking hands and said, "Don't be afraid, Thamarai. We have been through so much."

The rod was now very close to Kanchipurathan's eyes.

"No, don't," screamed Thamarai and Chennamma.

Chennamma and Thamarai turned away, unable to witness what was about to happen. But just in the nick of time, the horror was averted, when a woman called out to the guard with the heated rods in his hands.

"Hello, my dear husband. I've brought your lunch," she said.

"Go away... Is this the time for me to be eating?" the man asked his wife angrily.

"Now what's more important than eating at the right time, my darling?" she asked, and came down the steps.

When she saw what was about to happen, she snatched the rods from her husband's hands, and threw them away. She then knelt before Thamarai and said, "Forgive me."

The prison guard lifted her up, and said, "Do you want me to get killed? I was about to do my duty. Do I need your permission to do my duty?"

"You call this your duty? This is nothing but treachery and treason. How could you keep the Queen tied up and in a prison?"

"Shut up! She is no longer the Queen. She has lost the throne. Deivanayaki is our Queen now. Raghunatha told me that. And he was the one who gave the order."

"What order?"

"To put out the eyes of these prisoners."

"The Queen would never want this to happen. She has been crying not knowing what has happened to these people. Her servant told me so."

"All right. I compliment you for giving me such stories. But I deserve a pat on my back for being dutiful," the guard said, and picked up the rods.

His wife stood before Kanchipurathan with her arms spread out before her. "No, I am not lying, or telling you a story. I swear I am speaking the truth. If you have any doubts, ask the new Queen."

"All right. Come. We will go and ask her."

"Just wait for a day," his wife said. "The Queen is doing some special puja today. So she is observing a vow of silence. She has given orders that she is not to be disturbed today."

"Is this another of your stories?"

"Just wait for a day. And you will know the truth!" she pleaded.

"Have it your way," he said, took off his turban, and went to have his lunch.

"I speak the truth. Deivanayaki wants to see you all. Tomorrow you will be out of this prison," the woman said to the prisoners.

♦

Early the next morning. A worn out Thamarai was lying on the floor.

The prison guard walked in, followed by his wife.

"Are you happy now? I should never have allowed you to interfere in my duties," he said to her angrily.

He stuck the iron rods in the fire and began to heat them.

The woman came to the prisoners and said, "That rogue Raghunatha kept us from meeting Deivanayaki."

"How dare you take the name of the Queen so disrespectfully? Refer to her as Queen Deivanayaki," the guard chided her.

"Raghunatha refused to allow us to meet Deivanayaki. 'Have you not carried out my order? Go to the prison now and heat those rods. I will myself supervise the punishment being carried out,' Ragunatha said. We headed straight for the prison."

Kanchipurathan firmly gripped Thamarais' hands. "Never mind. You did your best," he said to the woman.

Suddenly a voice was heard from outside the prison, "Danger! Danger to the country! All of you, come out now."

Everyone, including the prison guard, ran out.

"Thamarai. Quick. That woman gave me the keys to the locks on the chains. Hold this key in your teeth and first unlock my chains. I will untie all of you," said Kanchipurathan.

Thamarai, who had been lying on the floor listlessly, grabbed the key with her teeth and began to open the lock on Kanchipurathan's chains.

"Quick. Hurry. They'll be back soon," Kanchipurathan urged Thamarai.

The few seconds seemed like ages.

Click! The lock was open. Kanchipurathan was free. He undid the chains that tied his sweetheart, and then freed Chennamma and Krishnappa. "That woman gave me the keys. That's all she could do. The rest was up to me. Luckily I hit upon the idea of shouting out that there was danger to the country," Kanchipurathan said.

"But that shout did not come from you. It came from outside," said Chennamma.

"No, it didn't. It came from me," said Kanchipurathan. And then it dawned on them that it was his skill in ventriloquism that had saved their lives. "Come on. Let's go out," said Kanchipurathan, and led the way out of the prison.

But the melee outside made him wonder if his ventriloquism alone had done the trick. Surely that couldn't have caused so much commotion outside the palace and in the streets of Singavaram. People were running helter skelter.

Kanchipurathan stopped a soldier and asked him what was happening.

"Don't you know? Rajaram, the King of Senji has laid siege to our fort!" the soldier replied.

THIRTY EIGHT

"I warned you. But you did not pay heed to me," said Peria Pedhu.

"What was it that I did not heed?" asked Raghunatha.

"I told you not to insult messengers from a King."

"Can't you see that the King of Senji is spoiling for a fight? He would have waged war against us anyway, even if we had treated his son with respect. There is just one thing I want you to do."

"And what is that?"

"Please do not interfere in governance." Raghunatha's face reflected his anger. "Whenever the country faces a crisis, the best brains in the country will come together to tackle the crisis. You don't have to worry."

Pedhu's face turned red with anger. "I thought I had some privileges too, as the father of the Queen," he said.

Raghunatha gnashed his teeth.

They could hear the sound of cannons going off in the distance. A ball of smoke rose, and they could guess that some house had been hit and was burning. On the streets, they could hear the cries of the people.

Raghunatha clapped his hands to summon a guard. "Where is the chief of the equestrian force? Where is the chief of the elephant forces?"

"One of them is in a drunken stupor. The other is sleeping in the arms of his paramour. I saw the officer in charge of the treasury this morning. He was on his way to some place and seemed to be in a hurry. The chief of the foot soldiers has been missing for many days," the guard replied.

Raghunatha hit the palm of his left hand with his right fist. "Traitors! Traitors! Ingrates! They have enjoyed privileges granted by the royal family for so many years, and this is how they show their gratitude!" he growled.

"Correction, master. They haven't enjoyed privileges granted by the royal family for many years. They are recent appointees. You appointed them only recently. They are from Chennai. The old generals are all in prison. If you order, they can..."

"Oh, so you want me to release them from prison, do you? Go away from here, you dog!" Raghunatha lifted his hand to strike the man. The guard made a hasty exit.

Raghunatha looked out through the window. He could see balls of fire in many places, which must all have been hit by cannon fire. His eyebrows merged in a frown. He looked round stealthily. And slowly made his way to the stables.

The horses were disturbed by the sound of the cannons and the screams of the people. But his horse Nityakalyani neighed almost as if it were welcoming its master.

Raghunatha patted it gently. He then peeped out. He gave a contemptuous smile. Even the guard of the stables was missing! He had run away and was probably hiding somewhere.

Raghunatha saddled Nityakalyani. He pushed aside sacks of hay and horse-gram, piled up at the other end of the stable. A door that had been hidden by the sacks could now be seen. He picked out a key, unlocked the door, and opened it. There was a passage that could just about accommodate a horse. He looked out just once, before entering the passage. "There are a few loyal generals. They should be able to hold on, until I return," he said to himself, and led his horse down the passage.

♦

What would a defanged snake look like? What would a crocodile with its nails cut off look like? That was what Zulfikar Khan looked like.

Aurangazeb's general was now camping near Vepery. He still sported a beard. But he had lost his arrogance. His eyes were still red. But gone was his cockiness. His sword was in its sheath. It hadn't been unsheathed for many days.

He hadn't got over his defeat in Senji. He had only one answer to the Emperor's questions. "Your son Kam Baksh is responsible for what happened. He joined hands with the enemy. He betrayed our army."

Aurangazeb was not a merciful king. "He is not to be spared simply because he is my son. Arrest him," the order came from the king.

Kam Baksh had been arrested.

"Now there are no more hurdles to your campaign. Get me Karnataka!" the Emperor ordered.

Zulfikar was fretting and fuming.

"The Emperor has no idea of the pressure I am under because of the Company. My men have become highway robbers," he said to himself, as he paced up and down inside his tent. He was interrupted by the entry of a soldier.

"Raghunatha from Singavaram is here," he announced.

"Singavaram? That is the country that borders Senji, isn't it? Bring him in."

"I bring good news," said Raghunatha and embraced Zulfikar. He was disappointed to see Zulfikar looking worn out and dejected. But his face didn't show his disappointment.

"Good news? If there should be good news, I am not even sure I can identify good news. Anyway, go ahead, and tell me what tidings you bring."

"The King of Senji is busy attacking Singavaram. Now is the time for you to capture Senji. Come on, bring your horses and your army," said Raghunatha.

But Zulfikar did not respond enthusiastically. "Horses? Army?" he spat out angrily. "Raghunatha, I don't care what happens to the King of Senji. Do you know what I want to hear now?"

"What is it?"

"I want to hear the clinking of gold coins. My men have gone away. I need gold. I need money to get them to obey my orders. Do you have gold coins?"

"That is not a problem for me. I knew such a situation might arise. Send for your men. Tell them to saddle their horses and be ready to ride to Senji. All I have to do is to go to Chennaipattanam. When I return, I will bring you the gold you need."

"Glad to hear that, Raghunatha," said Zulfikar, but his tone of voice betrayed a compete lack of belief in Raghunatha's words of assurance.

Raghunatha sped away on his horse, and the dust from the horse's hoofs settled on Zulfikar's face. He wiped his face, spat on the ground and said, "If only this man is able to do what he claims he can…"

♦

Peria Pedhu's men bowed before Raghunatha. They knew he had been an honoured guest of Peria Pedhu. Raghunatha made his way to Pedhu's guest house. That was the place Raghunatha had stayed in during his previous visit. He walked towards the abandoned well. He looked for the rocks that had been marked. When he tried to move them, he noticed the shadow of someone behind him. He turned. "You?!"

"Why, what's surprising about that? This is my house, isn't it?" asked Pedhu. A mocking smile played about his lips.

"Have you left the Queen alone there?"

"Queen? In times of peace she was the daughter of an ordinary merchant in Chennai. But when war breaks out, you make her the Queen."

"Stop making light of a serious situation. If we abandon the people of Singavaram in this moment of crisis, they will never accept her as their Queen!"

"I have got to grant it to you. You are a glib talker whenever you are caught on the wrong foot. But you don't have to worry. My daughter is cleverer than either of us. She is braver too, I would say. She consulted some of the army chiefs about how to fight the enemy and she is safe in the palace."

"And so you followed me, I suppose."

"Even a shadow could not have followed so closely."

"Reason?"

"I was curious. You said some great brains were going to come together to find a way out of the crisis. I wanted to be witness to this coming together of brains. You first looked for those great brains in the palace. Then you looked for them in the horse stable in Singavaram. Then you searched for those brains in Zulfikar's camp. And then you have come here to search for them. I just wanted to know if you would be successful at least in my house."

Raghunatha laughed. "You are a merchant, but you do not know the value of the yellow metal. Look!"

Raghunatha moved aside the rocks. Hidden were many wooden jars. Raghunatha removed the cloth covering the mouth of a jar.

"I will pull out some coins for you now."

He stuck his hand inside the jar, and looked up, a shocked expression on is face. The jar was empty. He opened more of them, and every one of them was empty.

Raghunatha turned pale with fear. The snakes he had let loose there to guard the coins lay dead. They had all been killed.

"Big brains—did you find them here?" mocked Pedhu, but stopped when he saw the expression on Raghunatha's face.

"Gold coins! Thousands of them! Coins of the Company! They are the only legal tender here. I had hoarded so many!"

"You've lost them. Now can you hire soldiers without money? There is only one place where you can get help."

He pointed to the fort. "You mean from the Company?" asked Raghunatha.

"Why not? What have you to fear?"

The two of them set off for Fort St. George.

But disappointment and shock awaited them at the fort.

It wasn't easy to meet the Governor—Elihu Yale. "Directors of the Company have come from England. They are having a banquet tonight," they were told.

The Governor, who stepped in for a few minutes, said to the two waiting men, "Oh, it's you—Raghunatha and Pedhu!"

Why did he sound so contemptuous?

"Raghunatha, tell me what happened to the gold coins which you had hidden in Pedhu's mansion? You had put counterfeit coins in circulation, and had saved the Company's coins, hadn't you? Now tell me, what happened to those coins? Don't tell me they were eaten by termites. Or were they perhaps washed away in a flood?" the Governor asked.

Raghunatha did not reply. Pedhu was shocked. He was loyal to the Company and he was furious that Raghunatha had dared to cheat the Company, and had tried his tricks in Pedhu's own backyard.

"I didn't believe Kanchipurathan at first. But later we searched for and found the coins. We checked them and found they were genuine. I couldn't inform the two of you, because you were not in town. I hope you were not disappointed when you found the jars were empty," continued Yale.

"Let us forget the past. If only you could help us against the King of Senji..." said Pedhu.

"And what if we did help? Anyway, I'm sorry Pedhu. Only someone who is unaware of the policy of the Company will put such a request before me. Did you not know that we will not openly fight either the Mughal Emperor or the Maratha King?"

"You needn't fight them openly. But..."

"Well, we could work clandestinely. But that depends on what there is in it for the Company. Come with me."

Yale led the two men out of the room. He pointed to a map. "Do you see this fort? That is the Kunimedu fort. We built it on land that the King of Senji gave us."

"We too will give you land for a fort," Raghunatha and Pedhu said.

No sooner had the two men made their promise to Yale, than a horse sped away towards Singavaram. So what if Sivachidambaram was no longer there? There were still many patriotic people, who had been trained by him. One of them was now on his way to Singavaram, to inform the people about Raghunatha's treachery.

THIRTY NINE

Freedom! The shackles were gone! But there were more obstacles in their way.

Four people rushed out of the prison. There was chaos in the streets. The sound of explosions all over the city.

When they entered the palace, the servants fell at the feet of Krishnappa and Thamarai, and cried, "Save us, please."

"They fled when the enemy attacked, instead of staying on to defend the kingdom. The scoundrels! May they rot in hell!" wailed an old woman.

"What! Has my father run away?" Chennamma asked.

"Yes, along with that man from Chennai."

"What are you waiting for? You must take charge, since the experienced generals are no longer in charge. We have to defeat the enemy..." said Chennamma to Krishnappa.

She turned around and asked Thamarai, "Thamarai, where is he? Where is Kanchipurathan?"

Thamarai had just noticed the absence of Kanchipurathan. "Amma, don't worry. He trusts his sword. He doesn't indulge in boastful talk. He is a man of action. Even while we are having this conversation here, I am sure he is out there in the battlefield, fighting off the attack," said Thamarai.

"And I am just as good a warrior as Kanchipurathan. Don't underestimate me, my child. My sword loves to taste enemy blood," said Krishnappa.

Three horses, galloping like the wind, screeched to a halt outside the palace. The soldiers came in panting. "Danger! We can't keep the enemy away for much longer. The northern gate has fallen. The enemy forces will breach the other gates any time now."

"Don't be afraid. I'll join our forces soon," said Krishnappa. "Which gate is Kanchipurathan defending?"

"Kanchipurathan? You mean the former General? We haven't seen him anywhere," said the soldiers.

"Who knows where he is, in what disguise? Even God will not be able to anticipate his plans. He must be somewhere out there, fighting for us," said Chennamma.

◆

Krishnappa stood on the ramparts of the fort, and looked down. What he saw there made him shudder. Singavaram had never expected an attack from Senji. That was why they had never strengthened the northern gate. The moat there was shallow and narrow. The Senji king had capitalised on this weakness. They had used huge logs to bridge the moat. Every time a log was thrown across the moat, the crocodiles rushed to the place, jaws open, expecting to find someone who had fallen in. Occasionally, one careless step, and a soldier would go crashing into the water. His screams as the crocodiles fastened their powerful jaws over him, made one's blood freeze.

Arrows went flying from the Singavaram forces towards the invading army. A Senji soldier was loading a cannon with ammunition.

Krishnappa summed up the situation in just a second—the cannon was the most dangerous enemy that Singavaram faced. He summoned a few soldiers, and told them all to throw spears at the man who was loading the cannon, and the man who was waiting to light it. Both fell to the combined assault. Immediately, many soldiers surrounded the cannon, and quickly piled up boulders around it, thereby protecting it from attack.

"Great. It is clear that they depend mainly on that cannon to do the damage. That is the most important weapon in their arsenal. Destroy it," Krishnappa said to his men.

In his enthusiasm, Krishnappa stood up, exposing himself, and a spear thrown by a Senji soldier pierced his right arm, and exited through the other side.

Krishnappa let out a scream. He tore a piece of his dhoti, and tied up the wound tightly, and got up to give directions to his men.

"We will manage. Please go to the palace, and get the wound treated," said one of the generals.

At first Krishnappa refused to budge. But his men could not staunch the blood flow, and reluctantly, he agreed to leave.

Thamarai was waiting for news about the battle.

"Did you see Kanchipurathan?" she asked anxiously.

"No," said Krishnappa.

"He never pays heed to anyone. What is he up to now," she said.

The Deputy General who had brought Krishnappa to the palace, said, "You must forgive me, Your Majesty. Our former General—Kanchipurathan—never came to the battlefield."

Thamarai laughed. "To him a battlefield is as dear as a mother's lap is to her child. Just because you didn't notice him there, doesn't mean he wasn't out there fighting."

"We checked all the gates, Your Majesty. He wasn't in any of the four places where fighting is going on."

"Is that true?" Krishnappa moaned in pain. "He is not a coward. He probably has some plan to defeat the enemy..."

The Deputy General gave a mocking smile. "We should never have trusted his plans."

A soldier barged in in, with a message for Thamarai. "Your Majesty. Our former general Kanchipurathan is in the house of the palace nagaswaravidwan. I told him about the danger Singavaram faced. But he refused to leave."

"Stop blabbering. Speak clearly. Where did you see him and when?" Chennamma asked the soldier sternly.

"We face a shortage of men to fight. So, the chief of my division said that every family had to send one man to fight the enemy. I saw Kanchipurathan seated on the pyol outside the nagaswaravidwan's house. I was surprised to find him there. I explained the crisis to him. But he just walked in quietly."

"All right. You go back to your division," said Krishnappa. "What is wrong with Kanchipurathan? Has he lost his mind?"

"I will go and check what has happened," said Thamarai.

"Your Majesty. Why should you go to fetch him? One doesn't use a stout stick to kill a small chick. Give me an order, and I will bring him here," the Deputy General offered.

"Thamarai. It is dangerous for you to leave the palace now," warned Chennamma.

"I am prepared to take the risk. Take me to the nagaswaravidwan's house," she ordered the Deputy General.

♦

The whole village was wailing and mourning its dead. But from inside the house came the strains of Mohana raga.

The Deputy General hammered on the door. A huge crowd had gathered outside the house. The Queen was here, standing before the house of an ordinary citizen of the country. Why? That was the question they asked themselves.

Kanchipurathan came out with a nagaswaram in his hands. He was surprised to see Thamarai there. He smiled at her, and said, "Come in, Your Majesty."

"Come out. I didn't believe the man who told me you were here. I never expected that your levity would go so far."

"Levity? What do you mean?"

"This- this act of playing a musical instrument, when people are out there dying for the country. Pick up your sword and come and fight. Don't forget your duty to the people," Thamarai said angrily.

"Duty? What duty are you talking about? I was prepared to die to save them from the rule of a tyrant. But what did they do?"

The people hung their heads in shame.

"Let me remind you. We were careless and a usurper occupied the throne. Enraged, I appealed to the people. I asked them if it was fair. But my voice was like a lone voice in the wilderness. It was like the voice of an orphan. I was ignored. The people sold their dignity for a piece of cloth and some money. They thought that food was more important than their self-respect. Why does independence seem so important to them now? Why don't they turn for help to the men who gave them bribes? Let those men help the people now. Tell them to wait patiently for help from those who gave them bribes."

Thamarai was speechless. Kanchipurathan had always rushed to the help of people. How hurt he must have been to speak so dejectedly!

She didn't know how to pacify him.

"Forgive us, general."

"You are like an elder brother to me... Won't you forgive me?"

"Let bygones be bygones. Forgive us."

The people fell at Kanchipurathan's feet, seeking forgiveness.

There were tears in Kanchipurathan's eyes.

"Are you happy now?" asked Thamarai.

"No, no. Please stop. You mustn't fall at my feet. I was hurt and I spoke rather harshly. Forgive me. I am your servant. You, the people, must command me, not beg me for help. Order that I should fight, and I will fight gladly," said Kanchipurathan.

"Long live Kanchipurathan!"

"Long live the general!" The cries of the people rent the air.

♦

"Open the doors," thundered Kanchipurathan.

The men guarding the gates of the fort were taken aback. "Our enemies have already managed to cross a moat. They have not been able to break down the gates. The gates are the only things standing in their way. How can we open them?

"Do as I say. Open the gates," ordered Kanchipurathan.

Kanchipurathan mounted an elephant.

"General. You haven't taken your spear and sword," the soldiers pointed out.

"Only a man who is going to confront an enemy needs weapons. But I am now going to meet... Wait and watch," Kanchipurathan laughed.

The gate fell to the Senji forces, and they charged into the fort.

A spear missed Kanchipurathan by an inch.

"Come on, my friends. Kill me. Why do you hesitate?" Kanchipurathan said to them.

"No, no. We are not here to kill you."

A general of the Senji army stepped forward. "We are here not only because we were insulted. We are here because we heard that you were in danger. We are here to save you, our dear friend," he said.

"Thank you, my friend. Please tell your king that the traitors are no longer in charge in Singavaram. The people of Singavaram have risen against the traitors. We no longer need help from Senji. We need your good wishes."

Again the crowd shouted enthusiastically, "Long live the General of Singavaram!"

"Long live the friendship between Senji and Singavaram!"

The Senji forces gradually withdrew from Singavaram. Bloodshed had been avoided. The ground was not red with blood. As the sun went down, only the sky was red.

"Traitor! Traitor!" Loud cries of anger could be heard.

"Who is it?" Kanchipurathan asked.

Two horses could be seen on the road from Chennai.

The Singavaram soldiers surrounded the horses.

"You idiots! You made that woman from Chennai our Queen. Do you know what her father has done? Right now he is trying to sell your country to the Company. The Company has promised him their forces. He has promised to give them land in Singavaram to build a fort."

"Traitor!"

"Quiet, please," Kanchipurathan pacified the crowd. "Why should we care what the cowards who have run away are up to?"

One of the men from Chennai said, "Run away? Who has run away? Peria Pedhu and Raghunatha are in Chennai. But that woman—Peria Pedhu's daughter Deivanayaki is still here, in the Singavaram palace."

"Our palace?" shouted the crowd. "Let's find her and kill her."

They rushed towards the palace. "Come out, Deivanayaki! Where are you hiding?" they shouted and tried to enter.

"Stop right there," said Thamarai.

FORTY

The people pushed ahead. "Don't let the traitor escape. She's inside the palace," the crowd shouted. But Thamarai blocked their way.

"Step aside, Your Majesty…"

"I want you all to go away. I am responsible for every person who is inside the palace. It is my duty to protect them."

"But the woman you are shielding is a traitor."

"When I said I have to protect everyone inside the palace, I meant her too."

"We are patriots, and we have a duty…"

"I am your Queen, and my duty is important to me. I am not beseeching you. I am ordering you—go away. If you take just one step forward, I will no longer be your Queen. I will step down. I am serious. I mean what I say."

The people were taken aback by her sternness.

"Here comes the General. Let's ask him what to do," they said.

Kanchipurathan dismounted from the horse, and said to the people, "Your anger is understandable. But sensible people will pay heed to their Queen. However, I can promise you one thing."

"And that is…?"

"That woman from Chennai will no longer be in this palace. Before dawn tomorrow, she will be on her way to Chennai, where she belongs."

The people were not pleased with Kanchipurathan's words. They had come expecting some action. They were not inclined to listen to lectures on ethics. But there was a certain firmness in Kanchipurathan's voice, which held them back. They dispersed.

"In which secret chamber is Deivanayaki?" Thamarai asked Chennamma.

Krishnappa laughed. "In all the years that I was King, I didn't learn how to administer the country. But I did learn all about secret passages and chambers. Come on General. Let's look for Deivanayaki."

They didn't have to search for long. Deivnayaki was waiting in the secret passage right below the throne. She knew nothing of the latest developments.

"Have the enemies been defeated? Have they run away?" she asked Kanchipurathan.

"They were defeated, and they have run away, but they are not the enemies you have in mind," said Kanchipurathan. "Singavaram is rid of two curses. One is Raghunatha and the other is your father."

Joy and sorrow—Deivanayaki experienced mixed emotions. "I told my father that only one who had a right to be on the throne should rule Singavaram. But he didn't listen to me. What is to happen to me, now? Those who try to usurp the throne will be beheaded. I am ready to take my punishment. Take me, General, to the place where traitors are executed." Peria Pedhu's daughter smiled, and extended her hands, expecting to be handcuffed.

"Your honesty has won you forgiveness. Come on. Let's go," said Kanchipurathan.

"Go? Where?"

"To Chennai. To your father. The Queen has ordered that I should escort you up to the border of Singavaram. Some soldiers from Singavaram will come with you all the way to Chennai."

"Thank you," said Deivanayaki. She didn't speak to anyone. She embraced Thamarai. She fell at Chennamma's feet respectfully. When she took leave of them, there were tears in everyone's eyes.

Singavaram was like a country that had been ravaged by a storm. It was less noisy now. But it still bore the scars of fighting. Houses were still burning; soldiers were going to have their wounds dressed; women were sobbing.

Deivanayaki looked round in silence.

"Do you know that the people were furious with you? It was the Queen who saved you." Kanchipurathan told her what had happened.

They were getting close to the moat. That was as far as Kanchipurathan was to escort her.

"I am ashamed of my father," said Devianayaki.

"And yet, you have to go back to him."

Deivanayaki was silent for a few minutes, and then said, "General, can you do me a favour? I don't want to go back to my father's house. It has become a meeting place for treacherous men. Can you arrange for me stay elsewhere? And later…"

"And later?"

"Go to the Company's fort, and by some means…"

"By some means?" Kanchipurathan could guess what she was about to say, and that made him uneasy.

"Rescue Sivachidambaram, and bring him to me. If I can have him beside me, I am prepared to live in a hut or even out in the open, with a simple meal of gruel. All I want is to live with dignity and self-respect."

Kanchipurathan usually never showed his emotions, but now his eyes turned misty.

"Don't you know what your father did?"

"What did he do?"

"Sivachidambaram has been dead for a long time."

Deivanayaki let out a scream and collapsed in a heap.

◆

All arrangements had been made in Fort St. George. Peria Pedhu was pleased. A mocking smile played around Raghunatha's lips. The officials of the Company indulged in daydreams.

Cunning was in the blood of the men of the Company. They didn't have the courage to take on the King of Senji openly. They had been making secret plans. Raghunatha and Peria Pedhu would leave either today or tomorrow…

"There is a messenger from Singavaram. He has brought something along," a guard informed Governor Yale.

"Excellent! The King of Senji must have been defeated, even without our help," said Raghunath gleefully.

"The guard said they have brought something. What could that be?" asked Peria Pedhu.

Four men brought a chest in and put it down before Peria Pedhu. One of them handed over a palmleaf manuscript to Yale.

PeriaPedhu felt uneasy. And when the chest was opened…

"Deivanayaki! My darling child!" Pedhu screamed.

Inside the chest was Deivanayaki's body, cut up into many pieces. "Tell me, who is responsible for my daughter's death. I will kill him," Pedhu said to theguards.

"Be happy you have her body, even if it is in pieces. And if you must punish those who are responsible for her death, then you should be the first to be punished," said a guard.

Raghunatha had turned pale with fear. He could see that his plans had gone horribly wrong. But he tried to put on a brave front and said, "Tell us what happened. I want all the details."

"We tried our best to bring her to you safely. She didn't seem to know about Sivachidambaram's death or Pedhu's role in his death. When she heard about Sivachidambaram's fate, she said, 'Is my father such a wicked man?' And then she jumped into the moat of crocodiles. Our general Kanchipurathan…"

"Kanchipurathan? Has he surfaced again?" asked Raghunatha.

"He jumped into the moat and tried to save Deivanayaki. All he found were these pieces. He told us to bring these pieces to you."

Pedhu was holding the chest and sobbing.

"We should see that these men are punished," said Raghunatha angrily. He said to Yale, "We have to leave at once. We have to teach those arrogant people a lesson."

But Yale didn't seem perturbed by the turn of events. "The Maratha king of Senji has sent this palm leaf manuscript. He says that we are trying to foment trouble in his kingdom. He says we should not try to drive a wedge between Singavaram and Senji. He says that if we interfere in their affairs, then Mangamma, the Sethupathi of Ramanathapuram, Ekoji of Tanjore, and Mysore Chikkadevaraya will all join hands with the King of Senji and they will all turn against us," Yale said to Raghunatha.

"Oh, so now Rajaram dares to threaten us. We must teach him a lesson," said Raghunatha.

"No, no. I think it is best that you sort out your difficulties," Yale said. Some of the Company's directors and officials were there and they concurred with Yale.

Raghunatha was seething. He could see that the men of the Company were not willing to take risks.

"History will say you are a coward," Raghunatha said.

"Better to be known as a coward, than to have the Company and its interests destroyed," said Yale.

Raghunatha could hardly control his fury.

♦

She lifted her eyes slowly. Her coral red lips twitched with desire. The veins in her neck stood out.

He stared hard at her. He ached to crush her in an embrace. He wanted to lift her chin, to run his hands down her silky tresses, to gently pinch her soft cheeks. He controlled himself with great difficulty. It was far easier to bridge the moat than to bridge the chasm between them.

"Your Majesty, I have done my duties. It is time for me to depart," he said.

"You might have fulfilled your duties. But that does not mean you have fulfilled my desires," she said with a smile.

"And Queen, your desire…"

"You know what it is…"

"What is it?"

"I wish you wouldn't address me so formally. Can't you call me Thamarai, as you once used to?"

"But you...I...I mean..."

"I told you there is something you have forgotten," said Thamarai, blushing.

"That's what we wanted to talk to Kanchipurathan about," said Krishnappa, as he entered the room with Chennamma.

Thamarai moved away from Kanchipurathan.

"What did you want to discuss with me?"

"You have to be the principal advisor to the Queen. My father-in-law, no, no, her father," he pointed to Chennamma.

"Don't defame me," said Chennamma angrily.

Krishnappa laughed. "All right. Let's just say Raghunatha, shall we? He used to be the principal advisor to the king. That position is now vacant. We want you to..."

"Me? How can I be the advisor, when there are more experienced people like you?" asked Kanchipurathan.

"I'm going to be in Singavaram. You can always turn to me for advice," said Krishnappa.

"My best wishes to you," said Thamarai to Kanchipurathan.

"My blessings to you," said Chennamma.

"Looks like you have all conspired against me," said Kanchipurathan.

"Yes, yes. It is a conspiracy by the whole country," laughed Krishnappa. "Look at the flag there flying proudly on its mast. Can't you hear musical instruments being played?"

Kanchipurathan looked at the faces of the three people before him. He knew they had great regard for him. He walked towards the palace slowly.

Suddenly the sound of musical instruments sounded nearer. He realised that he had come to the place where the regiments of the army were going to be on parade. As he stood behind an almond tree—

"I was told that one man wouldn't be here. I want to know if he will be late, or is he staying away?" one of the Deputy Generals thundered.

"He is heartbroken. He says his mother is on the verge of death."

"How does that matter to us? We are here to honour the gentleman who is going to assume office tomorrow as principal advisor to the Queen. Every soldier must be here. Do you know where he lives?"

"Yes. He lives in the oil merchants' street. His house is to the West of the Ganapathy temple."

"Bring that ass here."

Two soldiers jumped on to their horses. But Kanchipurathan was already on the way to that house!

FORTY ONE

The soldier was wailing. His mother's life was ebbing away. She was stroking his hands affectionately.

"I have to go, mother," he said, his voice choked with emotion. "I cannot disobey a royal order. I have to go to pay my respects to the newly appointed principal advisor to the Queen."

His mother's last words were accompanied by tears. "Can you not tell them your mother is about to leave this world?" she asked.

"It will be of no use, mother. There is no one there to lend me support."

"I am there for you."

The startled solider turned round to find the principal advisor to the Queen. He welcomed Kanchipurathanin.

"You have done the right thing. You are paying respects to the one who deserves it. Queens, Generals, not even God—is as important as your mother. You don't have to come for the parade. Stay here, beside your mother," said Kanchipurathan.

But the door was now pushed open by a group of soldiers, who grabbed the soldier's hand and said, "How dare you disobey an order? We've been asked to bring you to the palace, even if we have to use force," they said. It was almost twilight and they hadn't noticed Kanchipurathan standing in a corner of the room.

"My son!" shouted the old lady, and tried to get up. The effort proved too much for her, and she dropped down dead.

"Mother!" shouted the soldier, fell upon her body and broke down.

"Are you satisfied now?" Kanchipurathan asked the soldiers.

They moved aside as if they had stepped on fire. They did not know what to say. They didn't have the courage to leave either.

"Will you let this man perform the last rites for his mother? Or will you say that paying respects to Kanchipurathan is more important than performing the funeral rites for his mother?" There was no anger in Kanchipurathan's voice, but there was bitterness and sorrow.

"I just heard that you had come here," said Krishnappa, as he entered the house. "You are the advisor to the Queen. Think of your status. Is it proper that you should visit the houses of commoners? Come on. Let's go back to the palace." Krishnappa held Kanchipurathan's hand.

Kanchipurathan slowly disengaged his hand. He didn't utter a word. He picked up a palm leaf and a stylus and began to write.

To the Honourabe Queen, Kanchipurathan's respects. I do not have the courage to face you, and hence this letter.

When I left Kanchipuram, the town to which I belong, I had only one desire. I wanted to see the world of the poor. I wanted to rub shoulders with the poor. Whenever I happened to help them, it was not something I did consciously. It just happened. My strength and enthusiasm come from the common man.

When you suddenly entered my life, you were like one of the poor people I had come to love. I felt I had met my soul mate.

Later I came to know that you were a Queen. I fought those who were out to deprive you of your rights. But that was not a fight I waged on your behalf. It was a fight against injustice. I never aspired for a position in the palace.

Respected Queen! The journey that I undertook when I left home, has taken many unexpected twists and turns. I am now in a position that I never dreamt I would be in. People use my name to strike terror in the hearts of the people. I have been witness to one such instance. I don't blame anyone. It is something that goes with power. There may be people who are willing to accept this as something inevitable, if one holds power. But Kanchipurathan is not cast in that mould. How many injustices will be committed in my name, if I were to be your advisor? Even if I do come to know of them, I will have to put up with them. I shudder to think of this.

Honourable Queen, please forgive me. You should be free of worries. At the same time, I do not wish to be shackled. I wish to go my way.

Wherever I go, whatever I do, the Queen of Singavaram will be enthroned in my heart. If you ever think of this ruffian called Kanchipurathan even for a few seconds, I would consider it my good fortune.

Kanchipurathan.

He fell at Krishnappa's feet, handed over the palm leaf to him, and left.

The evening breeze caressed him. He walked on, savouring his independence.

♦

The water of the Kapaleeswara temple tank glowed like a gem in the early morning sun.

A woman washed her hands and feet in the water. Her silk saree and jewels suggested that she was wealthy. But there was a look of sorrow on her face. She looked up at the temple tower and sighed.

She opened a pot of curd rice. "Goddess Karpagavalli!" she whispered, with closed eyes. When she was about to put a ball of rice into her mouth, she heard someone say, "Can I have some curd rice?"

Startled, she turned! Could it really be…? Was it his voice?

"My son! Is it you? How could you leave us and run away? Your father and I have been distraught."

"Mother, I am hungry and want some rice. Instead of giving me some of that rice, you are lambasting me."

"My dear child! Of course, you can have the curd rice. You were the one who left saying you didn't want rich food, or even a cot to sleep on. You have lost weight, my dear child!" The lady rolled balls of rice and ladled them on to Kanchipurathan's outstretched palm.

"Mother, haven't you added enough salt in the rice? Why are you adding more through your tears? I just saw two drops drop into the rice," Kanchipurathan said.

She wiped her eyes. "Now tell me, you must have been to many places. What have you brought me?"

"I... haven't... I," stammered Kanchipurathan.

"Why do you hesitate? Why don't you tell her you've brought her a daughter-in-law?" said a sweet voice from behind Kanchipurathan.

"Mother, will you not give me some rice too?" Thamarai sat down and stretched out her hand for some rice.

"Thamarai! Sorry. Queen" stuttered Kanchipurathan.

"No, no. Not a Queen. A slave. Your slave," she smiled. "The moment my uncle gave me your letter, I left the palace and followed you."

"Thamarai... The kingdom..."

"Where was Sita's kingdom? I too think like Sita. My uncle and aunt are used to the trappings of power. Since you were keen to make me the Queen, I didn't want to stop you. But whatever you like, that's what

I like too. Wherever you want to live, that is heaven to me."

Kanchipurathan's mother cleared her throat. "My son, have you forgotten that I am here?"

"Forgive me, mother. If I were to tell you about this naughty girl, it will take hours. Have you come in a bullock cart?

"Yes. Look- there is our cart, son."

"We'll leave this evening, mother. You rest now in that choultry." Holding hands, the lovers walked jauntily.

♦

The entwined fingers exchanged many messages of love. Unmindful of the stares of passers-by, the couple walked on.

"Thamarai, what a huge sacrifice you have made! Am I deserving of such a sacrifice?"

"I wish I could have given up much more than just Singavaram for your sake."

"Thamarai, shall we go along that road?"

"Why? What's there to see?"

"The place where you and I first met."

Thamarai shuddered at the recollection. "Please do not remind of that place. It is the abode of death."

"You may not want to go to the abode of death. But what if Yama, the god of death comes to take you to his world?" said a voice behind him.

"Who is that?" Kanchipurathan turned round, to find Raghunatha standing there, sword in hand.

FORTY TWO

Kanchipurathan ducked. Else Raghunatha's sword would have run through his chest. He spun round, grabbed Raghunatha's arm, and twisted it.

"I am surprised," laughed Kanchipurathan. "I've never seen you attack anyone after announcing your presence. That isn't your style. You always attack silently from behind."

"Let me go, you dog," Raghunatha broke free from Kanchipurathan's firm grip.

He again raised the sword. By now a crowd had gathered there.

Thamarai shouted, "Is there no one to question this man? Is there no law to stop him? He is attacking an unarmed man."

A man stepped forward and said, "Yes, this is unfair. If there is a duel, both men should be armed."

"Hello, priest! Where is Moses?" smiled Kanchipurathan.

"I am going to be the referee. So please don't try to be friendly with me," said the priest who had a chameleon for a pet. He asked a Maratha solider for his sword and gave it to Kanchipurathan.

"All right. On the count of three, you start fencing. One... two... three..."

Thamarai was wringing her hands in anxiety, and said to the priest, "I was hoping you would stop Raghunatha. But you are now presiding over a duel."

The swords clashed—thrust, parry, thrust, parry. "Ayyo," screamed Raghunatha, and fell bleeding to the ground. Kanchipurathan's sword had tasted blood.

Thamarai covered her eyes with her hands, not wanting to see the gory sight before her.

"Murder! Cold blooded murder!" Peria Pedhu pushed the crowd aside! Since he was well known in Chennai, people stepped aside respectfully. Kanchipurathan felt sorry for him. He was a broken man. He no longer looked regal. Even his moustache seemed limp.

Kanchipurathan said to Thamarai, "Come on. Let's go."

PeriaPedhu looked from the bleeding Raghunatha to the two departing lovers, and shouted, "They are my slaves. You can see my initials branded on their backs. Capture them! Don't let them get away. Here come the Company's soldiers."

Pedhu shouted out to the soldiers, "You are the custodians of the law. You are not like the people of Chennai, who have no sense of justice."

The soldiers came close to Pedhu. The Christian priest gave a meaningful smile.

The soldiers struck a drum, while another nailed a cloth banner to a tree. The man with the drum read out the words on the banner,

The East India Company, who are here as representatives of the Crown, have an announcement to make. From today, owning slaves has been declared illegal in Chennaipattanam and in Ezhumbur, Mylapore, Tiruvallikeni, Vepery and Purasaiwakkam. Anyone who buys or sells slaves will be punished severely. No mercy will be shown to them. Recapturing slaves who have run away, or shipping slaves to other countries have been declared illegal too.

The crowd mocked Pedhu and had a hearty laugh, and dispersed.

The priest also took his leave of Kanchipurathan. "I suppose you are responsible for this law."

The priest smiled. "I am not responsible. Give the credit to Christ."

Kanchipurathan and Thamarai continued their stroll. The fort could be seen in the distance. The fort built by men who had come as traders and had ended up as rulers. The Company flag could be seen flying atop the fort.

The two lovers, who had escaped slavery, had just one thought. This land would see many Kanchipurathans. Many revolutions, many sacrifices, many scares, many uprisings—Tamil soil would be witness to it all.

Man will be caught in these upheavals. He will fall, be insulted, and will shed tears. But in the end, he will rise. He will rise with strength in his arms and courage in his heart.

Failure will yield to success as night yields to day.

Yes, yes, said Kanchipurathan's fingers, which clutched Tamarai's hand. Yes, yes, concurred her fingers.